OUT OF
Time

OUT OF
Time

AMANDA M FLEET

Also by Amanda Fleet

The Wrong Kind of Clouds
Lies That Poison

The Guardians of The Realm
Aegyir Rises
Aeron Returns
War
Invasion
Chaos

For everyone who has believed in me

1

She had six months. At best. Then everything she had worked so hard for would be gone.

Nausea prickled Ellie's stomach, and tears burned her eyelids. In desperation, she re-did the calculations. It didn't make any difference. She slumped back in her seat, chewing her thumbnail. Her yarn and knitting business had been her dream, and she'd worked her fingers to the bone for all of it. But there were no two ways about it: if business didn't pick up hugely, *immediately*, she would have to wind everything up. She'd already borrowed from her brother, Joe, and although he would happily give her more money, she couldn't ask him to bail her out when she had zero chance of paying him back.

She shivered and tugged a knitted woollen wrap tighter around her shoulders, allowing her focus to drift away from the laptop screen. Her minuscule flat was cold at the best of times. With the increased cost of living, and fuel bills skyrocketing, it was now even colder.

How could her landlord justify charging so much for this cramped place, let alone raising the rent? Her laptop perched on the unit separating the tiny kitchen from the living area. That unit was her 'office'. Her dyes and other chemicals for the yarn-dyeing process filled the cupboard at her knees, and piled in the corner were the pans and kettles she used to create glorious colour combinations in her yarns. Finished skeins lived in the living room until sold, stored according to the weight of the yarn and the colour, along with any undyed skeins. The last remnants of floor

1

space held a lumpy sofa and a telly on a filing cabinet. At least she was fairly petite. Whenever Joe came over, he struggled to negotiate the space with his rangy, six-foot build, graceful as he was.

The business *had* been ticking along nicely. The arrival of covid and subsequent lockdown sparked a surprising interest in knitting and crafting. Part of that boom had included an uptick in demand for the things Ellie made: bespoke hand-dyed yarn with a focus on biodegradable, eco-friendly yarns and dyeing processes, plus knitting patterns that showed off her yarns well. She wasn't rich by any stretch of the imagination, but she was doing what she loved and keeping her head above water. Just.

Or at least she *had* been. Now, she faced going under. Bespoke hand-dyed yarn wasn't an essential, and with the increased cost of living, sales had taken a definite nose-dive recently.

She rubbed the back of her neck, her nose tingling. Half of her wanted to tell her landlord where to stick his rent rise. The other half knew that everywhere else would be exactly the same. She sighed. If she could expand the business and get a couple more projects up and running, things would almost certainly turn the corner. But to expand, she needed a bigger place, which would cost more in rent.

Her phone buzzed on the table next to her. She scrubbed her knuckles under her nose, turned the small radio on the desk down, and peered at the screen. Joe.

"Hey there," she said, easing her shoulders out as she answered.

"Hey. Has Mum rung you?"

"Mum? No. Why?"

"It's Granny Molly. She's had a huge heart attack."

Ellie swallowed, closing her eyes. "Granny Molly" was actually their great-aunt. She'd had no children of her own, but had been like an extra grandparent to Joe and Ellie, all of their lives.

"Oh, no. Will she be okay?"

There was a long pause on the line, and her heart sank.

"I don't think so," said Joe eventually. "She's getting discharged tomorrow and will be at home, but the prognosis isn't promising. Mum's gone there to be with her when she gets out.

I'm going to go too. Did you want to come?"

Images of holidays at Granny Molly's danced through Ellie's brain. She and Joe had loved going there for holidays because Granny Molly and Grandpa John had spoiled them and let them run wild. Just outside Masham in Yorkshire, the large, old house had an untamed garden, perfect for children to get lost in. Losing Grandpa John to cancer was tough, but Granny Molly had always seemed immortal.

"Ellie? Did you hear me?" Joe's voice snapped her back to reality. "Would you like to go down together?"

"Yeah. Yeah. When?"

Did it matter when? She wasn't exactly snowed under. The bills weren't going anywhere.

"I have to shift some things, but we can go this weekend." Another pause before he came back, his voice cracking. "I don't think we should leave it too long before going."

"Sure."

They rang off, and she stared unseeing at her laptop, her accounts forgotten. Losing Granny Molly would almost be worse than losing the business.

2

They took Joe's car for the trip down to Granny Molly's. Allegedly, Ellie was navigating, but given that she couldn't read a map, Joe had driven the route umpteen times, and his sat nav was cradled on the dashboard, she'd spent the journey either staring at the rain-lashed scenery, or chatting to Joe. As they skirted around Leeds, she told him about the business and how she thought it was going to fold.

"You know, you could always move back in with me. Use the money you saved by not having to pay rent for the business. It's not like I need all those rooms," said Joe. "Maybe if you just had a bit of breathing space with the business, things would be okay?"

Ellie's eyes flicked as she tracked the passing trees. Much as she loved her brother, she wasn't sure she wanted to move back in with him again. It had been one thing to be there for him after his wife had died in an accident. Then, he'd needed putting back together when his grief almost demolished him. Now, her moving back in would be a badge of failure.

"Ellie, I'm serious. There's plenty of space."

There was plenty of space because Joe and Hayley had planned on having a big family. And then she'd been killed by a hit-and-run driver, and the rooms had never become nurseries.

"If it's too big, you could always move somewhere smaller," Ellie suggested carefully.

Would he ever be able to let go of the house with all its memories?

"I want your business to take off," Joe said softly. "And if that

4

means you move back in with me for a while, then fine."

Ellie didn't reply. Several miles passed in silence.

"Do you think you'll see your tawny-haired boy again?" Joe said finally. "At Granny Molly's?"

Ellie blinked. She'd almost forgotten about him. Everyone had teased her about the imaginary play-friend she'd claimed she had, way back when she was small, but he'd been absolutely real to her. When Ellie had stamped her foot and insisted he was real, her parents assumed he was a kid from the village. Granny Molly had smiled knowingly, saying that perhaps he was a ghost from the past. The house dated back centuries, after all. At the time, the thought of the house being haunted had been thrilling. There had been no sign of him since she was about twelve, presumably because she had grown out of having imaginary friends.

She conjured a memory of him – a boy a couple of years older than her, with hair the colour of whisky, mischievous hazel eyes, and a wiry build. He'd told her his name once, but she couldn't remember it now. He had a large birthmark over the left side of his face, making it look as if someone had slapped him hard. She'd teased him about it once, and he'd been so upset and self-conscious, she'd regretted it immediately.

"Granny Molly thought he was real," Joe added, breaking into her memories. "Even if the rest of us didn't."

"Granny Molly was entertaining a small child with an over-active imagination," muttered Ellie. "That's all."

Joe gave her a sly look, and she turned away to track rivulets of rain down the window.

"Do you think she'll die?" Ellie blurted out when they were about ten miles from Masham. She'd been chewing over the question for some time.

Joe's dark eyes saddened. "Everyone dies, Ellie."

She flapped a hand. "I know that! I meant, do you think she'll die while we're there?"

He kept his eyes on the road, shrugging. "I don't know. I just hope that when it happens, it's peaceful."

Ellie chewed her lower lip. Hayley's death hadn't been peaceful. She'd died in the ambulance. Joe hadn't been with her.

The posh woman on the sat nav gave them the last few

instructions, and Joe turned on to a narrow road leading to the house.

"You have reached your destination," stated the sat nav, almost as soon as he made the turn.

Joe snorted at the empty road with no sign of a house nearby. "Good job we know where we're going."

He drove on, turning right immediately after a large oak tree. Granny Molly's house lay a short distance from the southern edge of Masham village, on a quiet side-road. Ellie craned her neck, peering ahead eagerly for the first signs of the house. Bang on a hundred metres from the turning, the familiar gates loomed – one large wooden one with a smaller one to the side. A sign attached to the stone wall read "Rose Cottage", although everyone always informally called the place "The Old Forge". There hadn't been a blacksmiths here for well over two hundred years, as far as anyone knew. There weren't many roses nearby, either. Beyond the gate lay a large gravel area in front of a substantial stone-built house. Ellie's heart lifted at the sight.

"I'm driving. You have to open the gate," said Joe smugly, as the rain lashed the windows.

Grimacing, Ellie hopped out of the car and opened the gate, turning up her coat collar to shield herself from the rain. She huddled in the lee of the house while Joe parked next to their mother's car, then she scurried back to close the gate again, rain trickling behind her collar and down her neck.

It still didn't quite feel real that they were here, despite the frenetic packing and the drive. The gate closed, she dashed to the house. Behind her, Joe retrieved their bags from the boot of his car.

"Knock on the bloody door then!" he urged. "I'm getting soaked!"

He shifted his arms to demonstrate that he didn't have a free hand since he was carrying all the bags. Ellie rapped the brass door-knocker, squashing herself into the porch to allow Joe some respite from the rain.

Their mother must have heard the tyres on the gravel, because the door swung open almost immediately, revealing a square hallway with a comfortable-looking leather chair, a shoe-rack, and a series of hooks for coats. Laura Stewart grinned broadly and pulled Ellie into an enormous hug.

"Oh, you're here. At last!"

Joe shouldered his way past them, dumped the bags in the hallway behind them, and waited for their mother to free Ellie. She released her, then opened her arms to her son. Laura had the same petite build as her daughter, and Joe swamped her with his hug.

"Ugh, you're both wet!" she said as he stepped back, her smile negating her words. "Come inside and get a tea or coffee."

"How's Granny Molly?" asked Ellie, her voice almost a whisper.

Laura's face fell. "She's doing okay. Very frail. She went to bed when she got back from the hospital. I'm not sure if she'll make it back downstairs again. She's sleeping at the moment."

"Is that the children?" a reedy voice called down from above them. Clearly, Granny Molly wasn't asleep.

"Children?" Joe arched a brow. "I'm nearly thirty and she's twenty-six. Are we still children?"

Laura punched his arm affectionately. "Go up and say hello while I get the kettle on. You're both in the back rooms."

Ellie sucked in a long breath, then shrugged out of her damp coat and hung it up on one of the pegs. The years peeled away, transporting her back to long childhood holidays spent here. Joe picked up the bags again, and they crossed the small porch to a larger, wooden-floored hallway. Faded Persian-style rugs covered the boards. To the right lay the lounge; to the left, the dining room. The hallway continued, passing through an archway to the kitchen and a study that overlooked the gardens. There was a utility room between the kitchen and study, with a door leading to the back garden. What had once been an outdoor toilet now adjoined the house, accessed via the end of the utility room. Absolutely nothing had changed since Ellie had last been here a couple of years ago.

Joe and Ellie headed up the stairs. The upper floor was split over two levels – two bedrooms and a tiny bathroom at the back; two bedrooms and a second, larger bathroom to the front, up another few stairs. Ellie and Joe had always stayed in the back bedrooms on their visits.

Granny Molly's bedroom was at the front of the house, above

the lounge, and Ellie waited on the landing while Joe deposited their bags in the back rooms. She poked her head around the half-open door, her pulse quickening. Just how ill *was* Granny Molly? A frail old lady's head poked out from under the covers, her grey hair tousled by the pillow.

"Hi!" Ellie said brightly, crossing to the bed, Joe right behind her.

Granny Molly shifted herself until she sat up straighter, wheezing and panting as she did so, her lined face creasing as she beamed at them.

"You came! Oh, it's so lovely to see you. And Joe, too!"

Ellie leaned over to kiss her papery cheek, then perched on the edge of the double bed. Joe reached past her to kiss Granny Molly, then sat behind Ellie.

"You've given us quite a scare." Ellie's fingertip traced around a flower on the old quilt on the bed.

"Oh, tush. It's something and nothing!"

It wasn't. Granny Molly's skin had a bluish tinge to it and her skin was almost translucent, the veins of her hands showing dark blue against the white.

"Mum's putting the kettle on. Did you want a cuppa?" Ellie said.

Granny Molly shook her head. "No, thank you." Suddenly, all the stuffing went out of her and she sagged. "I'm sorry. I'm always so tired these days."

"Shall we leave you to rest?" said Joe. "I'm absolutely gasping for a cuppa. And no doubt Mum will want to hear all our news, even though we only spoke a few days ago."

Granny Molly's face softened. "If you don't mind. I'll feel better after a nap."

"Okay. Deal. You grab a nap, we'll catch up with Mum, and we'll see you later."

The bed creaked as Joe stood up. He leaned over to kiss Granny Molly again, then withdrew. Ellie was about to follow his lead, but Granny Molly caught her hand. "He's waiting for you. Though he doesn't know it yet."

Ellie frowned. "Sorry? Who are you talking about?"

But Granny Molly's eyes had closed and her breathing

8

deepened. Ellie adjusted the pillows behind her and drew the quilt a little higher. Who had Granny Molly meant?

Back downstairs, Joe and Ellie found Laura in the kitchen, pouring boiling water into a teapot.

"I assumed you'd both take tea," she said over her shoulder. "But there's plenty of water if you'd prefer coffee."

"Tea's fine for me, thanks." Ellie pulled out a chair at the scarred pine table in the kitchen. Joe sat beside her.

"How was Granny Molly?" Laura plonked the teapot along with a carton of milk on the table, then turned to retrieve mugs from the cupboard behind her.

"She looked blue," said Joe, pulling the teapot towards himself. "Shall I be Mother?"

"We'll both ignore the sexism implicit in that question," said Laura, putting the mugs next to him. "Yes, you can pour." She sat down. "Granny's pretending hard, but she's not well."

Ellie poured milk into the tea Joe passed over to her. "Can we do anything to help?"

Laura shook her head. "Just keep me company for a couple of days. Oh, thanks, Joe." She stirred milk into her mug, then clasped her hands around it. "How are things, Ellie? Last time we talked, you said it was a bit difficult."

Ellie's gaze spun out to the hallway beyond the kitchen, her attention caught by kaleidoscoping colours dancing at the edge of the hallway. She blinked, and the colours disappeared.

"Still difficult." She let her focus drift back to her mother.

"I've told her she can move back into mine." Joe set the teapot down on the table with a thump and faced his sister. "See how things go. Worst-case scenario and you do give up the yarn business, you could get a job in the city, live with me, and still do the designing."

Ellie stirred her tea, tension prickling her neck. "I know. I'll keep it in mind. Thanks. Are you able to test-knit something for me?"

Like her, Joe was a keen knitter. Granny Molly had taught them both to knit one summer when they were children. She'd actually been teaching Ellie, but nosy as ever, Joe wanted to know what she was doing and had taken to it with alacrity. If Ellie was being honest, while he might not have enough artistic flair to design anything, Joe was a better knitter than Ellie, especially with multi-coloured pieces, and she invariably asked him to test-knit for her.

"How big is it?" he asked.

"A hat. Fret not. It'll barely take you an evening, the speed you knit. I brought needles and yarn. You could do it while we're here."

They lapsed into silence, and questions flowed unbidden through Ellie's brain. How long would Granny Molly live? What would happen to the house when she died? Since Granny Molly had no children, the house would probably go to Laura. But what would she do with it? Ellie poured herself another cup of tea. Laura would probably sell the house. No one in the family lived close enough to live in it and continue in their jobs. An old house, so far from everyone's jobs and life, was no use, however beautiful it was and for however long it had been in the family.

The dancing colours reappeared in the hallway, making Ellie frown. What was causing them? The door between the front porch and the main hallway had a stained-glass panel, but the colours in it were different. And anyway, the rain still lashed down outside, so no sun shone through it. Ellie searched for a light-catcher or prism or something that could be casting the colours, but there was nothing.

"Penny?" Joe nudged her with his foot, pulling her attention back to the kitchen.

"Oh. I was thinking about the house and all the amazing holidays we've had here." She finished her tea. "I'm going to go and unpack, but then can I make dinner, Mum? Give you a break."

Laura smiled. "Yeah. That would be nice."

"I'll give you a hand," said Joe.

As Ellie stood to put her mug next to the sink, the faint image of a man crossing the hallway mixed with the colourful lights. She turned to look properly, but as she did, the lights faded, then disappeared. The hall was empty.

3

The following morning, Ellie took Granny Molly a cup of tea. Her heart lurched as she set the cup down on the bedside cabinet. Granny Molly's skin resembled parchment, and a slight rattle had developed in her breathing, but she still had a smile for Ellie.

"Ellie, darling. Pull that chair over. It'll be more comfortable than sitting on the bed."

Ellie carried the wicker chair from the bedroom window to the bed.

"It's good of you and Joe to come," Granny Molly said as Ellie sat down. "I know how busy you both are."

"Well, I'm not so busy these days. People need to spend their money on food and heating more than they do on expensive wool."

"But you're still designing? Your designs are so beautiful."

"Mm. I'm still designing."

Granny Molly wheezed, and patted at the corner of her mouth with a lace-trimmed handkerchief. "Do you still see him? He's all grown up now and *so* handsome. Mind you, he was a bonny lad, so that's no big surprise."

Ellie blinked at the change in direction. "See who? Who's all grown up?"

"Your little boy."

She laughed. "I think I imagined him."

Granny Molly shook her head. "No, no. He's real. You spent a whole day with him when you were very little. Your mum went frantic. She was convinced you'd wandered off and been killed on the road or kidnapped."

Ellie leaned forwards, resting her forearms on her thighs. "When was this? I don't remember being lost."

"Oh, you were three, I think. Four? But then you got too big to go."

"Go where, Granny Molly?"

"To see him!"

Granny Molly must be getting wandered. Best to humour her?

"Well, I'd certainly be too big to see him now."

Granny Molly shook her head. "No. No. That's not what happens."

Ellie laughed lightly. "You know the future?" It had been a family joke that Granny Molly could.

She pinched her lips together disapprovingly. "You know I can. Look in the cupboard. That's where you'll find all the answers."

"Which cupboard?" The conversation was wriggling away from her.

"The one in the study."

Ellie did a mental scan of the study downstairs. A desk under the window, some shelves, a comfy chair... absolutely no cupboard.

"Okay."

Granny Molly closed her eyes. Ellie waited a moment, then got up to leave her to sleep. As soon as she moved, Molly stirred.

"I wish Joe would find someone. He can't keep loving a ghost."

Ellie sat down again. "I know. I think he's getting there."

"He'll find someone down here."

Ellie let it pass. Why would Joe move down here? His life and work were a two-hour drive away, and she couldn't see her brother spending four hours a day in a car.

Granny Molly peered at her and patted her hand, her skin cool and dry. "He is a *lovely* man. I know you'll be happy together. You'll find a way. I know you will. Just don't let the mob get him. It wasn't him. And make sure you take a room at the front for your bedroom, or who *knows* what will happen."

Her eyes held a mischievous glint.

Ellie frowned, not following the conversation. "What do you

mean?"

Granny Molly didn't reply. Ellie watched her for a few minutes, wondering if there would be any more gnomic statements, but her breathing slowed and her eyes were shut tight, so Ellie tiptoed away and left her to sleep.

Downstairs, she found Joe knitting in the back garden, sitting at a round ironwork table with Ellie's pattern pinned down on it with a couple of stones. The rain of the previous day had disappeared, unveiling a stunning late spring morning.

He looked up, the wooden needles clicking together. "How was she?"

"A bit wandered. She still claims my tawny-haired boy was real. Apparently, I spent a day with him when I was three or four." She pulled the spare chair out and sat down, stretching her legs in the fresh sunshine.

Joe's brow creased. "I vaguely remember you wandering off when you were little. You said you'd been playing with someone. We all assumed you'd got lost on the path down to the village and then got caught up with another family or something."

"I can't remember any of that." She jutted her chin at the knitting. "How's it going? And *how* do you knit so quickly without even looking at it?"

He laughed. "Practice. The pattern's fine. I found one slight mistake, but nothing major. Your maths is rubbish and you can't add up stitches properly for a stitch count. I've marked it."

She watched him knit for a few minutes, her shoulders sagging. Earlier that morning, she'd taken a walk into the village and come back buzzing with ideas for a new collection, based on the patchwork of colours in the old stonework of the houses. Would she ever turn her ideas into yarns?

Almost as if he could read her mind, Joe asked, "How bad *is* business? Surely there's still demand? Slow fashion and so on?"

She chewed the inside of her lip. "Yes, and no. I would be better off if I could expand and offer all the colours in all the yarn weights and blends. Just before my landlord said he was upping the rent, I'd been talking to some small-holders about doing an undyed range, showcasing the natural fleece colour of some heritage breeds. I think the market is there for that, but I don't have the space or the capital to set it up. I'd been saving as much as I could, hoping to get that up and running this summer, but that's all been gobbled up. My costs have also gone up, but there's no way I can increase my prices to match and I've nearly run out of savings."

She leaned on her arms on the table. "I had so many ideas for the undyed stuff. Traditional gansey patterns, some colourwork sweaters making great use of the subtle shading between the natural colours. I'd planned to do kits, and all sorts."

"Maybe Granny Molly will leave you a bit of money? Tide you over. Or I could lend you it."

She tucked her hair back behind her ears. "I can't afford to pay you back what you've already lent me. And I don't want Granny Molly to die."

Joe's dark eyes settled on her. "But she will. And soon, in all likelihood."

Ellie turned away, blinking tears back.

"If you didn't pay rent on your place, could you afford to expand and get on to a better footing?" asked Joe. "Get this new project going?"

She pinched her nose, sniffing. "Probably."

"Then give notice to your landlord and run your business from my place for a bit. You can use my kitchen for the dyeing. Or my shed."

"I'll think about it. Thanks." She pulled a face. "You can add it to my tab."

"No tab, sis. I still owe you everything after you put me back together."

His voice was gruff, making her reach over to squeeze his wrist.

"If I drop stitches, I'll blame you," he said, but his eyes were warm.

She sat back. "You realise how much knitting I'll be getting you to do, if I manage to expand?"

"As long as I can knit them in my size and get to keep them afterwards, I don't mind."

She snorted. "Joe, of course they'll be in your size. You'll be *modelling* them for me. Your pretty face will be on all the kits!"

"Jeez. Then you'll *definitely* go under!"

14

She shook her head. If only he could see what others did. Despite him being her brother, even she had to admit he was good-looking, and all of her female friends at school had swooned over him.

"Anyway. Yes, you can knit them in your size and keep them, but you need to test the patterns in other sizes too. Mind you, the way things are looking, I'm probably going to go back to waitressing."

He raised his gaze to her again. "Can I be blunt?"

She folded her arms, a smile tickling her lips. "Why are you asking? You will be even if I say no."

He acknowledged the point with a tilt of his head, then turned serious. "You're so tired and stressed at the moment, but I know my funny, creative, amazing, annoying little sister is in there *somewhere*. Stay with me and focus on the business. For as long as you need to. Talk to your landlord. See if you can get out of your lease early."

He peered earnestly at her and her objections crumbled.

"Okay. I'll think about it."

If she kept her head above water long enough to get the new projects up and running, could she turn things around?

***

Ellie stood in the hallway, waiting for Joe to join her for the drive back. Tears rolled down her cheeks. Would she ever see Granny Molly again? Would she see the house again? They'd talked about it over dinner the previous night. Laura had said she would consider renting it out as a holiday cottage, but that was all still up in the air. As if that hadn't been depressing enough, Ellie had then worked through her finances with Joe. They'd come to the conclusion that either the business folded and she found a job, or she moved everything to Joe's and used the money saved on rent to keep the business afloat. After breakfast that morning, Ellie had emailed her landlord to discuss ending the tenancy early. Failure wrapped around her shoulders like a lead blanket.

Movement caught the corner of her eye, and she glanced up the stairs, expecting to see Joe. Instead, the strange colour-effect was back. Bright blues, reds, and greens flickered together, along with yellow and orange highlights. As the patterns swirled, the back half of the house shifted, making Ellie blink. Close to the kitchen, another set of stairs appeared at the back of the rear hallway. She rubbed her eyes, but the mirage remained.

Joe clattered down the main stairs to join her and she indicated the patterned lights.

"Joe, what's causing that? I can't see any prism or stained-glass that would make that."

Joe peered in the direction she pointed. "Make what? What are you looking at?"

"The coloured lights. There's a swirl of them, about level with the archway."

Joe craned his neck, then bobbed down to match Ellie's height and angle. "I'm not seeing anything."

The lights faded, then disappeared.

"No. Neither am I now." She looked up at her brother. "Are you ready to go?"

"Yeah. Just waiting for Mum to come down. How was Granny Molly with you?"

"Okay. Sad we were going. Still telling me that she knows I'll be happy with my ghost-boy."

Joe huffed. "Mm. She told me I would be really happy here and start a new life."

Ellie twitched her shoulders. "Guess she's not so good at seeing the future, after all." A lump lodged in her throat. "Do you think we'll see her again?"

Joe tipped his head up, breathing hard. "No. She told me she wasn't scared. That she was ready. That she'd known it was coming for a long time."

"She's not *that* old!"

Joe didn't answer. Instead, he hooked his arm around the back of Ellie's neck and pulled her against his shoulder. She bit her lip, resting her face against his neck, tears burning her eyes. He squeezed her, releasing her as Laura came down the stairs.

"That you off?" she asked.

"Yes. Sorry we couldn't stay any longer, Mum," said Joe

She flapped a hand. "I'm glad you could come down at all. And Granny Molly was pleased to see you both."

They exchanged more hugs, then Joe loaded their bags into the boot, and Ellie settled behind the wheel for the first shift at driving. Joe slid into the passenger seat next to her and wound down his window to wave.

"Do you think we'll ever see this place again?" asked Ellie, as they pulled away.

"Let's not think about that right now. Maybe Mum and Dad will keep it as a holiday home and we can come up and stay." He swallowed. "I guess we'll see it again at the funeral."

Ellie *really* didn't want to think about that. Maybe they were all underestimating Granny Molly and although she'd had a bad turn, she'd recover and be back to her usual self.

She glanced in the rear-view mirror at the disappearing house. A tawny-haired man crossed the gravel, just behind Laura.

4

A week later, Ellie parked a little way down the street from Joe's, squeezing her car into the only available space on the road. No doubt she'd taken someone's favoured spot, but there was only space outside Joe's for one vehicle, and his car currently occupied it. She grabbed the shopping bag and strolled down towards Joe's house, the plastic handles cutting into her hands.

She'd offered to cook Joe dinner as a thank you for him agreeing to test-knit a sweater pattern. And so they could talk about her moving in. She rapped on the door, her brain doing an imaginary walk through his two garden sheds. Would they be big enough to take all of her dyeing equipment? Possibly, but they'd need a good tidy. Maybe he might let her use his kitchen instead.

Joe swung the door open, and she grinned at him. He swallowed, his face full of pain, and her smiles vanished.

"What? What's happened?" She dropped the bag and hurried to him.

"Your phone's off. Mum's been trying to call you." He broke off again. "It's Granny Molly."

Ellie scoured his face, hoping he was just telling her she'd had another bad turn, but the look in his eyes confirmed her worst fears.

"Oh, no. When?"

Joe pulled her into a hug, sniffing. "In her sleep, peacefully. This afternoon."

She scrubbed at the tears on her cheeks. Joe reached around

her to pick up the shopping and she stumbled after him into the house. In the kitchen, she turned to him, a sob catching in her throat.

"Joe, I need another hug."

He wrapped her up in his arms, holding her tight. "I know. It's horrible. But we knew it was likely. At least it was peaceful and in her own home." He kissed the side of her head. "Coffee? Or something stronger?"

"Oh, much as I'd love something stronger, I need to drive home tonight. I'm out at stupid o'clock tomorrow morning." She pointed to the discarded carrier bag of food. "There's some sparkling juice in there. I'll have some of that."

He released her slowly, and she headed to the lounge and flopped down on the sofa while he got the drinks. Her gaze scanned the photos adorning the room.

"When are you going to move on, Joe? Granny Molly thought you should let go of your ghosts."

Joe's wife, Hayley, had died almost four years ago, killed by a hit-and-run driver. Above the fireplace in the living room hung a large studio photo of Joe and Hayley, laughing together. The photographer had caught them looking relaxed and happy. More photographs littered the windowsill – some of them together, some of Hayley alone. One of Joe and Ellie larking about, which always made her smile.

Hayley's death broke Joe. And Ellie. Joe had collapsed into himself. At the time, Ellie had been living at home, trying to save up to afford a place of her own. She'd moved in to Joe's, making sure that he ate, keeping him together as well as she could. Over the second year, he'd emerged from his cocoon and re-entered the world a quieter, more subdued man. The old Joe was still in there somewhere, but his colours had faded, as if an internal light that made them glow had been dimmed. Four years later, he was finally returning to his old laid-back and lively self; the man who seemed to be the centre of any party, with an easy laugh and a wide grin. Would he ever be ready to share that with anyone new? Ellie eyed the pictures again. How could *any* woman share his life while Hayley adorned so much wall-space? And when would he finally take his wedding ring off?

Joe returned, carrying two glasses and a bottle, dragging her out of her thoughts. He set them all down on the low coffee table, poured a glass out for her, and slumped down on the sofa.

"To Granny Molly," he said, clinking glasses with her.

"To Granny Molly."

She kicked her shoes off and tucked her feet up, letting her head drop back. "Man! I'm tired." She checked the clock, surprised to see it was still only half-past six. "How was Mum when she rang? Does she want me to call her?"

"Upset. Give her a ring. I take it we'll be going there together for the funeral?"

Ellie nodded. "Mm."

She took out her phone from her back pocket and switched it on. It logged several missed calls from her mum, and a message asking her to call. She pressed the screen and settled back.

"Hi, Mum. How are you doing? Joe told me about Granny Molly."

"Holding up. I'm hoping that we'll hold the funeral next Saturday. Will you and Joe be able to make it?"

"Of course. Is Dad joining you?"

"Yeah. He's coming down tomorrow."

"Mum, can we do anything? I feel bad that you're dealing with all of it on your own."

Laura sighed. "No, not really. I'm seeing the solicitor tomorrow; get the ball rolling on the will. I'd already gone through most of the paperwork, and your dad can help me with that when he gets here. We're seeing the funeral director the day after tomorrow, so we'll be able to finalise the date of the funeral then."

Laura's voice caught, making Ellie's heart ache for her. "Mum, are you okay?"

"I'm fine. Ellie, darling, I have to go. I'll ring you again soon."

"Okay. Love you."

"Love you too."

They rang off, and Joe cocked a brow at her. "She okay? Did she say when the funeral will be?"

"Next Saturday, she hopes."

"How does that fit in with you leaving your place?"

Ellie let her breath out slowly. "My landlord agreed a month's notice. I'll move in after the funeral, if that's okay? I don't think I can cope with Granny Molly dying, the funeral, *and* moving."

Joe gazed steadily at her. "Move in whenever you want. Stay for as long as you want."

"Thank you."

Tears needled the backs of her eyelids. Granny Molly. Her independence. Quite probably her business.

What else was she going to lose?

5

The following morning, Ellie leaned back in her seat at the kitchen worktop and stretched, her brain whirring with ideas. Her online call with two amazing women at The Wool Library had flooded her with enthusiasm, and thoughts crashed in her head, sparking new idea after new idea. The pad at her side was covered in so many scribbles that she could barely see the paper. She turned to a fresh sheet and dashed off more notes about a potential project to pair her designs with some small yarn producers.

Kits. My designs, their wool.

More furious writing.

All natural colours? How does Cheviot compare to Masham? Which is better for stitch definition? Or is that more from the spinning?

Her phone rang, scattering her thoughts to the four winds and making her swear softly. She grasped at the threads of her ideas, desperate to keep hold of them, but they had vanished. Maybe she could just ignore whoever was calling; try to find the zone again.

A glance at the screen told her it was a three-way call with Joe and her mum, and she answered it.

"Hi. What's up?" Three-way family conversations usually happened at weekends, not the middle of the week.

"Hi," said Laura. "Um. Are you both able to talk?"

Joe nodded at the same time as Ellie, a quizzical expression on his brow. From his background, he was in his office at work.

"I'm just back from the lawyers." Laura's mouth tightened.

22

"Granny Molly's will."

"Has she left everything to the cats' home?" asked Joe, hal[f] smiling.

"No." There was a long pause. "She's left everything to yo[u] and Ellie."

The siblings stared at each other across the ether.

"She's done what?" asked Ellie.

Their mother inhaled sharply. "She's left it all to you two. Th[e] house, its contents… There's no money, really. Only a li[ttle] assurance policy to cover any inheritance tax. There was a coverin[g] note saying that you two needed it more than me, and I quote, '[to] bring you both the happiness you deserve'."

Bitterness tinged their mother's voice.

"Are you angry, Mum?" asked Ellie. "We didn't know. W[e] didn't ask her to do this."

Another sigh. Laura rubbed a hand through her hair, her fac[e] drawn. "I know. And she had no children, so she could leave th[e] house to whoever she wanted. It's just a surprise, that's all. [I] suppose I'd assumed she would leave it to me, but she'd nev[er] actually said anything about who was getting the place. Th[e] solicitor will contact both of you about it. They'll send on all th[e] information." Another pause. "Anyway, I needed to let you kno[w.] I'll ring you again later."

Before they could even say their goodbyes, she had rung off.

Joe blew his cheeks out. "We have Rose Cottage!"

Ellie struggled to get her head around it. Why on earth ha[d] Granny Molly left it to them?

"Do you think Mum will ever talk to us again?"

Joe shrugged. "She'll come around. The bigger question i[s] what do we do with it? Because love you as I do, sis, I don't kno[w] if I want to live with you in Masham. My job is here, and I'm n[ot] commuting *that* far."

Ellie eyed him. It wasn't his job keeping him here, it was [a] ghost. And perhaps it was time for him to leave it behind.

"Yeah, but your current contract's ending in a few months, s[o] you could move after that. I'm assuming Yorkshire need[s] hydrologists, too."

He pulled a face.

Her spirits sank. "So, do you want to sell it?"

Joe laughed lightly. "No. I was actually thinking that it would be a brilliant opportunity for you."

Her heart fluttered. It *would* be an amazing opportunity, but where did that leave Joe?

"I can't afford to buy you out."

A soft smile crept over his lips. "I know that. I know *exactly* how skint you are!" He picked up a mug and took a sip from it. "It would be a shame not to keep the house in the family and it would be perfect for your business, wouldn't it?"

"Yes." Ellie cast her mind over the house and the outbuildings. It would be absolutely ideal for the expansion she wanted to do. "I mean, the house will be a bit big for only me rattling around in it, but there's space for a proper office, and the outbuildings would be perfect." She fiddled with the edge of the mouse-mat at her side. It might all be perfect, but the idea of moving somewhere where she knew no one terrified her. "It would be a big change, though."

Joe tilted his head to one side. "I know. But you could just as easily run your business from Masham as from here, so the sensible option is you move to Granny Molly's rather than move in with me. You have a waiting list for orders. You could expand with minimal risk. Weren't you talking to some people this morning about something new?"

"Mm. But I can't have the place and you have nothing. That's not fair."

"Why don't we talk to a lawyer about it? Maybe I could be a sleeping partner in the business or something. Or you could pay me tuppence ha'penny as rent. Ellie, we'll work something out. Neither of us wants to sell the place. And Mum would slaughter the pair of us if we even suggested it!"

The weight on Ellie's shoulders lightened slightly. "Thank you. I don't want you out of pocket, though."

His gaze shifted upwards and to his right, and someone murmured something to him. "Okay." His focus returned to Ellie. "Sorry, I have to run. Let's talk some more about the house soon? Lunch tomorrow? We'll figure something out."

He rang off. Ellie doodled on the corner of her discarded

notes, her thoughts racing. Why had Granny Molly left the house to them? Had she realised how precarious Ellie's business was? Was that what she'd meant about the house bringing her the happiness she deserved? She gnawed at the end of her pencil. Moving to Rose Cottage would be a significant change, albeit one full of opportunities. Would she find new friends? Would she end up lonely there? She wasn't like Joe, who could happily go into a room where he knew no one and come out with ten new friends. She needed to screw her courage up to even *start* talking to people.

Her excitement refused to be crushed, and ideas raced through her head. Could she turn the embryonic plans she'd made that morning into reality, after all?

***

Ellie grabbed a table in the corner, took her jacket off, and shook the rain off it. The cafe was busy with people escaping the weather and she'd nabbed the last free table. A steady hum of chatter mingled with the chink of cutlery on porcelain, and the smell of toast hung in the air. Ellie sat down and sneaked a glance at her watch. Joe wasn't late; she was early.

As she pulled her sleeve back over her wrist, Joe arrived in a flurry, rubbing rain out of his dark hair and turning heads. He plonked himself down opposite her. "Hi. Have you ordered?"

Her gaze pointedly scanned the two menus on the empty table between them. "Not yet."

The waitress scurried over, all smiles. For him. She'd studiously ignored Ellie. Most people did. Clearly, she didn't have enough aura or something. Joe had it in spades, and he didn't even realise. If he wasn't her brother, she'd probably find it less annoying. Probably.

"Soup and a sandwich?" Joe flicked a brow at her, and she nodded. He turned to the waitress. "A tomato soup and a ham sandwich, please. Is there pickle in the sandwich?"

"No." She looked as if she'd personally go and secure the best pickle available, just for him, if she could.

"Oh, well. Never mind. Thank you."

Ellie put her order in – exactly the same as her brother, but she didn't care about the pickle – and the waitress shimmied away.

Joe rested his chin on his hand. "Shall we talk about the house? Have you drawn up a gazillion plans of what you'll be able to do once you move?"

Ellie shook her head. "Not yet. We need to figure out what *you* get from this before I can even think about moving. I don't have enough money to pay you rent. Not at the level we could get if we rented it out. And it all feels too daunting to even consider."

"We'll sort out something. You can pay me a percentage of profit or something. I'd far rather you had the place and your business flourished than you stayed here and went under! Why is the idea of moving so daunting?"

"It's a big upheaval. I'm based here."

Joe scratched his jaw, and she braced herself for tough questions. "Where do you want the business to be in five years' time? Or even in a year? Can you achieve those dreams more easily if you moved into Granny Molly's? A simple yes or no to the last question."

Ellie rolled her eyes. "Yes. Of course I could. The outbuildings are great. There's a lot more space in the house. It's closer to a new project I'm hoping to get up and running. But that's not the point. It's a big move. Me, the business—"

"Your business isn't location-based," Joe interrupted. "The wool you dye comes by courier. In fact, all of your raw materials are delivered. You have sales at fairs, but the majority of your income is through online sales, either of your patterns or of your wool. So, your concerns are your friends being here, and the fact you hate change. Right?"

"Mm."

Her brother had a useful, albeit annoying, habit of being utterly practical over everything.

Joe settled back in his seat and folded his arms. "If you moved the business to Masham, what disadvantages would there be?"

"Getting to some of the fairs would be more of a trek."

"True. But you already travel the length and breadth of the country to attend those, and others will be nearer. What else?"

She struggled to come up with many. "My support base here. You. Friends."

He waved his hand, dismissing them. "They're not business-related. Not directly. And if 2020 taught us anything, it was that it's possible to keep up with friends and family without actually seeing them physically. And I know you can have wallflower tendencies, but you *will* make new friends."

She chewed her lip. "Would you stay for a bit? If I move. I don't know anyone there."

He pulled up his diary on his phone, scrolling through it. "Were you intending to stay up after the funeral? Move in then?"

She shook her head. "No. It'll take me longer than that to get everything sorted. Instead of coming to yours at the end of my lease, I'd go there."

"Okay. Well, it's only a couple of hours away. I should be able to grab a week or so when you move in and I can come down at weekends for a bit. Be the chatty sibling for you."

"Thank you."

He reached across to squeeze her hand. "Ellie, this could be brilliant for you. A fresh start. Build something amazing."

The weight on Ellie's shoulders lifted a fraction. Could this be the break she needed?

6

Ellie drank in the soft greens and ochres of the countryside as she drove, plotting how to achieve the colours in the dye bath. Between them, she and Joe had managed to cram all of her meagre belongings into their cars, and they were now driving down to Rose Cottage in convoy. Joe had promised to help her unpack and stay for a while, but he had to return home for some in-person meetings eventually.

As Ellie followed Joe on to the lane leading to Rose Cottage, butterflies flapped in her stomach. The last time she had seen the house had been at the funeral. Joe pulled up next to the gate, hopped out, and opened it, waving her through. She parked on the gravel and got out, fidgeting with the keys as she waited for her brother. A few moments later, he stood beside her, looking up at the house, a bag of groceries in his hand. He stretched his back, flexing first one way, then the other.

"Well, here we are. Are you going to unlock the door?" he said.

Was this really theirs? After long discussions, they had finally agreed that Ellie would pay Joe rent for his share, though it was less than she'd been paying her old landlord, and Joe was very much accepting it under sufferance.

She stepped forward and opened the front door. The air was chilly and a little musty, with a faint remnant of furniture polish. Joe slid his arm around her shoulder and squeezed her. "It's pretty special, isn't it? I'm still struggling to get my head around the fact it's ours."

"Mm. Me too."

She crossed the wooden-floored hallway to stand next to the stairs, then circled slowly, drinking in the house. Joe gazed around, his eyes bright.

"You know I said I didn't want to live with you? I might change my mind about that!"

She laughed. "Paws off. I'm renting your half from you, remember."

"Cuppa, before we fetch everything in?"

"Mm, hm. Can you make them? I'm going to have a walk round."

Ellie opened the door to the dining room. It was a nice enough room, with a solid table and chairs in the centre and an old dresser against one wall, but Ellie couldn't imagine ever eating in there. They never had when they'd been to visit. They'd always eaten at the scrubbed pine table in the kitchen, sitting on the hard wooden chairs in there. That would be where Ellie would still eat, in all probability.

She strolled back to the lounge, smiling at the cosy-looking room with its squashy sofas, small bookcase, and wood-burning stove. Trailing her hand over the back of the nearest sofa, she reluctantly turned back to the hall to go and help Joe with the tea.

In the main hallway, she stopped dead in her tracks. A man, maybe Joe's age, stood outside the study door, staring straight at her.

"Hello?" Her voice rang across the space.

The man didn't react.

"Hello?" repeated Ellie, waving her arms at him. Surely he could see her?

He turned and walked into the study. Ellie followed him, her footsteps echoing on the wooden floor. "Excuse me? Hello? Who are you?"

She hurried through the open door, but the study was empty. She frowned. There were no other exits from the room, and the window was shut tight. Where the hell had he gone? She moved to the window and tried to open it, only to find it locked.

Joe stuck his head around the doorway. "Who are you talking to?"

"There was a man here. Tall. About your age. Light brown hair.

Dressed a bit weirdly."

In fact, he'd looked like he'd just stepped out from a historical re-enactment of the 18th century.

"Where is he?" asked Joe.

"I don't know! He was in the hallway and then he came in here. You didn't see him?"

"Nope. And if he came in here, where's he gone? And how did he get in, in the first place?"

Ellie cast around her. The room had floor to ceiling bookcases covering one wall, a fireplace with a wood-burning stove, a large desk in the window, and a comfy chair in the corner, but no sign of the man she'd seen. She rubbed her face.

"He definitely came in here."

Joe arched a brow. "It's not your tawny-haired boy again, is it? Only all grown up."

Ellie stuck her tongue out at him.

"Anyway," Joe went on. "Tea's made and I've unpacked the shopping. The pantry is almost empty, so we need to do a proper shop tomorrow. Mum said she'd left anything that was in date, but that clearly wasn't much."

"Okay." She took one last look around the study, then followed Joe to the kitchen, still perplexed.

A large brown teapot sat on the square table, along with a couple of china mugs of tea. Ellie sat, still wondering who the man could have been and where on earth he'd gone. Joe sat opposite her, his hands clasped around the mug.

"Have you decided which bedroom you want?" he said.

Ellie hadn't even thought about it. "No. Want to check them out while these cool?"

As Ellie walked through the hall, her neck prickled and she looked behind her. For the briefest of moments, she thought she saw the strange man again, but the hall was empty.

"Don't say Granny Molly was right all along and this place is haunted," she thought. *"That would be par for the course. Comes to us out of the blue, saves the business, but the catch is there's a restless soul marauding through it."*

The bedrooms facing the front of the house each had a double bed, along with a chest of drawers and a wardrobe. Laura had cleared all of Granny Molly's belongings out, leaving both wardrobes and chests of drawers empty. Neither bed was made. The bathroom that sat between the two front bedrooms had a claw-foot tub and a separate shower. Again, all traces of Granny Molly had been removed.

Ellie joined Joe on the lower level at the rear. There, all the rooms were slightly smaller. The bedrooms had the same furniture as when Ellie and Joe were children: a single bed, a wardrobe, and a chest of drawers – all empty except for spare blankets and pillows in one wardrobe. Next to the small bathroom on that level was a linen cupboard and a hot-water tank. Ellie rummaged under the cladding to touch the tank. Cold.

"The hot water's been off since the funeral, hasn't it? Is the boiler in the utility room?" she said.

"Yep, I think so. It's not in the kitchen, anyway."

"Okay. Let's see if we can get that switched on and then make the beds up. I'm going to sleep at the front for a change."

Whenever they'd visited, she and Joe had taken rooms at the back, but the others were larger and airier. She didn't want to sleep in Granny Molly's room, though. That could be a guest room. Or Joe could take it. She looked up through the skylight above the stairs, peace settling over her. The summer solstice was only a couple of weeks away, and the sun cast a golden light over the upper hallway.

Back downstairs, they retrieved their mugs of tea and peered at the boiler controls in the utility room.

"Well, the clock is right, and the on and off settings look right, it just needs switching to 'on'. That button?" suggested Ellie, pointing.

She pressed it and waited. A low rumbling sound emerged.

"Well done," said Joe. He shivered slightly. "I know it's June, but the house feels cold."

Ellie stuck her bottom lip out. "Shall we light the stove in the lounge? As I recall, it kicks out a ton of heat, so we could leave the doors open. Take the chill off the place."

"Are there any logs in the house?"

"If not, there are plenty of logs in the store at the back."

A quick scout around the rooms revealed a handful of logs in the basket in the lounge.

"We'll need more than that," said Ellie. "Should we get some in for the study, too?"

"Might as well."

She unlocked the door at the back of the house. Across a gravelled area lay a large outbuilding – the one Ellie intended to use for the business. Slightly nearer to the house was a separate building, one half of which was a garage, accessed from the front of the house. The back area widened out and held a substantial log-store. Joe retrieved log-baskets from the lounge and the study and loaded one up.

"You going to manage this much?" he asked, his brow wrinkling.

The basket had a handle on each side and she grabbed the nearer one, nodding. "Yeah. I may need to do it in stages."

"Okay."

She started towards the door, only Joe pulled in a slightly different direction.

"Where are you going, Ellie?"

"Through the door!"

"Uh, huh? It's not that way!"

She looked up. The door was definitely in front of her and she was about to argue back, but then the whole of the back of the house shimmered and redrew itself in a slightly different conformation. The door back into the house shifted a metre or so to the left.

"What the…?" She put the basket down and rubbed her face. When she re-opened her eyes, the house seemed perfectly normal.

"Ellie?"

"I just had a bizarre vision of the house. The back door was there." She pointed to the kitchen window. "And it was tiny."

"Right." Joe didn't sound convinced. "Can we get these in through the actual door now?"

They staggered with the basket through the back door and across the hallway, before plonking it down next to the stove in the lounge.

Back out in the log-store, they loaded the other basket. Ellie stared at the house, waiting for it to shift and morph again, but it didn't. She shook herself. The light must have been playing tricks, making it appear different. She helped Joe carry the log-basket through to the study.

As they tucked it into the alcove next to the fireplace, Joe scanned the room. Mirroring the upstairs, the rooms at the rear of the house were smaller, with lower ceilings than the rooms at the front. The study window looked out over the gardens and had a prettier aspect than the dining room or the lounge, which only had views of the drive and the road.

"I bet you spend all your time in here. Shame it's not south-facing. Mind you, you could move the dining room stuff in here and have one of the front rooms as your office."

Ellie wrinkled her nose. "I don't think the table would fit in here. It seats about ten and fills the dining room."

"True. Right, I'll go and grab some kindling," said Joe. "I think there was some next to the logs. Pour me another cuppa?"

Ellie poured more tea, then sat at the kitchen table while he dashed out. As she raised her head to sip her tea, the man she'd seen earlier locked gazes with her across the kitchen, then strolled through the wall, exactly where Ellie had thought the door was. A shiver shot down her spine and all the hairs on her arms stood up. Joe breezed back in, then pulled up short.

"Ellie? Are you okay? You're white as a sheet! You look as if you've just seen a ghost!"

She laughed dismissively, but deep down, she knew she'd done exactly that.

7

The following morning, a loud clattering from the kitchen woke Ellie. She pattered downstairs to find Joe rummaging through the kitchen cupboards. Sunlight from the front of the house streamed through the kitchen door, picking out dust motes, and the smell of toast filled her nose.

"Morning. Toast?" Joe asked as she sat at the table.

"Ooh, thanks. Is there still tea in the pot?"

"Yep." He scruffed up her hair as he passed, and she swatted at his hand.

She poured herself a mug and splashed in some milk while Joe located plates. He slithered two rounds of toast on to one and put it on the table in front of her, along with a tub of butter and a jar of jam.

He joined at the table with a second plateful. "Battle plan?"

Ellie buttered her toast. "Business stuff first. I want to have as small a break in that as possible. I have a notice up on the website to say orders won't be going out until next week, but I want to get everything up and running as quickly as possible. Could you set the study up as an office for me? And I might send you out for groceries."

"Study and groceries I can manage. Did you want me to go to Ripon and get some storage for you?"

"Mm. I know we stacked everything in the workshop, but I'm not a hundred per cent sure that's going to be where it stays. I need to check out sockets and everything. Plan where things might go. It might end up more of a design studio."

"Okay. I'll get storage stuff and groceries, while you check out the outbuilding. Then you can unpack all your yarn and get your storeroom how you want it, while I set your office up. We could get it all done by this evening."

She smiled, grateful. "Thank you. I'm not sure I could have done this on my own."

After breakfast, Joe set off to Ripon. Ellie grabbed a notebook, and skirted past the log-store to the other, larger building at the back of the house. It sported new double-glazed windows and doors, but much of the rest of the building could have been there since the original part of the house had been built. Stone-built, it stretched away from the house, with a door at each end. Granny Molly had originally had the place done up to use as a summer-house, and a wicker sofa and two chairs still sat at one end. The previous day, Ellie and Joe had piled all the boxes of yarn at the other end.

Her footsteps echoed on the concrete floor as she walked around. She scanned the walls, but there were no radiators or any other form of heating. Although the morning sun made the space warm, it would be cold in there come winter. The rough original stonework hadn't been plastered, but the building had electricity. All the wiring was external to the walls, in neat white trunking. She counted sockets, mentally plugging in all of her equipment. It wasn't over-furnished with sockets, but there were enough. There was no water supply, though. If she converted this building to a dyeing workshop, it would require some renovations. She circled slowly, trying to figure out where the nearest water supply would be.

She strolled down to the far end where the wicker furniture lay, talking to herself. "If I could get water to here, I could use this area for the dyeing process. I think it's going to be too cold in here for drying or for storage in winter, though, unless I add some form of heating. Maybe I should store yarn in one of the rooms in the house."

She jotted some notes and drew some sketches, then turned to go back to the house. She froze. The ghost she'd seen the day before stood less than a metre in front of her, though, of course, he couldn't see her. He strode purposefully towards the other end of the workshop, passing straight through Ellie. She felt nothing as he walked through her, but something made her stumble. She turned in time to see him stagger and look behind him, as if searching for what had caused him to lose his footing. He stared directly at her, making her heart race. Then he vanished.

She shook herself. "Why on earth would he be able to see you? He's either your over-active imagination playing tricks, or he *is* a ghost. But what kind of ghost trips over the people he's haunting?"

***

By late afternoon, they had finished most of the unpacking. In the morning, while Joe had constructed the flat-pack storage he'd bought, Ellie had unpacked all her clothes. After lunch, Ellie carried all the boxes of yarn to the back bedroom. Her legs ached from going up and down the stairs so many times, but now she'd unpacked and sorted all the yarn, her stress levels had dropped. The sight of all her yarns, sorted by colour and weight and neatly organised in the new storage, warmed her heart.

Joe popped his head around the door. "I've done as much as I can. I've emptied what was in the desk into boxes and they're on the dining room table. The Wi-Fi is up and running, and your laptop and printer are ready to go. You need to clear the bookshelves if you want to use them, and there's one box of your paperwork that I haven't unpacked, but you can get online, check orders, print stuff, and generally run things from there."

She stretched out a leg as she stood, wincing at the pain of the blood recirculating. "Thank you. For coming up; for shifting so many boxes; for setting everything up."

He smacked a kiss on to the top of her head. "Isn't that what big brothers are duty bound to do? Right. I need a beer. Want one?"

"Glass of wine?"

She eased out her other leg and followed him downstairs. As she turned at the bottom of the stairs, she caught her breath. The ghost stood in the middle of the back hallway, looking straight at her. She shook herself. He couldn't see her. How could he?

Nonetheless, she waved at him, waggling her fingers. "Hello."

His eyes widened, and he took a step back, bringing his hand

36

up to cover a birthmark on the left side of his face.

And then he returned the wave.

Ellie dropped the notebook in her hands, and it clattered to the floor. The man's eyes followed it. She leaned on the wall, her heart pounding. *How* could he have seen her? And the birthmark… the little boy she'd seen when she was a kid also had a birthmark on their face. Granny Molly's words came back to her: *"Do you still see him? He's all grown up now and so handsome."* Was she seeing the same little boy, only now a man? She raised her head. He hadn't moved. He stood, the whites of his eyes showing, chewing his lip. Before she could wave again, a series of colourful lights filled the space between them and the image of the man dissolved.

She steadied her breathing. Surely, she'd imagined it. She scoured the hallway, but the illusion had gone, as had all the coloured lights.

"Get a grip, Ellie," she muttered.

Joe leaned out from the kitchen. "Ellie? Who are you talking to?"

"No one. Just myself."

She picked up the dropped notebook and joined him in the kitchen. He poured her a sizeable glass of wine and she picked it up, her hand still unsteady. Joe clinked his glass of beer against it. "To new beginnings."

"To new beginnings," she murmured, her mind still on the ghost.

"You okay?"

"Mm." She rubbed the back of her neck. "I think the place might be haunted."

His brows crept up. "Seriously?"

"Yeah, seriously. He's about your height. Light reddish-brown hair. Looks like he's from history."

"From history?" Joe frowned. "What do you mean?"

"He looked like he was from a re-enactment or a film or something. He had a waistcoat on over a loose shirt, trousers that stopped just below his knees, long boots, and his hair was tied back in a ribbon. I dunno. I got the impression he was from the seventeen hundreds or something."

"Was the house even built that long ago?"

"Maybe."

The house was Georgian and Victorian, according to the papers from the solicitors, and 'Georgian' covered a lot of kings and a lot of years. Including the seventeen hundreds.

Joe sipped his beer, his dark brown eyes on her. "There's no such thing as ghosts. Whatever Granny Molly said."

No, her scientific, everything-has-an-explanation brother wouldn't believe in ghosts.

But she'd just waved at *someone* who had waved back at her and then vanished.

8

At lunchtime the next day, Joe and Ellie sauntered down to the village. Light clouds scudded past and a fresh breeze ruffled their hair as they walked. It might be sunny, but the day wasn't warm and Ellie was glad to have grabbed a cardigan before they left.

They strolled along a road lined with foaming Queen Anne's Lace, or 'cow parsley' as Ellie thought of it, the birds twittering away in the trees in the hedgerow drowning out the rumble of the odd car that passed.

Joe glanced up at the canopy of leaves. "I'd forgotten how noisy sparrows could be."

He sounded gruff, but his shoulders and face had softened. Was he becoming more enamoured with the idea of living in the country? Would Granny Molly's prediction come true? He did contract work as a hydrologist, and although Ellie was never entirely sure she understood what he did, there must be similar work near here, surely.

They pottered through the village together, reminiscing about childhood holidays. The two of them had always loved the place, with its history and soft vanilla-coloured stone buildings. A cross in the centre of the square commemorated the village's first charter, allowing a market to be held in 1250, although the village went back further. Ellie and Joe paused to read the plaque on the side of the town hall, describing the discovery of an ancient cemetery dating from the 7th century.

"I remember this," said Joe. "There was a telly program about it, wasn't there?"

"Mm."

Ellie glanced around. Only a portion of the cemetery had been excavated. More bodies were believed to lie under the surrounding buildings. Presumably, everyone had forgotten about the cemetery when they were built. She shivered at the thought of all the skeletons under the houses.

Some of the buildings had remained largely unchanged over the years, though the roofs must have been thatched originally and now were slate. The village wasn't large, but it had an impressive variety of shops and small businesses. One had a board displaying index cards in the window, and Ellie peered at them. People offering their services; someone asking everyone to look out for a missing cat; reminders about various local activities. The main part of the village clustered around the market square. The village had newer houses further out, but the buildings in the centre dated back to the 18th century.

"Shall we have lunch in the haunted cafe?" asked Joe, grinning at her.

Ellie gave him a pointed look. "I didn't think you believed in ghosts."

'The haunted cafe' sat in the corner of the market square, with tables inside and out. The front of the cafe faced north, and it was a touch too chilly in the shade to sit out, so the two of them went in. Joe needed to duck sharply to avoid the low lintel. According to legend, the ghost of Janet Shaw, a murdered young woman, was said to run screaming through the building. Something about the story tickled Ellie's brain, but she couldn't quite pinpoint what.

"Hello, you two!"

The woman at the counter beamed at them as they entered, giving Ellie a warm feeling. Jill, who was roughly the same age as Ellie's mum, had run the cafe for years. As Ellie sat, she remembered Jill had a daughter about her age, but she couldn't recall her name.

Joe took the seat next to her. "Hi, Jill. How are you?"

"Oh, mustn't grumble. Is that you both moved in then? I heard on the grapevine that Molly had left the house to you."

No, there were no secrets that could be kept in a village.

40

"Well, Ellie has. I'm just helping her settle in."

"You not moving in too? I'd heard the house had been left to the pair of you."

Joe smiled his 'my business, not yours' smile and said nothing. Jill pinched her lips together and nodded.

"Soup today is lentil, and the quiche is ham and cheese."

A plastic stand on the table held a printed card, outlining the ghost story. Ellie picked it up and read. Janet Shaw lived in the building during the late 18th century when it was a bakery. The local blacksmith had asked her to marry him, but Janet had cheated on him before the wedding and got pregnant. Knowing the child wasn't his, the blacksmith had bludgeoned her to death with one of his hammers. The village had been so angry about her death – Janet being the salt of the earth, as all murdered people are as soon as they're dead, regardless of whether they'd been horrible in life – that they'd rushed to the blacksmith's forge and killed him.

The Old Forge was now Rose Cottage. Presumably an attempt by subsequent residents to distance themselves from the stories.

Ellie passed the information card to Joe, who read it, then smirked at her. "Maybe our house *is* haunted – by the murderous blacksmith! Maybe that's who you saw last night!"

She took the card off him and put it back on the table. "As I said, *you* don't believe in ghosts. And anyway, if he *was* going to haunt the house, wouldn't he be wailing or screaming, echoing when the mob attacked him, not just wandering around looking normal?"

A bell jangled as the door opened, and a slim woman around Ellie's age, with wilfully wavy light brown hair, entered. She'd been at Granny Molly's funeral and had been visibly upset throughout, but Ellie couldn't quite place her.

"Hi, Liz," said Joe, startling the newcomer.

"Joe! And Ellie! Hello. Is that you both here now?"

Liz, Jill's daughter. Ellie sifted back through her memories. Hadn't Joe and Liz had a holiday romance when they were teenagers? Liz's cheeks had a faint blush, but then, many women seemed to react that way to Joe.

"I've just moved in." Ellie found her tongue.

"Oh. I'd heard the house had gone to both of you."

41

Neither sibling responded. Liz turned to her mum and handed her a bag. "Salad. Like you asked."

"Thanks, Liz."

"You knew Molly well, didn't you?" asked Joe, catching Liz's attention before she left. He nodded to the free chair at their table, inviting her to join them.

"Oh, thanks, but I have to run. I just popped in over my lunch break to drop that off." Liz flapped a hand towards the counter. "Yes. Molly asked me to help her research the house. She was a lovely woman."

Her blue eyes brightened with tears and she blinked hard.

"Did you want to come over some time?" said Ellie. "I'd be really interested in what you found out."

"Sure." She fished out her phone. "Give me your number?"

Ellie held her hand out for the phone, called her own mobile, then hung up and handed it back. "There you go."

"Thanks. Sorry. I have to run. See you soon?"

Was it Ellie's imagination, or had that been directed at Joe more than her? "Yep. See you soon."

Liz dashed out, making the bell jangle a second time. Joe raised his brows at her.

"Get you, being all sociable. Normally, you rely on me to do all the talking."

Ellie punched his arm. "Shut up. It's not like I don't know her at all. We played together as kids. And what she's found out about the house might be interesting."

"What do you want to know about the house?"

She shrugged. "Just general stuff. It's a bit of a weird layout and I wondered if Molly was right that the back half was the original building and the front half had been added on afterwards."

Joe stuck his lip out. "Maybe. That would explain the double hall and the fact the ceilings are different heights. I wonder how old the place is."

Given the history of the area, she would bet that the oldest parts of Rose Cottage had been built in the 18th century. Maybe Liz would know more.

"Did you and Liz have a thing? When you were teenagers?" asked Ellie.

Her brother pinked lightly. "Um. Mm." He rubbed his index finger under his nose, then rested his chin on his palm. "Yes. I was sixteen, she was fifteen. All very innocent, as I recall. She probably doesn't even remember."

Oh, she remembers alright.

Jill came over with a pad and pen. "Are you ready to order?"

Ellie was. Joe scoured the menu while she ordered. Once Jill had returned to the bar area, Joe tilted his head at her. "I can't remember when I last saw you look so relaxed. Must be the country air."

"That. Or the fact I've jointly inherited an amazing house with space to expand the business," she murmured, fiddling with the edge of the plastic stand on the table.

"Either way, it's good to see you happy."

Jill brought over drinks and Ellie took a sip of locally produced apple juice, savouring the cool crispness on her tongue. "What about you? At least twice now you've mentioned coming down here. Would you consider moving?"

He shrugged. "I don't know. Not immediately. I've too many things going on."

"Long-term?"

"Maybe. I'd forgotten just how beautiful it was down here." A slight shadow crossed his face. "It almost feels like home. Weirdly."

Ellie nearly choked on her drink. For Joe to consider *anywhere* other than his house with Hayley as 'home' was a major shift. She chewed things over. Could this be a fresh start for *both* of them? If Joe moved here too, could he finally leave his ghosts behind?

Had she moved here only to acquire one?

9

A couple of days after they'd walked into the village, Joe had encouraged Ellie to call Liz.

"You need to make friends here. I'm not going to be staying here forever. You knew each other as kids, so it's not as if she's a total stranger," he nagged. "And you said you wanted to ask her about the research she'd done on the house for Granny Molly."

Ellie threw her hands up. "Okay! I'll call her."

So, she'd called, and now they were sitting in the lounge, waiting for Liz to arrive. Warm morning sun bathed the room with golden light and made the room cosy and welcoming. It had rapidly become Ellie's favourite room in the house, and she often took her laptop out of the study to work in there. Ellie checked the clock, her nerves fluttering. At least Joe was there. He could always talk for Britain.

Bang on time, the doorbell rang. Joe glanced up from the sofa opposite. "Are you going to get that? Or am I?"

She scrambled up to answer the door.

"Hi, Liz! Come on in."

Liz beamed at her, crossing the threshold into the small outer hall and unwinding a Paisley-print scarf from around her neck. "Hi. God, it's weird being back here."

Ellie's heart sank. "Oh. Of course. I didn't think. Sorry."

She should have asked Liz to meet in the village, rather than here. The place must be full of memories for her. For a moment, Ellie froze. Neither she nor Joe had moved anything much. Was

44

that worse? Would it feel less like Liz was walking back into Molly's house if Ellie had changed things around a bit?

"Do you mind coming here?" Ellie asked. "I'm so sorry. I should have realised. We could have met in the village."

Liz smiled reassuringly. "It's fine. It's just a bit odd after not being here for so long."

"Come on through. Joe's in the lounge. Can I make you a tea or a coffee?"

"A coffee would be great. Just milk, thanks."

Ellie showed her into the lounge. Joe jumped to his feet, holding his hand out. "Hello again."

"Hello."

Ellie glanced between them. *Both* of them had blushed.

"I'm making Liz a coffee," she said. "Do you want one?"

He nodded, then indicated for Liz to sit on the sofa opposite him. Ellie left them to it, glad to escape to the kitchen and let Joe break the ice.

As she spooned coffee granules into mugs in the kitchen, Joe's laugh boomed out from the lounge, filling the space. What had amused him so much? He hadn't laughed like that since Hayley died. Ellie finished making the drinks, her heart lifting. Joe was still laughing when she carried the tray of coffees through. She put it down on the wooden trunk that served as a low table, then passed Liz a mug.

"You sound happy," Ellie murmured, handing him a drink and easing into the space next to him.

"Liz was reminding me of when we'd all gone with her brother Sam to hunt for some mythical mill building and Sam fell in the beck. Do you remember? You helped me fish him out."

Ellie's turn to laugh. "Yeah, I remember. Though, as I recall, you did most of the work. Mum was less impressed with your heroism when you paddled muddy water through the house."

Liz chuckled, then peered around the room. "You haven't changed a thing. Mind you, you only got up here about a week ago, didn't you? Have you got plans? Are you staying? Or will you sell?"

"Stay," said Joe. "We both love the place. And Mum would kill us if we sold it."

"Are you both moving in?"

Joe shook his head. "Just Ellie. My work's keeping me further north."

Liz blew on her coffee. "What do you do? If you don't mind me asking."

Joe ran a hand through his hair, then flattened it back down. "I'm a hydrologist. I study rainfall patterns and water – rivers and so on. Predict flood risks, or drought risks. Amongst other things. Honestly, it's too dull to explain."

"No, I know what one is. I'm a geography teacher in Ripon."

A slow smile crept over Joe's face. "Finally! Someone who will understand what I'm on about if I talk about work!"

Liz turned to Ellie. "What about you?"

Ellie swallowed, her pulse rate rising. "I dye yarn and design knitting patterns. Joe's jumper is one of my designs."

Joe sported a Fair Isle patterned sweater with intricate designs, and Liz pulled an appreciative face.

"In fairness, Joe knitted it," said Ellie. "But I designed the pattern."

"*Joe* knitted it?"

"*Another one who believes knitting is only a hobby for women,*" mused Ellie.

"Mm. He's an excellent knitter," she said. "Better than me. Especially on stuff like that."

"We have a Knit and Natter group in the village. It meets in the cafe every other Monday night. You'd both be very welcome. Our next meet-up is this Monday coming."

"Thank you," said Ellie.

"I'm not here for long," added Joe. "But I'll come along this week. What time?"

"We usually start about half six, and stop for tea and biscuits about half seven. It officially finishes at half eight, but it can be a bit variable." Liz caught Ellie's eye. "You never know, you could get some new customers for your yarn and patterns."

"Maybe. I'd prefer to just go for the chat, though. I don't really know anyone here. It would be nice to meet a few more people."

"Come along on Monday and I'll introduce you to some people. There are about a dozen of us who go. About half are under fifty and the other half are over seventy. I don't know why

46

people in-between don't knit." She looked sheepish. "It's all women. I'm not sure I've met a bloke who can knit before."

Joe grinned and sipped his coffee. His wedding ring glinted and Liz's slightly flirtatious body language towards him immediately switched to more reserved. Ellie didn't think her brother had registered either the flirting or the change.

"Do you have kids?" Liz asked Ellie.

"No. Neither of us do," she said, heading off a question that Joe wouldn't want to answer. He and Hayley had been trying for children when she'd been killed. Joe flashed her a grateful look. Liz's gaze rested on his wedding ring, but she didn't pry any further.

She turned back to Ellie, a mischievous gleam in her eye. "Have you seen the ghost yet?"

Joe snorted.

"Did Molly say the house was haunted to you, as well?" Ellie ignored Joe's scoffing.

"Mm. Though I never saw anything myself. She said that she saw someone she believed was one of the original occupants of the house. She asked me to help her trace who'd had the house over the years and we went back to pretty much when the place was built. I suspect she either got muddled with that, or had an over-active imagination."

"Ellie thinks she's seen a man dressed in old-fashioned clothing," said Joe.

"It must just have been a trick of the light." Ellie fired a 'Shut up!' look at him.

"Oh, Molly said she saw someone very like that description," said Liz. "But then, she also said a lot of other things that were clearly nonsense, like being able to see the future."

Joe smiled sadly. "Mm. She always told us she could see the future. Apparently, Ellie's going to fall in love with a tawny-haired man."

"And you?" Liz raised her brows.

Joe shut down, and Ellie stepped in swiftly. "As you say, it's all nonsense. Do you know when the house was built? We know it's from the Georgian era, but not which King George."

Liz finished her coffee and put the mug back on the tray.

"There's certainly information that there was a forge here in the late seventeen hundreds. The documentation is fragmented, but it seems the forge fell into disuse by the early 1800s."

"Is that because the blacksmith was a murderer who got killed by an angry mob?" asked Joe, a sparkle back in his eye.

Liz laughed. "Ah. You've read Mum's ghost story in the cafe. There may be some truth in it all, but who knows? There are no records of that. It's all just folklore. I don't believe there's even a ghost in the cafe building. All I could find out for Molly was that this place was in a state of disrepair before being renovated and extended in the 1800s." She glanced around her. "As far as I could work out, the back half of the house – the kitchen and study, and the two bedrooms at the back – were the original part, and all the front half of the house was added later. The building next to the garage and the log-store was where the forge was. So Molly said, though I couldn't find any documents that showed that. I don't know where she got her information from."

Ellie's heart-rate quickened. "Did she document her research?"

"I don't know. I think so, but I've never seen any notes or anything. Molly kept a diary. I think they're all in the study."

They were, high up on the bookshelves. Ellie hadn't looked at them yet.

"If you *do* find anything, maybe you could think about donating it to the community heritage group?" said Liz.

"Oh. Um. Let me think about it? I mean, other than her diaries, I don't know that there *is* anything. I don't think it would be right to give her diaries to the group. Not so soon."

Liz flapped a hand. "No, no! I meant her history research. If you find anything interesting, let me know? I'm absolutely sure that Molly knew far more about the house than she let on." She peeked at her watch. "I'm sorry, I'm going to have to go. But you'll both come to Knit and Natter on Monday?"

"We'd love to," said Joe. "Thank you for inviting us."

At the door, Liz twisted her scarf around her neck again. "See you Monday. Honestly, Ellie, feel free to bring stuff with you – patterns and wool and so on. Or at least wear your designs! Joe's sweater is amazing."

"Thanks."

Ellie waved Liz off and returned to the lounge, where she found Joe back to working on a sock, the needles clicking rapidly. She sat on the sofa opposite, a faint scent of Liz's perfume puffing up from the cushions as she did so.

"When are you going to take your wedding ring off?" she said, hoping that Joe wasn't going to end up grumpy with this conversation.

Joe put the sock down in his lap and took his glasses off, unsmiling. "Where's this going?"

Ellie sighed. "It's not 'going' anywhere. I'm just asking when you might move on. You're a nice guy. You're kind, you're smart, you're *fairly* good-looking." She pulled a face to show him she was teasing him. "And you're still young. Liz clearly liked you. And then she saw your wedding ring and closed up."

"I'll take it off when I'm ready to." He put his glasses back on and picked his knitting up, his way of signalling that he considered the discussion was over.

Ellie drew in a long breath, not quite done. "I haven't heard you laugh the way you did with Liz, for *ages*. And your body language was open. Not like a married man would have been. The messaging can be a bit mixed."

Joe hadn't looked at her while she said all this, and his jaw bunched as he gritted his teeth.

"Joe, you're my brother, and I love you. I'm not meaning to upset you. I want you to be happy. And only the other week you told me you were lonely."

The needles clicked furiously. Ellie waited him out.

"I am lonely," he said, eventually.

Ellie's heart surged, but she kept quiet. He laid the sock down again and drew a deep breath.

"I miss coming home to someone. I miss talking." He closed his eyes and screwed his face up as if in pain. "And I *yearn* to have children. Deep down in my bones, Ellie." He blinked hard. "But I still feel like it would be cheating on Hayley."

She moved to sit next to him and slipped her arm around his shoulders. "Hayley would never have wanted you to be lonely. It's four years, Joe. No one could ever accuse you of moving on too soon."

Joe stayed silent, and Ellie rubbed circles on his broad back.

"It's your house," she said. "You'll *never* be able to have another woman in it, because it will always be yours and Hayley's. It's a huge anchor, tethering you. But you have this place now. You could move."

He tilted his head to look at her. "I know. I've been thinking about it. It just feels like a huge step."

"Yeah, I get that. But there's more than enough space for both of us here. Come and take an extended break down here when your current contracts finish? Perhaps a bit of space away would help."

He nodded, his face still drawn. She squeezed him. Was he *finally* going to move on? If he really wanted kids, he would have to, though at least men had less of a biological clock to worry about.

"What about you?" asked Joe, interrupting her thoughts. "When are *you* going to find someone new?"

She should have known he would turn it around and ask her the same thing.

"It's been over two years," he went on. "You can't *still* be moping about Simon."

Her turn to grit her teeth. She'd been engaged to her only long-term partner, Simon, and then, two months before the wedding, she came home to find him in bed with someone else. Ellie moved out just before covid hit the world and lock-down started. The only saving grace had been that she'd had more time to focus on the business.

"I don't think I *moped* about Simon. I just wanted to kill him."

Joe snorted. "Nah, you moped. I mean, we *all* wanted to kill him, but you can't claim you weren't hurt. And there's been no one since, has there?"

"That's less because I still have feelings for Simon and more because I'm happier on my own."

Joe's gaze zeroed in on her. "I thought *you* wanted kids, too."

She looked away.

"Hey! You're the one who brought the subject up. If you're going to ask me about when I might start dating again, don't be surprised if I ask you about when you're going to move on from

Simon!"

She held her hands up. "Fine. Sorry."

He was right, though. She couldn't keep on assuming all men would treat her the way Simon had. At some point, she had to have the courage to let someone get close again; had to allow herself to be vulnerable again.

She sighed. It was just so much easier to keep the barriers up. People can't hurt you if you don't let them in.

10

" Come on! This is your tribe! If you'll fit in anywhere, it's with a group of people who meet up for knitting, tea, and cake!"

Ellie scowled at her brother, but he was right. If she couldn't make friends at a Knit and Natter group, she wouldn't make them anywhere.

Joe shook his head at her and leaned his shoulder against the door to the cafe. Ellie tried to unwind the knot in her belly and followed him in.

About a dozen people sat at tables around the room and they all looked up, eyes curious, especially at Joe's presence. Ellie scoured the room, hoping to see Liz, finally spotting her at a table towards the back.

Liz scrambled up. "Oh, brilliant! You came. Ladies, this is Joe and Ellie. They're the ones who've inherited Molly's place."

The siblings waved and Ellie shot a desperate glance at Joe, her tongue frozen. He half rolled his eyes.

"Hi, everyone," he said. "Is there allocated seating, or can we sit anywhere?"

"Oh, just sit anywhere," said Liz.

Joe made his way over to Liz's table and sat, making space for Ellie next to him. Liz rattled through everyone's name, and Ellie promptly forgot all of them. Her palms were clammy as she unpacked her wool.

"Do you both knit?" asked one of the older women, peering at Joe over the top of her glasses.

52

"Yep. Ellie's a designer, and she hand-dyes yarn, too. This is one of her designs." Joe tugged on the bottom edge of his sweater to show more of the design.

The room filled with oohs and ahs and interest switched from Joe to Ellie. Her stomach tightened, and she sat down.

"Are all of your designs Fair Isle?" asked a woman knitting a complicated lace shawl. "I'm Carol, by the way. I'm sure you'll have forgotten all our names, they came in such a rush."

Ellie's words crawled out. "Hi. Er, no. Some are cable, some are plain. I have some shawl patterns, too."

Joe winked at her, opening his bag and retrieving the sweater he was working on, along with a wide selection of Ellie's yarns.

"Ooh, are those your yarns?" A woman their age craned her neck to get a better view. "They're fabulous. Can I have a squish?"

Joe passed them over, and the knots of tension in Ellie's chest eased a fraction. Joe was right. This *was* her tribe.

Over the evening, she learned everyone's name and had a long chat with Carol about the qualities of different yarns. Joe talked to everyone, but more to Liz than anyone else. One woman asked if Ellie could bring her patterns to the next meeting, and two women asked if they could come up to the house to see the full range of yarns.

"Of course." Ellie handed over her number. "Just ring ahead in case I'm not in."

"You're in The Old Forge, right?" asked Rain, a woman with purple hair and tie-dyed clothes, crocheting what appeared to be a bag in a lurid orange yarn.

"Yes. Well, it's actually called Rose Cottage."

Rain clicked her tongue. "That house has a really odd aura. It's been built on two ley lines."

Next to her, Joe stifled a guffaw, dipping his head and pretending to focus intently on the knitting in his hands.

"Molly said it was haunted," chipped in Liz.

"Wouldn't surprise me. You shouldn't build on nodes," said Rain darkly.

Joe swallowed another laugh, and Ellie kicked him under the table.

"Have you been up to the house? Did you know Molly?" Ellie

53

said. The house always felt welcoming to her, not odd.

Rain shook her head vigorously. "No. It would unbalance my energies."

Joe spluttered, earning him a sharp look from Rain.

"How do you know it has an odd aura if you've not been in it?" he asked, composing himself a fraction.

"You can just *tell*. It's built on a node!"

"Well, it feels fine to me," said Ellie, wanting to end the topic.

Rain muttered to herself, and the conversations around the room moved on.

All too soon, the two hours were up and the group dispersed. Rain had studiously ignored both Joe and Ellie since her proclamations about the house, and she stomped off across the village square as soon as the meeting finished.

Liz paused by the entrance to the cafe. "Hope you enjoyed coming. It's nice to have fresh faces here. And maybe you can sell some of your amazing patterns and wool."

"Maybe. But I was here just to meet people. Thanks for inviting us."

"Are you okay getting home? Did you want us to walk you back?" asked Joe.

Liz laughed. "You're fine. I'm only up there. But thanks. Goodnight."

She waved and set off across the square.

Joe tilted his head at Ellie. "Well done. You survived."

"So did you. I thought you were going to choke to death about the nodes."

They turned towards the road out of the village which led to Rose Cottage, Joe still sniggering. "Ley lines my arse. And how the hell can you claim a house has an 'odd aura' when you've never set foot in it?"

"I honestly thought you were going to implode when she said her energies would be upset."

"Mm. I suspect she is *not* going to be a customer. Mind you, she was crocheting something with the most horrible acrylic that I think I've ever seen, so she wouldn't like your stuff."

"She didn't like wool at all. She's vegan. She wouldn't even touch the skeins I took."

Joe tipped his head skywards, holding his breath for a moment. "Don't get me started."

They walked down the road, the sun still an hour from setting, gilding the edges of the flowers. Ellie sneaked a peek at her brother. "You and Liz were getting on well."

"Oh. Were we? Um, she's nice. I like her."

Ellie chewed the inside of her cheek, trying to remember the last time she'd seen Joe so flustered. "She is. I like her too. I think we might be friends."

"Oh. Good."

They reached Rose Cottage and Ellie opened the door, smirking. "Well, here we are. Home sweet home. Built on a node and ready to upset our energies."

As she stepped into the hall, the ghost disappeared into the kitchen, surrounded by a pattern of coloured lights. Ellie caught her breath. Maybe Rain had a point, after all.

11

That weekend, Ellie finished collecting together the last of the yarns for a large order that had come in overnight. She scanned the racks of skeins in the back bedroom, mentally noting which were getting low, and planning when she would need to dye new batches. Joe had gone out walking for the day, leaving her on her own.

Not entirely on her own, she thought. The ghost had appeared a few times since they'd waved at each other. Once, he walked through the door to the study, even though it was closed. Another time, he'd been working at a bench in the outhouse, although Ellie couldn't quite determine what he was doing. Sometimes he appeared only briefly – barely more than a shimmer. Other times, the entire room kaleidoscoped, disorientating her and making it hard for her to tell reality from mirage. Mostly, he appeared somewhere in between – there, but semi-transparent. He'd always seemed oblivious to her. He certainly hadn't waved at her again, and she was wondering if she'd imagined that.

Joe had found an old OS map in the study and taken himself off for long walks each day. He'd claimed it was so that Ellie could focus on work without tripping over him, but she knew it was because he needed to think. He'd confessed to being lonely, and said it had cut deep when Liz had asked if they had kids. If he was ever going to have children, he *had* to move on, and he had to figure things out for himself. Hence all the walking. She'd worried that the house would be lonely with him out all day, but each time she'd seen the ghost, the house felt *right* somehow. Less empty.

56

Which was daft, because he wasn't really there. *Was* he the infamous blacksmith? His clothes suggested he could be from around the time of the story, and in a couple of glimpses of him, he'd been hammering away at something. She tried not to think of the girl being beaten to death with a hammer.

The yarn order sorted, Ellie grabbed a notebook ready to plan what dyeing she would do. Scenery had always inspired her, and the colours of many of her yarns reflected the wild moors and hillsides of Northern England and Scotland. Now she conjured images of the soft colours in the stonework of the buildings in Masham, and the flower-rich meadows. Having woken early that morning, she'd walked down to the village and captured a series of pictures with her phone, and she scrolled through them, noting down which dyes she might use to recreate them. Some of the dyes she had; others she'd need to order in.

She headed downstairs to order the dyes. She sat at the desk in the study and booted up her laptop, the notebook open next to her. Her favourite spot in the room was the comfy chair in the corner, next to the stove, but that wasn't great for getting any work done. While her laptop warmed up, she looked out over the garden. A gravel area lay near the wood-store and outbuilding, and the garden then extended away to a small grassed area and flower borders. The garden contained mostly trees and shrubs, with a small greenhouse and vegetable plot nearby. There was also a weedy area next to the vegetable plot. Not entirely inspirational, but not distracting, either.

A sound caught her attention, and she frowned. Was that a *horse*? It sounded as if it was at the front of the house. She pushed away from the desk and strolled into the rear hallway, ready to go and peer through the front windows of the house, then blinked, her feet faltering. The archway that led to the front hallway had disappeared. Instead, there was a solid wooden door, as if the outer wall of the house was where the archway should be. She breathed steadily, waiting for the illusion to fade.

It didn't.

Her heart racing, she stepped towards the door and placed her hand against it. Solid. The house smelled different, too. Wood smoke… no… charcoal smoke.

Before she could think about it, a sound behind her made her whirl on the spot.

"You again!" the man said, just as she thought the same thing about him.

The 'ghost' stood on the far side of the kitchen, framed by the back door. Except that wasn't in the right place. He wore mouse-coloured, knee-length trousers, conker-brown leather riding boots, and a woollen waistcoat and jacket. His longish auburn-brown hair was neatly tied at the nape of his neck with a ribbon. A birthmark stained the left side of his face, partially hidden by his slightly scruffy beard and a wavy lock of hair that had escaped from the ribbon.

"Who are you?" He stared at her, his brow crumpled. "Why are you always in my house?"

She hadn't heard his voice before. He had a rich baritone, with a strong Yorkshire accent. She scanned the hallway. The layout was still wrong. What was happening?

"I'm Ellie Stewart. Who are you?"

"Kit Greenwood. What are you doing in my house? How did you get in?"

She paused, her mind reeling. The house... him... how he was dressed. Surely she was dreaming? She pinched her arm. It hurt. An impossible possibility crystallised in her brain.

"What year is this, please?"

He scratched his forehead. "What did you ask?"

Her voice quavered. "What year is it, please?"

He angled his head to the side, his brows knitting. "It is 1762."

The world tilted, and her knees buckled under her. Kit Greenwood shot forwards to catch her. "Lass?"

When she came around, she lay on the floor in the back hallway, her skin clammy with sweat. She sat up cautiously, her fingertips exploring her scalp. No lumps or bumps. She counted her breath in and out, her mind swimming. She'd seen her ghost in the flesh. She'd *spoken* to him. He'd said it was 1762.

She shook herself. She'd fainted and then dreamed it. How could she *possibly* have been in 1762?

She picked herself up off the floor and walked back into the study. Her gaze drifted over the view out of the window, but her brain ran back over what had happened. Should she log everything? Maybe there was a pattern to when or where she had visions of the ghost.

She jiggled the mouse to wake up her laptop, and created a new document, where she wrote descriptions of all the encounters she'd had, from fleeting glimpses and the odd shifts in the house, through to today's experience. Once she'd finished, she leaned back in the seat. He had the exact same birthmark as the little boy she thought she'd seen when she was a child. Was her brain playing tricks on her? Imagining him as an adult, the way she'd imagined him as a boy?

1762.

Kit Greenwood.

Her tawny-haired boy, all grown up?

The blacksmith who murdered Janet Shaw?

He'd said that he kept seeing *her*. How? You couldn't haunt backwards, could you? How could she be a ghost to him in 1762 when she wasn't alive until centuries later?

Oh, heavens. Was Rain right? Did the house stand on crossing ley lines, causing it to whirl through time? She snorted. If that were the case, the house would be renowned.

Could she *choose* to see him? So far, it had seemed entirely random and accidental.

She finished her tea and took the empty mug through to the kitchen, then stood in the back hallway and squared her shoulders.

"Kit Greenwood? Are you there?"

Silence. She peered hopefully at the walls, willing the layout to shift and morph. Nothing.

"Who are you?" she murmured. "And why are you a ghost?"

Time to find out.

12

The order for new dyes temporarily abandoned, Ellie surveyed the bookcase in the study, her hands on her hips. Granny Molly's dog-eared notebooks filled an upper shelf, along with cardboard folders stuffed full of paper.

She retrieved a chair from the kitchen to stand on and lifted down all the notes. It took several trips, but she carried them through to the large table in the dining room. The books were filled with handwritten notes in Granny Molly's spidery writing, and the cardboard folders had print-outs of maps and articles from the internet, all jammed in together. Ellie leafed through it all, but found no rhyme or reason to the pages. She returned to the study to get the box of papers Joe had cleared from the desk. Maybe they might help.

She made a large pot of tea, and settled in for the long haul, starting with trying to date everything and sort it into different time-frames. Most of the ephemera was from the 20th century, and less interesting to her. Ellie gathered together all the old OS maps or print-outs showing the village's layout and changes over the years. Various photographs of the village and its residents spanned the century, and Ellie smiled at the costumes. No one was dressed like Kit Greenwood had been, though.

By the end of the morning, she had four distinct piles: Granny Molly's notebooks, a pile for bits and pieces relating to the 20th century, one for the 19th century, and a small heap for the 18th. The most interesting pile was the last one, but it was thin on contents. None of the maps showing the village in any detail went back as far as she wanted. One that purported to being from 1801 had stumped her for a few minutes until she realised that, unconventionally, the top of the map represented west not north.

It took a while for Ellie to get her eye in and be able to read Granny Molly's handwriting easily. The notebooks documented her research, tracing the house's owners back through the years. Ellie nabbed several sheets of paper from the printer in the study, to make her own notes. The most recent history had been straightforward, since much of it had been included in the deeds for the house. That vein of information petered out in the early nineteen hundreds, and Granny Molly had had to chase things through other sources. Some of the initial research also included information from census data, accessed via online genealogy sites, and Ellie got sidetracked reading about the livelihoods of those who had lived in the house over the years. Interestingly, none of them were blacksmiths. Ellie matched notes in Granny Molly's books with print-outs and photocopies in the ephemera, amused to read Granny Molly's grumbles about how annoying some of the online sites could be.

By late afternoon, she'd followed Granny Molly's research back to the early 1800s but needed to unkink her neck and stretch her legs before tackling the final stretch. So far, there had been no Kit Greenwoods amongst the names. She made a fresh cup of tea, grabbed a couple of biscuits, and took a walk around the garden to clear her head. She peered at the house and outbuildings, hoping to see the ghost, but to no avail.

Her break over, she returned to the dining room. The later parts of Granny Molly's research covered the late 1700s and included information on a Christopher Greenwood, also sometimes known as Kit. Ellie sat up straighter, but a little further reading revealed this was not the Kit Greenwood she thought she had met, but the son of someone called Thomas Greenwood. Next to Thomas's name, Granny Molly had drawn a star, linking the page to another, a little further on in the book. Ellie turned to the marked page, squinting at Granny Molly's writing.

"I think Thomas is the other Kit Greenwood's brother. He's the one who put up the stone for Kit."

Ellie frowned. What stone? She flipped backwards and

forwards through the book, trying to find anything more on it, eventually finding some notes on a Kit Greenwood born in 1735. Ellie did the maths. In 1762, he would be 27 and the man she'd spoken to this morning certainly appeared to be the right age. A chill rippled over her skin when Granny Molly's notes indicated he was a blacksmith. Ellie read on.

'I can find no death information for Kit. Thomas, yes. There is a family stone in the churchyard. But there is nothing on it for Kit. Just his 'disappeared' stone.'

Ellie rubbed her brow. What on earth was his 'disappeared stone'? After the mob killed him, had his body never been found? Was that why he was a ghost? But wouldn't he be trapped as a ghost more closely linked to his violent death? Shouldn't he be screaming or something? Not strolling around. Granny Molly didn't furnish her with any more information, and she closed the books, frustrated. She called Liz.

"Hi, Ellie. How are you?"

"Oh, fine thanks. I've been trying to sort Molly's local history stuff into some semblance of order for you, and wondered if you wanted to come over sometime and have a look at it all? There's nothing personal in it. She's mostly trying to trace the history of the house, but there are some photos of the village over the years that might be interesting."

"Oh, brilliant. Yes, please." A brief pause followed, then Liz asked, "Will Joe still be there?"

Ellie chewed the inside of her cheek, trying not to laugh. "Yes, if you come up before Saturday. He's going back home then."

"Okay. Um. Well, I'll maybe come over on Friday evening if that's alright?"

Ellie's grin broadened at Liz being so flustered, and she rolled her eyes. Joe *did* have that effect on women.

"Perfect. Walk up and we can share a bottle of wine."

Liz laughed. Ellie rang off, still smirking about Joe and Liz. Mind you, they were well matched. He'd not let out a belly laugh in years, and yet Liz had provoked several on her first visit, and they'd got on like a house on fire at the knitting group.

She took her empty mug to the kitchen. As she dumped it in the sink, the front door banged, and Joe called out a hello.

"Hi! I'm in the kitchen," Ellie called back.

His footsteps paused in the front hallway, then continued.

"What's all the stuff on the dining room table?" he asked as he joined her.

"Granny Molly's research. Liz is coming over on Friday evening to have a look through it all. See if there's anything her history group would be interested in. I don't think there will be much, but there are some old maps and photographs they might like."

"Oh, right. Friday?"

"Mm."

Ellie smiled to herself.

Joe shucked out of his jacket and draped it over the back of a chair, then retrieved a bottle of beer from the fridge. "Anything else interesting in Granny Molly's stuff? And do you want a drink?"

"No, to the drink. As for the notes, I think the murdering blacksmith *did* live here. There was certainly *a* blacksmith living here in the late 1700s, called Kit Greenwood."

Joe pulled a face. "Kit? Is that an unusual name?"

"I don't know. It's a nickname for Christopher, isn't it? Kit Marlowe. And that actor. He's a Christopher, but is called Kit, isn't he?"

Joe shrugged, opening his beer.

"Anyway, Granny Molly's notes said that he disappeared," went on Ellie.

"If he was the one who killed the girl, that's maybe not a surprise. I think I'd disappear if I'd done that." He took a long drink. "Wasn't he killed by an angry mob?"

"So the story goes, according to the thing in the cafe."

"And is this the chap you thought you'd seen? Don't tell me your sweet little boy grew up to be a murderer!" He stuck his tongue into his cheek, widening his eyes at her.

Well, that settled it. She wasn't going to tell him about her weird encounter today.

"How was your walk?"

Joe grinned. "Great thanks. There are so many footpaths around here. I must have walked miles."

"And did it help?"

Caution filled his eyes. "Help?"

"To think about everything. I mean, that's why you've been out tramping through the fields. It's nothing to do with being out of my way while I work."

He scratched the side of his neck, looking as if he was about to deny it, then his expression softened. "Yeah. It helped."

"Good. Now, away and get a shower. You're all 'manly'."

He poked his nose into his top. "Okay. Fair."

She watched him head upstairs, happy. Was he tiptoeing towards moving here when his contracts ended? She hoped so. It would be great to have him closer. And maybe he and Liz *would* get together. Granny Molly was convinced he'd find happiness here.

She chewed her lip. Granny Molly had also been sure she would get together with her 'tawny-haired boy'. How on earth could that happen? He was a murderer who had died hundreds of years ago.

And yet… she'd spoken to him this morning.

13

The following morning, Ellie sat at her desk and booted up her laptop, ready to put in the order for the new dyes that she'd abandoned the day before. Half her mind was on the task at hand; half still mused about whether she had *really* met Kit Greenwood. She leaned back in her seat, rolling her shoulders. As she tipped her head back, the view through the window shifted, as if there were two scenes, one superimposed over the other. The plants in the borders appeared semi-transparent, with a yard and a stable visible through them. The smell of a fire tickled her nose. She sat up and rubbed her face. When she re-opened her eyes, the illusion had gone, as had the scent of the fire.

She dipped her head, breathing deeply. Was she going mad? The house *couldn't* be shifting back and forth in time. Someone would have noticed.

She found her notes about what she needed to order and opened up the website, soon too immersed in the ordering process to worry about peculiar illusions.

As she was about to find her wallet to fill in payment information, a loud metallic banging distracted her. Her eyes flicked to the window. The flowerbeds had gone. The stable had returned. As had the scent of smoke.

Her heart pounding, she pushed her chair back and headed out of the back door by the kitchen.

The gravel area had disappeared, and she stood at one end of a cobbled yard. At the other end was a stone building with a large wooden door standing open to one side. Part of the building overlapped with the footprint of the modern workshop, but about half of it didn't. In the far corner, a raised fire glowed with furious reds, pinks, and yellows, and the scent of burning charcoal filled her nose. Close to the fire stood a solid anvil on a section of gnarled tree-trunk. A wooden batten at about shoulder height ran around the walls, with tools hanging from nails in it, with more tools on a bench in the area that overlapped with her workshop. On the floor by the anvil sat a wooden bucket of water.

Even from where she stood, the heat from the fire warmed Ellie's face. She tiptoed a few paces closer to the forge. A man stood with his broad back to her, pumping a set of bellows with his left hand, his other using tongs to hold a piece of metal in the fire. As she watched, he took the rod out of the fire, held it on the anvil, grabbed a hammer, and walloped the metal, making sparks fly. After several blows, he stuck the metal back in the fire and pumped the bellows again. The embers glowed hot, colour rippling over their surface. From somewhere in the depths of her brain, Ellie remembered that a blacksmith knowing how hot metal was just from its colour, had led to something important being discovered in physics, but she couldn't recall the details.

Was she dreaming? She poked at the cobbles with her toe. Real. She chewed her lip, her heart beating fast. Was she *really* in 1762 again? If so, how the hell did she get back?

As the man turned back to the anvil, Ellie called out, "Kit?"

His head shot up, and he almost dropped the tongs. He turned to face her, his eyes wide. Sweat darkened the neck of his cream shirt above a dark brown leather apron. Ellie's focus rested on the solid hammer in his hand and the muscles of his arms, fear flickering in her belly. She swallowed, her mouth suddenly dry and not from the heat of the fire. She was trespassing, albeit outside of her control, and he was a violent man, wasn't he? Why on earth had she called out to him?

He still stared at her, his rolled-up sleeves revealing tanned, grimy arms, thick with strength. He placed the meaty hammer he'd been wielding only moments earlier on the bench at his side.

"Where did you go? Yesterday," he asked.

"Back to my time."

His frown deepened. "What do you mean? Who are you?"

Her breathing quickened. This *had* to be the blacksmith from the story in the cafe.

"Do you know Janet Shaw?" she blurted out.

He nodded. "Aye, lass. I know Janet. Why?"

Her pulse throbbed, and the vision of the blacksmith's yard faded, layered over her modern workshop.

"Lass?"

The forge vanished, leaving her standing next to her modern workshop. She went in, tottered to one of the wicker chairs and sank down, shaking. She'd spoken to him. He'd heard her and answered. Given that there was no fire here, or anvil, she *must* have been to his time. But *how?*

She leaned on her knees, dizzy. He knew Janet Shaw. He *had* to be the blacksmith that killed her.

The door to the workshop opened, and she whirled around. Joe.

"Hey there. Where'd you go?" he said, coming in, carrying a mug of coffee. He sniffed as he reached her. "And why do you smell of smoke? Where's the fire?"

She stared at him. "You can smell smoke on me?"

"Mm. Have you started smoking?" He sniffed her again. "No, that's not fag smoke. More like charcoal." He hooked a foot around a leg of the other chair in the workshop, drawing it closer, then sat down, wrapping his hands around his mug. "Shame the house shades this place. It'll be bitter in the winter. Maybe you could do with a stove or something."

Ellie clutched the mug he'd brought her. She'd written off the experience of the previous day as her banging her head and hallucinating, and maybe she'd imagined things today, but if Joe could smell smoke on her, she had definitely been near Kit Greenwood's fire. In 1762.

"You okay, sis?"

She smiled weakly. "Yeah. I'm fine, thanks. I was miles away thinking about an order. Thanks for the coffee."

"So, why do you smell of smoke? We don't exactly have close neighbours who could be having a barbecue."

She shrugged. "No idea. Maybe it's from the last time I wore this jumper."

He pushed his bottom lip out, accepting the explanation. "Anyway, apart from bringing you a coffee, I was coming to tell you I'm going into Ripon. Is there anything you want me to get?"

"Food? Give me a few minutes to draw up a list." She stood. "Let's take these back to the kitchen so I can check the fridge and cupboards."

She let Joe lead the way back to the house, then took a long look at the space where she'd seen Kit Greenwood.

She was sharing the house with a murderer.

14

Over the next few days, although the kaleidoscoping lights appeared several times, the house remained in her time, not 1762. Twice, Ellie had seen Kit. He'd walked through the back wall of the kitchen and skidded to a halt when he saw her. The other time he had been working in his forge, though she couldn't work out exactly what he was making. She'd smiled and waved at him. He'd returned the smile uncertainly and had waved back.

So far, all the shifts had been at the back of the house, none in the front, as if the rear archway separating the front hall from the back formed a boundary. Perhaps because the house in 1762 had finished there? At least with the front of the house staying firmly in the modern day, there would be no issue when Liz arrived, as long as she stayed in the lounge. Ellie made a mental note not to end up chatting in the kitchen the way she normally would have in the past.

It was now early evening on Friday and Ellie found herself at her study desk, composing an email to a fellow dyer, asking her for details about the natural dyes she used. This was an aspect of the business that Ellie wanted to expand. She'd started the business using synthetic dyes, but over the last year, she'd pivoted away to focus on using natural plant stuffs and a much more ecologically friendly approach to it all, but there were so many plants and so many variables that affected the resulting colour. She'd been taking notes on how different mordants and modifiers affected the colour and now had a reasonable record with samples of yarn for each combination. However, whatever she tried, she struggled to get a vibrant red from a native plant, frustrating her. Hopefully, her fellow dyer could offer some advice for a method that would remain eco-friendly.

As she typed, coloured lights dancing in the garden caught her eye, and she groaned.

"Oh, here we go. Is the house just going to do its shimmery thing, or am I going to meet the blacksmith again?"

She rubbed her face, torn between wanting to see Kit again, and thinking she shouldn't, given that he was a murderer. When she opened her eyes again, the lights had gone. She breathed deeply, her nose hunting for any trace of a scent of burning charcoal from the forge, but finding none. Half of her was disappointed. The other half was relieved. She had no idea why she went back in time, or, more importantly, how or why she returned to the present day. And Liz was due soon. A time-shifting house was going to play merry hell with her social life unless she could figure out if there was any pattern to it all, and predict when the house would behave, and when it wouldn't.

She finished the email and closed her laptop down, then sauntered through the house, seeking Joe. She found him in the lounge, reading, and she perched on the edge of the sofa. "Liz should be here soon."

Had he just straightened up?

"She's coming to look at Granny Molly's notes, isn't she?" he said. Disingenuously. He knew just fine why she was coming.

"Mm. Though I suspect she chose to come tonight rather than tomorrow, because you're still here."

He didn't reply, but he had a softness about him she hadn't seen in a long time, that warmed her.

Bang on cue, the doorbell rang, and Ellie sprang up to answer it.

"Hi, Liz. Come on in."

"Thanks."

Liz shrugged out of her jacket and Ellie took it from her.

"Joe's in the lounge. Tea? Coffee? Wine? The sun *is* over the yardarm."

"Oh, wine! It's Friday, isn't it?"

Ellie laughed. "Go through. I'll get the drinks."

Liz joined Joe, and cheerful voices filtered through to Ellie. She smiled and took her time getting the drinks.

When she'd spun out getting three glasses and a bottle of wine for as long as she could, she joined them, settling the tray on the trunk in the centre of the room. "Here you go, Liz. How was your week?"

Liz wrinkled her nose. "Mostly okay. Year 8 can be a pain in the neck! How about you?"

"Um. Busy. I'm hoping to get into more natural dyes, so the kitchen has been a bit like a bad chemistry experiment this week, with pans of boiled leaves and some scummy-looking bottles of stuff."

Liz snorted. "Don't use that in your marketing, will you?"

Ellie laughed.

Liz turned to Joe. "And you?"

"Very good, thanks. I've done a lot of walking. Cleared my head a bit."

He didn't elaborate, and neither woman pressed him.

"Molly's notes are still out on the dining room table," said Ellie. "Though there's no rush. We don't use that room. I may convert it to a craft room and yarn store if the back bedroom gets too small, but not immediately."

"Can I have a rummage? Oh! And I brought you something in return. The pamphlet Mum used to write the ghost story from."

Ellie perked up. Maybe there would be more in it than the bare bones on the card in the cafe.

The two women took their drinks through to the dining room and Ellie waited while Liz perused the piles of paper. As anticipated, the old photographs and the maps caught her interest the most.

"Could I take copies of these, please? We have a decent scanner in the heritage group. I can get them done and give you them back."

"Sure. No rush. Take whatever you think will be interesting. Molly's research only really goes back to the beginning of the 19th century. There's not much from earlier than that. About the only thing Granny Molly found out is that the house *was* a blacksmiths originally, which would fit with everyone calling it The Old Forge, even though the house is now called Rose Cottage."

Liz widened her eyes, making a mocking face. "Ooh… you live in the *murderer's* house!"

Ellie rolled her eyes. "Go on. Pack up whatever you want copies of, then let me see this pamphlet."

She helped Liz parcel up the pictures and the maps, then they rejoined Joe in the lounge. Liz drew out a battered pamphlet from her bag. Two sheets of ancient, typewritten paper had been folded in half and stapled at the spine. The front cover boldly claimed it was "The True Story of The Wench and the Blacksmith" with a subtitle of "A Tale of Murder and Retribution". It had been compiled in the early seventies by a local man, though he hadn't indicated where he had got any of the information. Was there *any* factual basis behind it? Or would it all be fiction?

She took a seat next to her brother in the corner of the sofa and read. According to the booklet, Janet Shaw was the daughter of the local baker, who lived in the building that was now Liz's mum's cafe. She'd been a popular, pretty girl who'd agreed to marry the blacksmith, Christopher Greenwood. Before they had married, he'd found out that she'd cheated on him, and was pregnant. The pamphlet implied the father was the local landowner, Hugh Ellis, and speculated that perhaps Janet Shaw had been trying to get a better marriage offer than the blacksmith. If that *had* been her plan, it had backfired spectacularly.

When Christopher Greenwood had found out about the baby, he'd known it wasn't his, and taken up one of his hammers and battered the girl to death. Her body had been found on the outskirts of the village, beaten to a pulp. When the village heard about it, they rushed to the forge and set about the blacksmith, killing him. Janet Shaw's ghost then haunted the bakery, her soul unable to rest after such a brutal murder.

Ellie put the sheets down, feeling queasy. "That's all quite violent."

"Mm," said Liz. "The village must have been incandescent about the blacksmith. You didn't normally cross the blacksmith because he was so important in those days. He was the one who made all the nails, the axes, the knives… the blades for cutting

72

crops, the ploughshares. Shod all the horses. Everything! With no blacksmith, *everyone* would have struggled. Perhaps another blacksmith took up the forge, or there was another blacksmith in the village, but it was a big thing for them to have killed him."

"Shouldn't he have been tried?" asked Joe. "Were there police back then?"

Liz shook her head. "No. The local magistrate would decide on minor offences, but murder would have been a hanging offence and dealt with somewhere bigger, as far as I know. I guess the village didn't bother waiting for justice to work."

Ellie sipped her wine, puzzled. "Why is she haunting your mum's place? If they found her body on the outskirts of the village, presumably that's because she was murdered near there. Why isn't she haunting *that* place?"

Liz gave her a long look. "Ghosts don't exist. She isn't actually haunting *anywhere*."

"Yeah, I know. But the story needs to work. Why is she haunting her home? Surely her restless soul would haunt the blacksmiths, or be walking about where she was found?" She considered the layout of the village for a moment. "She'd be haunting one of the new houses if they found her body on this side of the village."

Liz grinned. "You realise that the bloke who wrote this was the owner of the cafe at the time? This is more than likely just a way of getting more customers."

"Ah." Ellie passed the booklet to Joe. "That was a bit of a step-up for a baker's daughter, thinking she might marry the local landowner, wasn't it?"

"I think you might be making the mistake of believing any of it is true," murmured Joe, reading.

Liz pursed her lips. "I think there must be a kernel of truth to it. There must have been an oral history of the story, even if nothing was written down. These things don't spring up out of a vacuum. There was presumably a young girl called Janet Shaw who was beaten to death, and presumably the village then attacked the blacksmith in revenge. Those kinds of things seem too specific to be invented. Why he did it could be made up or embellished over the years, but I suspect the core of it has at least a grain of truth."

73

Ellie shivered. She kept seeing him. He'd spoken to her. She had no control over when she would encounter him. Was she in danger?

"You okay, Ellie?" asked Liz.

Ellie forced a smile on to her lips. "Fine. Just miles away. Sorry."

Liz turned to Joe. "So, you go back home tomorrow?"

"Yep. Back to the city. No more sparrows waking me up at stupid o'clock."

Ellie chuffed at him. Only that afternoon he'd been talking to her about possibly moving here. All the walking had helped him to accept that if he ever wanted to move on, he needed a change. She also knew for a fact that he'd been scouting out job opportunities in the area because he'd used her laptop to do it.

"Well, we'll all miss you at Knit and Natter." Liz glanced back to Ellie. "Are you bringing more of your amazing yarn and patterns on Monday?"

"Only if people want me to. I don't want people to think I'm only there to flog my stuff."

Liz flapped a hand, making an array of wooden bracelets rattle. "No one thinks that. Bring them along and then, if anyone asks, you have them. What are these natural dyes you've been experimenting with?"

The last shreds of tension slipped off Ellie's shoulders. She could happily talk at length about this, and Liz seemed genuinely interested. She explained the process – how to pre-treat the yarn, what the dyeing process involved, what had to happen after dyeing, and how all of these things affected the resultant colour.

"I'm still struggling to get a good red. I need to find someone with pear trees and get all their prunings from them."

"Oh, I have pear trees. Well, I have two. Which bits do you need?"

"Ooh, do you? I need the bark. If you can give me a shout any time you're pruning, that would be fantastic!"

The evening passed in easy conversation and laughter, and all too soon the sun had dipped close to the horizon and Liz was ready to leave.

"Thanks for all the maps and pictures. I'll get them back to you as soon as I can," she said, gathering her things.

"Oh, no rush! Do you want this pamphlet back?"

Liz shook her head. "Keep it. Mum found an entire box of them in the back of a cupboard."

Joe stood gracefully. "I'll walk you home."

Liz's face lit up. "Thank you. Though I'm fairly sure I'd be perfectly safe getting back to the village from here."

"What kind of gentleman would I be to let a woman walk home on her own? I mean, there's a history of violent crime here." He jutted his chin towards the pamphlet, a grin broadening, and Liz laughed.

Ellie watched them leave, smiling. Joe and Liz would make a great couple. Maybe Granny Molly *had* been right about him moving here and finding happiness.

Was she right in her predictions for Ellie? She hoped not, if her lovely little childhood play-friend turned out to have a penchant for beating people to death.

Reality poked her brain, and she pinched the bridge of her nose, sighing.

"There are no such things as ghosts. Or ley lines. Or nodes. The house is *not* travelling back and forth through time. Get a grip!"

15

Ellie sat at her desk in the study, examining the knitting in her hands, checking back over the fabric for why her stitch count was wrong. A few rows back, she spotted the rogue stitch.

Sighing heavily, she opened her bag of notions and hunted for a crochet hook, ready to undo the offending few stitches and correct the mistake. As she did so, the bag vanished beneath her hands. She blinked. Her knitting had disappeared, too.

"You again!"

Her head shot up. The voice had come from behind her. Her heart thumping, she peered out of the window in front of her. The expected view of a grassy area surrounded by flower borders had switched to a stable-yard and workshop. She turned in the seat, shaking. A hard, wooden seat, not her desk chair. In the doorway to the study, Kit Greenwood leaned against the frame, his arms tightly folded as he stared at her, his hazel eyes full of uncertainty. He wore a rough wool jacket over a woollen waistcoat with a cream stock tied at his neck. As before, he wore mouse-coloured trousers fastened just below his knee, with shiny knee-high boots.

"Who *are* you?" he said. "Why do I keep seeing you? Are you a witch? A demon? A spirit?"

Ellie scanned the room, her palms clammy. The wood-burning stove had disappeared, replaced with an open fire. The shelves of books had gone, and a much smaller bookcase stood on the other side of the room. Two chairs flanked the fire, replacing the one squashy chair that lived in the corner of the room. The desk she sat at had moved a few feet to the side and was smaller. The chair was harder, and the surface of the desk was empty. No knitting, yarn, needles, bag… nothing. Underfoot, the thick carpet had become wooden boards with a rug over them. She took a deep breath. A trace of charcoal smoke tinted the air.

Swallowing, she turned back to Kit. "No. I'm not a witch. Or a demon. Or a spirit. Just a woman."

"Why do I keep seeing you?"

She almost laughed, then caught herself. "I keep asking myself the same thing about you. You keep appearing in *my* house."

His brow puckered. "What?"

She peered behind him to the hall beyond. The modern archway had become a wall with a heavy door in it. She got to her feet, and Kit Greenwood stepped back briskly, giving her pause. Was he scared of her? Shouldn't it be the other way around?

Her gaze drifted back to him. "Is it 1762?"

His posture tightened, and he took another step back. "Yes. Why do you ask that?"

How on earth could she explain things? She let her breath out in a huff. "Okay. For me, it was 260 years later than that when I sat down at the desk."

He bit his lip, his breathing rapid. His eyes swept her from top to bottom, widening as they did so, and he blinked a couple of times. What did he make of her clothes? Jeans and a cosy sweater. Not exactly what 18th century women wore.

"What do you mean?" His voice held curiosity, not aggression.

She drew in an unsteady breath. "I don't think I can explain. I live in this house in the 21st century."

He took another pace away from her. "You are a spirit."

She shook her head. "No. I'm not. I'm just a woman. I don't know why I'm here or how it happened."

He paused, his eyes wide. "Where did you go the other day? When you fainted."

"Nowhere. I came to on the floor in the same spot, but the house had returned to my time."

She hesitated. Did she *really* believe she'd gone back in time? How was that possible? But here she was, talking to Kit Greenwood, in 1762. Apparently.

"And in the forge?"

"The same. The coloured lights arrived, the buildings shifted, and I was back in *my* yard."

"Can you conjure the lights again and go?" It came out as a genuine question, not an order.

Fear chilled her skin. How *did* she get back? "If I knew how to return home, I would," she said, her voice little more than a croak. "I can't control it. It just happens."

Should she leave? His colour was high and his posture tight. If he genuinely believed her to be a spirit or a demon, would he kill her, the way he would kill Janet? Rocks formed in her stomach, and her chest tightened.

A thought struck her. She had no idea how she had returned to her time on either of the previous occasions; it had just happened, but it had always occurred in the property. If she left, would she stay trapped in 1762? Would she ever be able to get back?

He trembled. Fear? Or anger? Would he bodily throw her out? He had the height and strength to. Sweat slicked her palms.

"You cannot conjure the lights?" he asked.

She swallowed, her mouth dry. "No." Her heart pounded. "But I think I need to be in the house in order to get back to my time."

He didn't move for a moment, his gaze flicking over her, his shoulders bunching, then he sucked in a deep breath.

"Then you had better sit."

16

Kit indicated for her to sit in a chair by the fire in the study. Not the squashy leather chair she knew from her time, but a much more upright one, though the seat was well-padded. Ellie hoped that the room would morph back to *her* version, but it didn't.

"Thank you," she said, sitting nervously.

Kit sat at the desk, his face neutral. "Who are you?"

She sighed. "I told you already. I'm Ellie Stewart. I can't explain it any better than I have. I live here. In the 21st century. I don't know how I'm here in 1762. I see you occasionally in my time. You appear fleetingly, like a ghost. Sometimes I think you can see me, but I can't hear you when you speak. Other times you're staring right at me, but I don't think you see me. You walked right through me once and we both almost fell over."

He rasped his jaw with the back of his fingers. "I have had the same. Sometimes I see you, but you are completely unaware I am in the room. Other times I think you *do* see me, and now, you seem real. Not a spirit."

"Oh, I'm definitely real!" She paused. "Granny Molly always claimed the house was haunted." She studied him intently. *Was* this the same person as the boy from her childhood? "When I was small, I used to spend some of the summers here, and I kept seeing a child. He had the same birthmark. Was that you?"

He brought his hand up to cover the side of his face, then leaned forwards in his seat, peering closely at her. "That was you? You came and played once. I told my parents about it and was

79

punished for lying!"

So, Granny Molly *had* been right about her not being lost, but merely visiting her 'tawny-haired boy'.

"I think so. I was very young, so I don't remember much. No one else said they could see you. Except Granny Molly, but I assumed she was humouring me."

"Granny Molly? Is that the old woman I used to see?"

"Mm. Probably. About this tall—" Ellie held her hand up level with her eyes "—dark eyes, silver hair, cut short? Twinkly smile." A lump formed in her throat as she spoke.

"Yes. That is her. I thought she was another spirit. Where is she? I have not seen her recently."

Ellie gripped her fingers. "She died. She left the house to me and my brother."

"Your brother? I have seen no spirit of a man in the house. Ever."

"Oh. He was here. He's gone back to his home. It's just me here currently."

Kit dipped his head, worrying his lower lip with his teeth. "What is the date for you?"

"July 6th, 2022."

He peered intently at her, his brow wrinkling. "What is the house like on that date? Are the rooms the same?"

She drew in a deep breath, imagining the modern version of Rose Cottage. "Well, the house continues on, beyond that hall." She indicated the space behind him. "There are two more rooms at the front. Where your main door is, is an archway in my time, connecting the front and the back of the house. The stairs lead up from the front hallway, not from this one. And the kitchen and storeroom are slightly different. The door to the garden is a few feet to the left. Upstairs is split over two levels. There are two rooms and a bathroom above here, then another half turn of the stairs leads to two more bedrooms and a bathroom."

She ground to a halt. Did bathrooms exist in 1762? She didn't think so.

He closed his eyes, his shoulders slumping. "My head tells me this must be a dream. A waking dream. Or that you have put a spell on me. My eyes tell me that you are not from this year." He sighed. "For years I have seen the older woman you call Granny Molly. And then you. Always ghost-like. I see a different building, though it is not real, but a mirage. Doors move. Rooms appear. The furniture is different. The way you have just described." His gaze skimmed her legs. "The spirits are dressed differently. You say truly, that you believe it is 260 years hence?"

"Well, I'm beginning to believe it's 1762 right *now*. But half an hour ago, I was in 2022. I don't understand this any better than you do. We're in the same place, but somehow the year isn't the same. Is it July 6th for you?"

"Yes." He pressed his lips together tightly, his head dipped, then pinched up a fold of cloth in his jacket so that two buttons touched. "It is as if you are here—" he touched one button "—and I am here." He touched the other, then smoothed the fabric out again. "We would never meet, normally, but somehow… Here you are. In my house."

"I didn't mean to be. I was sitting at the desk, minding my own business, in *my* house. Though I accept that it's *your* house at this precise moment."

He chuckled, transforming his features and reminding her of the little boy from her childhood.

"I'm genuinely worried about how on earth I'm going to get *back*, though. I hope it doesn't involve me needing to be unconscious."

"No. That would *not* be helpful. I am not prepared to hit you to be rid of you."

Fear coiled in her belly. He might seem like the sweet little boy she knew when she was small, but he was a murderer as an adult.

He cocked his head, his eyes lively. "Is it customary where you are from for women to dress like men?"

"Mm. Most women wear trousers, at least some of the time."

"Trousers? Is that the name for your long breeches?"

"Mm."

"And do men wear skirts?"

She laughed, shaking her head. "No, not really. Well, the Scots wear kilts sometimes, but that's different." She stuck her bottom lip out. "Trousers are practical. Skirts aren't. Which is probably why men started wearing them in the first place."

He laughed again. She took a moment to study *his* clothes. When she'd first seen them, she'd thought them plain and slightly drab, but now she studied the woollen waistcoat he wore, a bright yellow thread running through the woven front caught her eye. Her fingers itched to touch it and investigate it more closely. As she raised her eyes back to Kit's face, his lips twitched and his eyes danced.

"What has transfixed you, lass? My buttons?"

Heat flashed into her cheeks. "No. The material of your waistcoat. The yellow thread in it. I dye wool. In my time. That yellow is a beautiful colour, and I'm trying to work out which plant had been used to make it. Sorry."

He smiled softly. "Take a closer look if you wish. I can see you are interested."

"May I?"

She stood and moved closer to him, studying the cloth, her dyer's brain twitchy. The remaining wool in the waistcoat was a soft beige and she couldn't work out if it was the natural colour of the wool, or if it had been dyed. She suspected it was the natural colour, as was the jacket. The yellow thread was a warp thread and she could imagine the weaver deciding to make the cloth a little more special, rather than using all plain wool.

She sat back down.

"You dye wool?" Kit coughed softly. "You do not smell as if you do."

She frowned, then understood him. "Oh! No! We don't need to use urine in my time."

"Ah. That must be welcome. Do you weave?"

"No. Knit. I designed and made this." She pointed to her sweater – a richly cabled Aran in navy blue.

He glanced over it, confusion flickering in his face.

Did people wear sweaters in 1762? Women probably didn't. And no doubt all women knitted domestically. 'Knitwear designer' was almost certainly not a thing.

"Your gansey fascinates me," he said. "May I look closer?"
"Sure."

He stood, the chair creaking as he did, and crouched in front of her, peering at her sweater.

"How do you make it resemble rope?" he asked as he sat back in his chair. "I have never seen that before."

"Oh, you cross the stitches over on the needle. It's easier than it looks."

Silence stretched between them. He tapped his fingertips lightly on the desk, tilting his head. "What do I do with you? You cannot stay here. Not overnight. Dressed as you are, you cannot go to the village, and I have no clothing which you could borrow. What do I do with you?"

Her fear rushed back. "I don't know. I'd quite like to go back to my time, but I don't know how to." Tension ground her neck and shoulders. "You have no sisters? A wife? No one I could borrow clothes from?"

"No. It is only me and my brother, Thomas, here. Our sister is married and has gone to Thirsk. Thomas is in Masham today." His finger traced the grain of the desk. "I do not know how to explain you. If I tell him you are from the future, he will summon the minister and condemn you as a witch."

"Okay, let's try to avoid that happening!" She fiddled with her fingers, twisting them together. "If I'm still here when he's due home, I can hide in your forge. I think that's within the area where the time changes."

A frown marred his brow, and he didn't reply.

"Well, hopefully I'll be gone again before then." What did they do until then? She took a deep breath, wishing she was better at small talk. "Um. Since I'm here, why don't you tell me about yourself? How long have you been a blacksmith?"

His shoulders softened, and he leaned back in his seat. "Since a boy. My father was the master blacksmith here, and I learned from him."

"I never see him. Just you."

His head lowered. "He died. A few years ago. I took over."

"Oh, I'm sorry. And your mother?"

"Also dead. In childbirth." He paused. "She was perhaps too old for another child."

"I'm sorry. How old were you?"

"Fifteen."

All his lightness had gone, and he'd closed up. Ellie was clean out of chit-chat and they lapsed into silence again.

He squared his shoulders suddenly. "Why did you ask me about Janet Shaw?"

She tried to swallow, but her mouth was like sandpaper. "Er... There's a story about you and her. In my time."

He grinned. "A story? What can we have done for people to still talk of it in your time?"

She didn't know what to say. Kit leaned forwards and rested his elbows on his thighs. "What? What is the story?"

"I don't know how much of it is true. How do you know Janet? Did you ask her to marry you? *Would* you ask her to marry you?"

He threw his head back, guffawing loudly. "Janet? No. That would be like marrying my sister."

She blinked at his reaction. "Why?"

"We have known each other since we were children. She was my sister's favourite friend before she married."

"So, you like her?"

He twisted one side of his mouth, wrinkling his nose. "She is lovely. But no. I do not want to marry her. Is that the story? That we are married?" His brow creased. "No, there must be more than that for there still to be a story in your time."

Well, yes. But I'm not going to say what!

"So, you wouldn't ask her to marry you, and she wouldn't prefer to marry Hugh Ellis?"

"Hugh Ellis? The magistrate?" He snorted. "He would never ask her and if he did, she would never accept him. He convicted her brother for poaching. Had him hanged. She loathes him."

"Oh." The story was falling apart already.

"Is that the story? That I asked her to marry me, but she married Hugh Ellis instead? It is not much of a story."

"If she *did* want to marry him, would you be jealous?"

"I would be astonished. And hope that she was safe. Hugh Ellis has a fearsome temper. He is also old enough to be her father. Your story seems very unlikely."

"Well, it's 260 years after the facts. It must have got muddled."

Kit didn't speak for a few minutes, never taking his eyes off her, his expression light, his lips quirking into a soft smile. Then he blinked a couple of times and straightened. "Forgive my lack of manners. Can I get you any refreshment?"

Her mind raced. Would the water be safe for her? Did they have tea or coffee easily available? Didn't everyone drink wine or beer as the main drink? Or was that before 1762?

"Some wine, perhaps?" he prompted.

"A small glass? Thank you."

He stood gracefully, dipped his head to her, and left the room. She leaned forward and buried her face in her hands, her hair sticking up between her fingers.

"What on earth do I do if it gets to nighttime and I'm still here?" she muttered. "He can't let me stay, but I don't think he would turn me out. How the hell do I get home?"

She massaged her temples, breathing deeply. From the kitchen came a clink of glass, then Kit's footsteps as he crossed the hall.

And then silence.

Coloured lights played around her, and she crashed to the ground with a thud. She was back in *her* study, and the chair sat in the corner, not next to the fire. Her heart pounded.

"How? How did I get back?"

Frustration seethed through her. Why had she gone back to 1762 in the first place? What had she done that could have triggered it? And what had made her return? She hadn't passed out. She hadn't fallen asleep. Was this going to keep on happening to her?

She picked herself up off the floor and sat in the chair in the corner. Kit's reaction to her question about marrying Janet had been absolutely genuine. And if Hugh Ellis had sentenced Janet's brother to hanging, it didn't seem likely she would have chosen him over Kit, if Kit *had* ever asked her. Especially not if Ellis was so much older than her.

If all of that part of the story was wrong, was *any* of it right?

17

A few days later, Ellie stood at the back of the house, surveying a large patch of weeds. As Granny Molly had got older and frailer, the garden had been too big for her to manage, and although she'd hired someone to keep on top of a neatly cultivated area close to the house, there was this large, wild area behind the workshop that had returned to nature.

Joe had suggested throwing several bottles of weedkiller over it and digging it all up, but Ellie recognised some of the plants as potential dye-stuffs. The bright yellow thread running through Kit's waistcoat the other day had sent her to her study to consult all of her reference books, trying to figure out what had been used to dye it. A lot of plants could be used to provide a yellow colour, some producing a brighter result than others. Many of them were fairly common in the area, not least dandelions, which could produce a range of yellows, depending on the dyeing process. Right now, the patch of ground in front of her at had plenty of dandelions in it, along with several less useful plants. She would dig most of it over, but leave the blackberry that scrambled over the boundary fence. She could harvest its autumn berries both for dyeing and to eat.

Ellie paced out the space. She could grow four or five different plants and get enough matter from each to make it worthwhile dyeing several batches of yarn. She loved using natural dyes, but it could take a lot of leaves, roots, or flowers, just to dye a few skeins, and they could be expensive to buy in. The patch faced southwest and was bathed in sun for most of the day. She pulled out her notebook and planned what she might grow where.

Although the colourful lights that preceded time-shifts had danced along the boundary of the house a few times, she hadn't returned to 1762 since her long encounter with Kit a few days earlier. She'd seen several glimpses of him when she'd been working, though, and the two had settled into a pattern of waving to one another whenever the two houses became superimposed, provoking smiles in both of them.

For the last couple of evenings, Ellie had scoured the internet, researching 18th century life, and what an average day might be like for Kit. Frustratingly, much of the information she'd found centred on London or other cities; little covered rural life. Based on his clothes and the furniture in his house, Kit enjoyed a high standard of living as a blacksmith. He'd certainly been busy at work most of the times she'd seen him, often shoeing horses. Although she hadn't been physically transported back to 1762, she'd been able to watch him for several minutes the day before. The horse he was shoeing had danced about and tossed its head until Kit had stood by its neck, talking to it, soothing it. After that, it stood docilely while he propped its sturdy feet on his thigh and hammered nails into its new shoes. As he'd finished, he'd looked up, wiping sweat from his brow, and caught sight of her. He'd grinned sheepishly, some of his wavy auburn hair escaping from its ribbon and framing his face, then he'd turned back to his work.

Fat drops of rain landed on her head. She snapped the band around her notebook and hurried back towards the house to make a cup of tea and continue her plans in the dry of the study. As she passed the end of the workshop, the sound of singing filtered out. She poked her head in, just as the room shifted from 1762 to the present day, and the singing faded.

"Damn! I wish I knew when this was going to happen!"

The colourful lights danced away to nothing, and Ellie bit her lips together, thinking. Where exactly did the boundary lie? She'd been at the patch beyond the workshop and had had no inkling of the time-shift. There must be a definite boundary. The whole of Masham didn't warp and change. The front of the house was definitely outside any time-shifting area, and the end of the log-store and the workshop were both within it, but she didn't know where the edges lay.

She booted up her laptop in the study and found a satellite image of the property via Google she could print off. Scouring her mind for all the times the house had shifted, she tentatively marked where the boundary might lie, then jotted down all the times the rift had opened and for how long. Clearly, it opened, then closed again. If she was inside the boundary, there was a chance she would be shifted back to 1762, only returning when the rift opened again. But she didn't always get time-shifted. Often, the lights appeared, and although Kit and Ellie could see each other, they stayed resolutely in their own times.

She scratched her head with the end of the pencil. Maybe Joe's scientific brain would spot a pattern in it all. Though quite how she would tell him that she periodically wandered off to 1762 without him scoffing was beyond her. Maybe he would see it happen and *have* to believe her.

She'd just finished making notes on all the time-shifts she could remember, when something Granny Molly said popped back into her head, finally making sense.

"Make sure you take a room at the front for your bedroom, or who knows what will happen."

She laughed to herself. At least *that* issue wouldn't come up, as she'd taken the other room at the front. A wave of grief billowed up, blindsiding her, and she swallowed.

"Oh, Granny Molly, I wish I'd asked you about all of this when you were still here. You knew, didn't you? You knew I would meet Kit."

And apparently be happy with him. But how? They lived in worlds 260 years apart. Would he ever come to her time? Or was she going to end up trapped in 1762? A chill shot through her.

What if she went back to 1762 and the rift never re-opened? How would anyone know where she was?

18

By the following morning, the rain had cleared, and Ellie put on work clothes and wellies, ready to tackle the overgrown plot. Behind the greenhouse with its algae-stained-glass stood a small wooden shed. Inside, Ellie found various garden tools, and a pair of gardening gloves that fitted and weren't so old that the seams had come apart. She grabbed them and a garden fork, along with a large bucket, then set to work on clearing a strip of the plot.

As she tipped the sixth bucket of weeds into the wheelie bin for garden waste, Liz called her name.

"I'm round the back!" she yelled back, pulling off her gloves.

She hurried towards the front of the house, meeting Liz en route.

"Hello!" Liz grinned. "You're busy!"

"Oh, I'm ready for a break. I'm clearing that patch at the back."

"The old vegetable plot? Molly hadn't been able to work on that in a long time."

"I can tell. Want a coffee?"

"Ooh, go on. I actually came up to see if you wanted to go out and do something. It's stopped raining, and I fancied a walk, but don't worry if you're busy."

Ellie blew her cheeks out. "Not that busy. There's a limit to how much weeding I can do in a day. Come on in."

Anxiety prickled her belly as they went into the kitchen. Was the house going to shift and dump her in 1762, leaving Liz behind wondering where she'd gone? Or dump *both* of them in 1762? As

89

swiftly as possible, Ellie made the drinks, then gestured towards the door. "Shall we take them outside? There's a bench at the front in the sun."

Liz took her mug of coffee and led the way through the hallway to the front door. As Ellie crossed the line of the 1762 house, she caught her breath. Coloured lights flickered faintly along the wall separating the two halls, making Ellie quicken her pace. She *really* needed to figure out when this was going to happen.

Liz perched on the bench, her hands clasped around her mug. As Ellie joined her, a silver-grey tabby cat strolled out from the side of the house facing the workshop. Liz reached down to fuss it.

"Hello. You're a handsome thing." She looked up at Ellie. "Is he yours?"

Ellie shook her head. "Nope. But you're right. He's a nice-looking cat." A thought struck her. "Oh, he's not the missing cat, is he? When I first arrived, I saw a card in one of the shop windows saying there was a lost cat. Maybe this is it."

"No, that's a black cat, I think. I'll check when I go home if you want?"

"Yeah, thanks." She blew on her coffee. "Where did you want to go today?"

Liz shifted, fidgety. "Um. This might sound weird, and feel free to say no, but I was wondering about looking at old gravestones. One of the maps that you lent me gives the names of the people who owned land around the village, and I was going to see if any of them were buried in the churchyard. Or is that a bit morbid?"

Ellie laughed. "Um, yeah, that's quite morbid, but it also sounds interesting."

Maybe she could look for anything relating to Kit while they were there. According to Granny Molly, he had a 'disappeared stone' but no indication of what or where that was.

The cat prowled around their feet while they finished their coffees, then wandered back towards the workshop. It didn't reappear.

"He's not been neutered, so I think he must be a stray," commented Liz, putting her mug on the ground beside her feet. "Though he's keeping himself well fed, if he is homeless. Mind that he doesn't come in and spray on everything."

Ellie drained her mug and stood, wondering what year the kitchen would be in. Should she risk taking the mugs in and disappearing? Liz resolved the issue by taking her mug from her.

"I'll take them in. Can I pop to your loo, too?"

"Sure. I'll grab a jacket."

She followed Liz through the front door, her heart beating wildly. The kaleidoscope of lights still danced over the rear hall and through them she could see Kit's kitchen, as clear as day, superimposed over hers. To her surprise, Liz marched straight across the rear hall and into the kitchen, walking right through a chair in Kit's time with no noticeable effect. She put the mugs next to the sink, returned through the chair again, then went into the downstairs loo. Ellie blinked. How could Liz just breeze through it all? Ellie didn't dare step into the rear hall in case she was whisked away almost three centuries, but Liz had been absolutely fine. Ellie was pretty sure there wouldn't even *be* a loo in the house in 1762, never mind one right there, but a couple of minutes later, she heard the flush, and Liz reappeared.

Ellie unhooked a jacket from the pegs next to her and pocketed her keys, her heart still thumping. "Okay. Let's go. Lunch in Masham afterwards?"

Liz smiled. "Perfect."

With any luck, the house might have stopped shifting time-zones by the time she came back.

***

The two women sauntered down to the village, past the fairly new houses on the outskirts of the village and into an older area, cutting down a narrow lane to reach the square. As they walked, Ellie scanned the buildings, trying to spot which ones might have been standing in Kit's time. Most of the buildings around the market square appeared old enough, as did some of the buildings they'd passed on the road leading to the square, though the outskirts were definitely more modern.

The Saturday market was on, and an eclectic mix of stalls had taken over the central area of the square normally used for parking, selling food and drink, artisan crafts, clothing, books, and plenty of other things. The Wednesday market had slightly different stalls to Saturday, but Ellie always enjoyed pottering around, whichever day it was.

They picked their way past the stalls and down the small lane to the church, passing Liz's mum's cafe. A blue wooden sign next to the wrought iron churchyard gates proclaimed that the church was open, and the gates to the grounds stood fastened wide.

"Whose gravestones are we trying to find?" asked Ellie. "I assume there are specific names you're after."

Liz pulled a notebook out of her bag. "Um, the surnames are Barker, Walker, Morton, Danby, and Lightfoot. I suspect the Danby will be related to Sir Abstrupus Danby, who was a wool merchant and who has a big monument in the church, but the map refers to a Mr Danby, which I guess will be a second or third son or something."

"And what kind of dates? Late 1700s?"

"Later than that. The map dates from 1801."

"Okay. Do you want to look together, or split up?"

"Let's look together."

The gravestones lay predominantly on the south side of the church, with a few to the north. They started on the north side and worked methodically along the rows. The graves were loosely arranged over time, with the older graves grouped more towards one area. Many of the headstones were made of sandstone, and time and weather had taken their toll, making the inscriptions hard to read. They walked slowly, studying every inscription, spotting family names as they did so. Akers, Blackburn, Rider. The oldest headstones dated back to the early 1700s, including one with Lightfoot as a surname, though Liz didn't think it was the person listed on the map.

"Maybe their father or grandfather," she mused, taking a picture anyway.

Warm sunshine bathed the churchyard, and birds cheeped and twittered from the trees. Ellie's heart lurched reading some of the stones, the grief reaching across the centuries to touch her. Whatever the century, losing children must be devastating, and some stones listed several children, none of them reaching more than two years of age.

As they strolled on, Ellie's eye snagged on a name from Liz's list. "Ooh. Here's a Barker. 1831. A possible?"

"Oh, a definite possible!"

Liz crouched down and took a picture.

They walked a little further, then Liz paused. "These are getting too old now, I think."

"Let's look, anyway? I quite like the really old ones."

She still hoped to find something with Greenwood on it and, to her delight, she spotted a tall stone, covered in writing:

In memory of Thomas Greenwood died 18 May 1806 aged 67 and his wife Esther died 22 October 1810 aged 68

And their son Christopher died 5 September 1825 aged 61 and their daughter Ann died 4 January 1826 aged 59 and their son George died 9 March 1837 aged 67

Ellie pulled her phone out of her back pocket and took pictures. Liz peered over her shoulder.

"Why are you taking a picture of this one?"

"I think it's Kit's family."

"Kit?"

Ellie froze, her heart racing. "Er. Christopher Greenwood. I think these people might be related to him."

"Christopher Greenwood, the murderer who lived at your place? Why did you call him Kit?"

Ellie thought fast. "Oh, I dunno. Isn't that what Christopher got shortened to in those days?"

"Maybe. You almost sounded like you knew him!"

Ellie laughed, cursing herself internally, and put her phone away. "Perhaps I'm thinking of the Elizabethan guy, actually. The playwright. Kit Marlowe?"

Liz's brow remained creased, and Ellie turned away, pretending to look at other headstones. Liz didn't pursue it, and the two women meandered through more of the cemetery.

An old headstone poked up near the stone wall at the back of the graveyard, protected from the weather. The edges of the lettering had softened with time and a crust of lichen and algae clung to the surface of the stone. Ellie made her way over to it and screwed her eyes up, trying to read the faded lettering. As the letters resolved, she caught her breath.

Erected by Thomas Greenwood, in memory of his brother Christopher who

The letters of the next word were particularly difficult to fathom. She assumed at first it said 'died', but although the word started and ended with a 'd', there were far too many letters. She traced the carved letters with her fingertip. An 's'? Was that a 'p'? After peering at it this way and that, she was fairly sure that it said 'disappeared'.

The date was equally difficult to read. Eventually Ellie settled on 6 September 1762 as the most likely. Her heart skipped a beat. When she'd last seen Kit, he'd said it was the same date as it had been for her – July 6th. Did he only have a few months left before he 'disappeared'? Was 'disappeared' a euphemism for 'ripped apart by a baying mob'? She wrinkled her nose. 'Killed' or just 'died' would have been better. Had there been nothing left of him to bury after the mob had attacked him? She breathed hard, nausea bubbling at the back of her throat at the idea of anyone being killed like that, never mind someone she'd met, however briefly.

She squatted down on her haunches, mulling it over. He'd said he lived with a brother called Thomas. How many Christopher Greenwoods with brothers called Thomas could there be in 1762? Surely, this was tangible evidence that the man she'd met had actually existed.

"What have you found?" Liz called across from the path where she crouched, photographing another stone.

"Oh. Nothing. Just an old stone that's interesting. Not one of the names from the map."

She pulled her phone out again and took pictures, trying to get the shadows to emphasise the words as well as she could. Finished, she joined Liz. "All done?"

"I think so. I mean, it's hard to be sure, but there are some with roughly the right date. You had enough?"

Ellie pushed her bottom lip out. "More that I'm getting hungry. Lunch at your mum's place?"

Liz tucked her notebook back in her bag, and they strolled to the cafe in the corner of the square. The combination of it being market day and a sunny Saturday meant they had to wait for a table to come free. They lurked close to the building, watching the sparrows darting out to steal crumbs from around the tables.

"Oh, I meant to tell you. Joe's coming back up again soon," said Ellie.

Liz's eyes lit up. "When?"

"Three weeks? That kind of time. He's been looking at job opportunities in the area."

"Oh? I got the impression he was pretty settled where he was."

A couple vacated a table, and Liz and Ellie hurried to take it.

Ellie picked up the menu card. "Hm. He is, and he isn't. I don't know if he told you, but his wife died. A few years ago."

Liz shook her head, and Ellie carried on. "Yeah. Hit-and-run. He was devastated. Absolutely broken by it. But he's a lot better now. I think he's finally realised how much he wants to have a family. To do that, he needs to date again. And for *that* to work, he needs to move house."

"And you two have inherited The Old Forge together."

"Rose Cottage, but yes. Though we're not going to share it forever! That would be as much of a dampener on any relationship as him living in the house he shared with Hayley!" She toyed with the menu. "I know he's the chatty, gregarious one, but he's unsure about this. It's an enormous step for him to leave the house he had with Hayley. I think he wants to move somewhere where he has *some* connection, not just move for the sake of moving. His contracts are coming to an end where he is, so if he *is* going to think about a move, the timing works. Anyway, the plan at the moment is that he comes up for a short while and stays at Rose Cottage until he's sorted with a job and a place to live."

Liz studied her. "And how do you feel about him moving in?"

"Fine. We get on well." She smiled ruefully. "Granny Molly always swore he would settle down here. We both thought she was wrong."

"And what did Molly predict for you?"

Ellie shrugged. "Nothing really. That I would find happiness with a man with reddish hair. I'm not sure I would have bought a lottery ticket on the strength of Granny Molly's predictions."

A glint formed in Liz's eye. "I know a man with reddish hair.

Maybe I should introduce you."

"Who?" said Ellie, wary. Too many friends had tried to set her up with men. That was how she'd ended up with Simon in the first place.

"One of the other teachers at school. John Edwards. Chemistry." She smirked. "He's single, and quite attractive. Shall I introduce you to him sometime?"

"No, thank you. I'm not looking for anyone."

"Let me know if you change your mind." Liz gave Ellie a long look. "You're too lovely to be single."

"I'm also perfectly happy being single," Ellie retorted. "If someone wants to share my life, they have to be better than my own company is."

Liz held her hands up. "Okay!"

Ellie pointedly studied the menu. She *was* happy on her own, though if she met someone who would treat her well, it wouldn't go amiss. She was fairly sure that Granny Molly hadn't meant Mr Edwards, chemistry teacher, as the man with reddish hair, though.

19

Ellie stood in the doorway to the utility room. Granny Molly may have barely used the room, but it had potential. The room held a washing machine and tumble-dryer, and shelves lined one wall, holding dry goods and tins. Above the appliances was plenty of space for more shelving, and it would be an ideal location for keeping washing powder and cleaning products. The walls had surface-mounted pipework and electrics, but Ellie checked and re-checked the area of the wall with a detector. No hazards. She eyed the surface apprehensively. How easy would the stone be to drill? It was the same as the other walls and *they* had shelves, so it was *possible*. Possible by her?

She unfolded the small set of steps and grabbed a spirit-level and a pencil. Standing on the top step, she measured up the wall, marking where she would need to put the fixings. As she did so, the shadows in the room shifted, disorientating her. Her breath caught in her chest. Was the house playing up again? As she scanned the room, the windows were superimposed over different parts of the wall.

Before she could get off the step-ladder to safety, she clattered to the ground, landing badly on her wrist. She swore, loudly and profusely, rubbing her wrist and checking the room. The spirit-level and the set of steps had vanished, and she sat in a crumpled heap on a stone-flagged floor. Where the door to the yard should be, there was a small window. She was amused to find some withdshelves roughly where she'd been marking up the wall. The other wall also had shelves a-plenty, loaded with stoneware jars and a variety of packets.

She flexed her wrist, wincing. How long would she be in 1762 this time? And how was she going to get back? A sound behind her made her turn.

"Are you stealing my food now?" asked Kit drily, leaning in the doorway, which was also in the wrong place according to the modern layout of the house.

He ducked inside the room and held out a hand to her to help her up, smiling. Ellie scowled, but accepted his hand.

"I was trying to put up some shelves in my time," she said, nursing her sore wrist. "And – naturally – the steps I was standing on didn't come with me to 1762. Hence me lying on the floor."

"You were putting up shelves?" His brows rose. "Does your brother not do those things for you?"

"He does, but he's still away. And I'm perfectly capable of putting up shelves myself. Unless the steps disappear from under me."

His gaze alighted on her wrist. "You are hurt?"

"Yes. I landed on it and twisted it."

Soft hands drew her arm towards him and he inspected the swollen joint. "Ouch."

"Mm." She flexed her fingers, flinching. Ice was an impossibility, and Tubigrip wouldn't be invented for 200 years or more, but maybe he would have a bandage?

"I don't suppose you have anything I could use to bind it? It needs compression, so it doesn't swell any more." She eyed his stock. That would work if all else failed.

He nodded, leading her out of the pantry and into the kitchen. There, he ushered her to a seat while he retrieved a wooden box from a shelf next to the fireplace. She looked around the room. It seemed smaller than her modern version, and the window in her kitchen was where the back door was in 1762. A simple wooden table sat in the middle of the space, with two wooden chairs next to it. Smoke tickled her nose from the fire for cooking. In her kitchen, the cooker was in the same space, although the chimney had been blocked off, and the modern cooker took up a fraction of the space that his fire did. Some pans and a blackened kettle sat next to the fire, and above it were hooks for hanging them. The

98

wall adjacent to the fire had two shelves with plates, earthenware mugs, and various other items on them. A wooden box hung from the wall next to the shelves, and a simple wooden dresser stood to one side.

Kit set his box down on the table in front of her and drew a roll of linen from it.

"Is this still a kitchen in your time?" he asked.

"Mm. The layout is different, and we don't cook over open fires in my time."

He frowned. "Where is the heat?"

"It's there. It's just done differently. It's hard to explain."

He unbuttoned the cuff of her shirt and rolled the sleeve back to expose her wrist. "And the pantry?"

"It has laundry equipment in it," she said, hoping she wouldn't have to explain washing machines or tumble-dryers to him. "And some food storage, too. I was trying to put up another shelf for cleaning equipment." She sucked her breath in sharply as he wound the bandage around her wrist.

"Sorry," he murmured, bending his head down again.

The same scent of cedar wood and leather that she'd encountered in the house so many times, drifted to her from him, overlaid with charcoal smoke. He was dressed the same as he had been the previous times she'd encountered him, except he wore no jacket. His waistcoat was wool at the front, but linen or cotton cloth at the back, and the back laced up, though the front had buttons. Were the laces in case he got fatter? Or thinner.

A glossy brown ribbon kept Kit's auburn hair tied back neatly, though some unruly waves had escaped, framing his face and partially obscuring the birthmark covering the side of his left cheek. The birthmark made it look exactly as if someone had slapped him across the face. His light beard also hid some of the birthmark and was less scruffy than the other day, as if he'd trimmed it recently. Light glinted off the gold highlights threading through his hair, and a smattering of freckles dotted his nose and cheeks. She was still admiring them when she realised he'd finished binding her wrist.

"Thank you," she stammered. Her cheeks burned.

A smile tickled his lips and his eyes sparkled. "It is no hardship,

Mistress Stewart. Might I suggest that if you are determined to break into my house, that you find a more surreptitious way of doing so? You make a terrible thief."

She tilted her chin up, amused. "I'm not a thief, Mr Greenwood. You're a terrible host, accusing me of things I haven't done."

His brows crept higher, and his gaze scanned her freshly bound wrist. "You are a forthright woman."

"Is that code for rude? That's rich, coming from the man who has just called me a thief."

"And trespasser," he added, mock-seriously. "Do not forget that I have accused you of that, too."

"I haven't." She smirked. "You also called me a witch. I'm starting a book. 'Things I have been accused of by an 18th century gentleman.' You *are* a gentleman, aren't you, Mr Greenwood?"

He laughed. "Well, I am not a rogue. And please, call me Kit. 'Mr Greenwood' makes me think I am my father."

"Only if you call me Ellie. And thank goodness you are not a rogue!"

He chuckled, and she caught herself. Normally she was completely tongue-tied when she met someone new, and here she was, teasing him as if they were old friends who had known each other for years. She couldn't remember that ever happening before, and clamped her mouth shut, averting her gaze.

"May I offer you a drink?" said Kit. "If you are staying."

She met his eye again, unsure. "I don't mean to be rude, but where does your water come from?"

"The well." He pointed through the doorway towards the back of the house. "Where does your water come from?"

"A tap." She paused. "Forgive me, but I don't know that I would be able to drink your water without getting ill."

He leaned back, his eyes locked on hers. "The well is only for this house. The water is sweet. But I could get you beer or wine if you prefer?"

"Perhaps a small glass of wine?"

He stood and retrieved a glass from one of the shelves of the dresser, then poured her some red wine from an open bottle. He slid the glass on to the table and she sipped from it. It was a distant cousin of modern wine – far drier and more acidic – but it was probably safe for her to drink.

He sat again, stretching out long legs and crossing them at the ankle.

She put the glass on the table. "What were you doing before I arrived?"

"My accounts. But then it sounded as if part of the house was falling down, so I came to investigate and found you in the pantry."

"Do you need to get back to work?"

"Eventually. But the accounts are dull and you are interesting. How is the wrist?"

She flexed her fingers. "Still sore, but it'll be okay. Thank you. I'm not sure I'm very interesting."

His mouth fell open. "You live in the future and have travelled through time! How can that not be interesting? I have been thinking about you since we talked and I have so many questions for you."

"Oh, please don't let them be about history. I was always rubbish at that."

He laughed loudly. "Do you not marvel that your history is my future?"

She thought of the stone in the churchyard. His future. History to her. Why did he disappear if none of the story about him and Janet was true?

"Tell me about the future?"

"If I do, maybe it won't happen."

He frowned. "I do not understand. For you, it *has* happened. How would that change if you told me?"

She sighed. "In my time, there are lots of stories that involve time-travel. No one can ever explain it properly, and there are always conundrums over actions in the past changing the future. There's one tale where a man goes into the past and does something that stops his parents from meeting. But if they don't meet, then he won't be born, and so won't be able to go back in time, so his parents *will* meet, because his time-travelling version won't have stopped them."

Kit blinked a few times, his brow puckering. "That is difficult

101

to understand!" He caught her eye again. "Do you think you will do something while you are here that will mean things are different in the future?"

"I don't know. I suppose I might tell you where to invest your money – things that will go on to be very successful – and your descendants could be rich."

He snorted. "I do not have any money to invest."

"Well, that's maybe for the best. The way the stories usually go is that I tell you where to invest, you put all your money into it, and then the business goes bankrupt and you lose everything, so…" She shrugged. "The moral of the story always seems to be: don't try to cheat fate."

He settled back more comfortably. "Do you believe that? That our path is predetermined?"

"I don't know. I don't think so. It would remove the whole idea of free will, wouldn't it? If I am predestined to be something, it wouldn't matter what I did, it wouldn't change that."

She wanted to get off this topic. What if the ghost story *was* right, and Kit *was* predestined to murder Janet and then be killed himself? He seemed lovely so far, but then, when neighbours of murderers were interviewed, didn't they often express surprise? Say they would never have believed it; that the person had always been so nice to them.

"Do you believe God has a path for us all?" Kit interrupted her thoughts.

She scratched her ear. "Um. Not really." Better not to say she didn't believe in any god. He'd accused her of being a witch once, and a lack of faith in 1762 was surely rare.

"If telling me the future is wrought with danger, tell me about life in your time instead. What is it like? I am sure telling me about *that* could not cause any difficulties."

She smiled. "Let's hope not. My life is very different. Easier, in many ways."

"Describe your day to me? Describe the house in your time?"

She did, and he marvelled at everything. It was so easy to talk to him. And he *listened*. Really listened. Simon had never paid her this much attention, frequently leaving the room while she was talking, and more often than not, cutting across her and speaking when she was still mid-sentence. Kit leaned forwards, resting his forearms on his thighs, taking in her every word, never interrupting, never taking his focus away from her. It almost made her cry.

He must have seen it in her face. "What is wrong?"

"Nothing. It's just wonderful for someone to be interested in what I have to say."

Surprise flooded his face. "You *are* interesting."

Her face grew hot and her skin prickled with sweat. She dipped her head. "I'm never normally this chatty!"

"Chatty? What does that mean?"

She met his eye again. "Talking a lot. I never normally talk so much."

"Chatty. Chatty." He rolled the word around in his mouth, trying it out. "I must remember that word." His gaze drifted over her patterned cardigan. "Did you make that?"

"No. I designed it. I made Joe knit it for me, though. He's better at colourwork than me."

"Your brother?"

"Mm. Granny Molly taught us. Well, she was teaching me, but Joe's not one to miss out on anything. And then he turned out to be better at it than me."

Kit laughed.

Self-consciousness caught up with Ellie again and she ground to a halt. She picked up her glass and took another sip.

"I have been trying to calculate when our worlds merge," said Kit. "I cannot fathom a pattern yet."

"No. Nor can I. It would be useful to know when it's going to happen. Then I wouldn't crash to the ground off a ladder. Or emerge in the middle of your fire!"

He blanched at her words, then recovered. "No. I think the fire is not inside the space where it first happens. There are colourful lights preceding the mirage, but they are always a few yards from the fire."

"Good to know."

She would fence off the area, though, just in case.

"I don't really understand it," she said. "The lights are in very specific places. They're never in the front of the house. *My* house—" she added "—which would be outside yours. And they appear in a part of the buildings outside, though far from your forge. If I'm inside the area where the lights are, I can end up here, but if I'm not, they are like an edge, and through them I can see you and this house, but I stay where I am."

He nodded vigorously. "Yes. I see the lights where you describe, and through them I see you, or the old lady who was here, but I never come to you. The lights only last a few moments for me."

"Mm. Me too. I think they're the doorway. If I stepped into the area when the lights are there, I might come here, but if I don't, I miss the opening." She sighed. "I wish I knew when it would happen. Or why sometimes I *am* within the area and I see you, but I *don't* come to 1762."

Kit's head shot up and he caught her hand. "It's happening now."

The kitchen flickered around them.

"What do you see?" he asked. "For me, there is a ghostly mirage of another room."

Ellie glanced around, seeing her modern cooker in the fireplace and her table and chairs, but superimposed over the reality, like a double image.

"That's my kitchen. I think our time together is up." She tried to put her glass down on the table.

Too late. Her surroundings blurred and her stomach flipped. For a moment, the room made a confusing jumble – part 1762, part modern – then it settled, and she lay on the floor, a small glass in her hands, its contents spilled.

"Okay. I prefer the walking back in and the building has switched. That shift was brutal."

She raised her head. He stood in front of her, but in a ghostly, silent form. He held her gaze for a few seconds, then faded away, leaving her alone in the room. She got to her feet and placed the wineglass on the table, staring at it. Tangible proof that she'd gone back to 1762. She fingered the linen around her wrist, thinking about how tender Kit had been, and how she had felt so at ease with him.

Frustration laced with loneliness licked through her. Had she finally met a man who made her feel valuable and interesting, only to be separated from him by more than two and a half centuries? Life could be spiteful.

20

Ellie finished packing the last of a sudden influx of orders, then leaned back in her seat in the study and stretched. To her dismay, time had stayed resolutely in the 21st century over the last few days and although she'd caught glimpses of Kit in the corner of her eye, she hadn't seen him in person. In some ways it had been a bonus, as she'd been run off her feet with the arrival of so many orders, but with Joe still away and no contact with Kit, the house could be lonely. She should call Liz and arrange to have a coffee with her, now she had cleared the decks.

As she contemplated hanging the washing out, the beautiful silver tabby cat strolled into the study. It stretched languidly, then peered at her, blinking vibrant green eyes.

"Hello again."

Ellie held out her hand, and the cat trotted over and rubbed its cheek against her fingers.

"Well, you're a very handsome chap, but where have you come from? In case you hadn't noticed, little one, we're the only house out here. I hope you've not come from the village via the main road. It's a bit too busy for cats to be strolling around." She tickled under the cat's chin, eliciting a loud purring. "Shall I see if there's any chicken left in the fridge for you?"

The cat trotted after her to the kitchen, then gulped down the tidbits of chicken Ellie put down for it.

"You're a bit too well cared-for to be a stray, but you seem quite happy to be here." Ellie stroked the cat again. "I wonder where you've come from."

She cocked her head to hear if the washing machine had finished. It had, so she headed for the utility room, grabbed the large wicker basket that lived on top of the machine, and unloaded the laundry. The cat followed her, sitting in the middle of the room, washing its face.

The washing line spanned the gravelled space outside the back door, running from the garage-cum-wood-store to the house. By the time Ellie had finished pegging out the washing, the cat had disappeared. When Ellie bent to pick up the basket, it had, too. As had the washing line and all the washing.

"Oh, okay. Hello, 1762." Her heart lifted at the thought of seeing Kit again.

Sounds from behind her caught her attention and she turned. Kit's workshop and stables filled the end of the yard, and the now familiar smell of charcoal smoke hung in the air. Low, tuneful humming filtered out of the open door of the forge, and she tiptoed to the corner to peer in. Kit stood at a bench with his back to her, and a smile came unbidden at the sight of him. She opened her mouth to speak, but then closed it again, choosing to watch him work for a while. He had a piece of metal in the fire, working the bellows with his left hand. His clothes were the same, with the addition of a leather apron protecting his front.

He removed the iron from the fire and turned to the anvil, hammering the hot metal in the tongs into a curve. He'd rolled his sleeves to the elbow, revealing muscled forearms smudged with grime. As ever, some unruly strands of hair had escaped from the dark green ribbon holding his hair back at the nape of his neck. Ellie rested her shoulder against the door-frame, happy.

In the yard next to the workshop, a grey horse snickered and shifted its weight from hoof to hoof. The silver tabby cat strolled across the yard.

"Hello, Shadow." Kit broke off from his work and reached down to fuss the cat. "Where have you been? Mousing?"

"He's been with me," Ellie said softly.

Kit whirled around, his face lighting up. "I was beginning to fear I would never see you again!"

"Hm. Me too. I wish I had some sign of when it might happen. How are you?"

"I am very well, thank you. How are you?"

"Better for seeing you. What are you doing? Making a horseshoe?"

He nodded, beckoning her closer. "For her." He pointed to the grey mare tethered in the yard, then pulled over a crate for Ellie to sit on, apologising for the roughness of it.

"It's fine. You're not going to have comfy chairs out here, are you?"

She perched on the crate, and Kit leaned his hips against the bench. "You get no warning that you are coming here?"

"No. I was in the middle of hanging out some washing and then the basket and all the washing disappeared, and here I am. I wish I *did* get a bit more warning! At least I haven't fallen today. Do you need to get back to work?"

"Yes. Sorry." He bunched his lips apologetically.

He returned to the fire and continued working on the horseshoe.

"Where's the horse's owner?" asked Ellie, hoping that they weren't about to return soon.

"In Masham. He left her here while he went to the market. It is Mr Barker's mare. He lives that way—" Kit pointed in a direction east of the village "—towards the mill. It is easier for him to leave her and come back for her."

Barker had been one of the names Liz had been scouting for in the churchyard, and a shiver passed down Ellie's back. He was alive and well in Kit's time; long since decayed and gone in Ellie's.

Kit peered at her, eyes wide. "Are you well, lass? You have gone pale."

She pushed a smile to her face. "I'm fine. It's strange when you talk about places here. There's no mill down there in my time."

"No? Tell me about the area?" He thrust the iron back into the fire, the colours of the embers gilding his face. "What is it like in your time?"

"The village is bigger, but many buildings from now are still standing. There's still a market on Wednesdays and Saturdays, though it probably sells different things in my time."

"And is this house still a blacksmiths?" He frowned. "No, it cannot be. You are no blacksmith!" He gave her a cheeky grin.

She laughed. "No. It's officially called Rose Cottage in my time, though everyone still calls it The Old Forge. I don't know when it stopped being a blacksmiths."

"Are there roses? There are none here now."

"A few. Not enough to warrant calling it Rose Cottage!"

He chuckled.

She shifted on the crate. It wasn't hugely comfortable, but there was no alternative. "How come you're so far from the village? I would have thought the blacksmiths would be closer in."

He shrugged. "We were, oh, before my grandfather's time. But then people did not want so much noise near to them." He pulled a wry smile. "They value the work done, but not *how* it is done. Where is the blacksmith in your time?"

"There isn't one. Well, there's one a few villages away. There isn't one in Masham."

Shock filled his face. "Where do people have their horses shod? Who makes nails? And the farm equipment?"

She paused, taking a breath. How on earth to explain the result of the industrial revolution and invention of the combustion engine?

"Um. Well. Horses aren't used all that much any more. Certainly not for farm-work or transport. A lot of what you do is now done in factories or by machinery. There are still blacksmiths, but not in every village."

"Horses are not used for transport? How do you get from place to place? What does the work of the horse?"

"Cars. Tractors. Machinery. I've never been on a horse."

He stared, his mouth falling open. "You have never ridden a horse?" He puffed out his cheeks. "Your world differs greatly from mine."

She lifted a shoulder and let it drop. "Yes, and no. People are still people. There's still love and hate and war and peace, even if a lot of other things have changed."

They lapsed into silence. He worked the horseshoe, using the curved end of the anvil to shape the metal, before putting it back in the fire.

"Where's Thomas today?" she asked. Was he about to appear and ask awkward questions?

Kit wiped some sweat from his brow, leaving a grimy streak behind. "At his work."

"What does he do?"

"He is a clerk."

"He doesn't help you here?"

A snort escaped from Kit's nose. "You have clearly never met Thomas. He might look like me in his face, but he is closer to you in strength! He could no more hammer iron than he could fly to the moon."

She laughed. "People *have* flown to the moon in my time."

The mirth evaporated from his face. "Do not mock me."

She held her hands up in peace. "I wouldn't. I promise. It's true. 1969. Two men walked on the moon."

He took a long look at her. "Your time is full of wondrous things."

She screwed up her nose. "Some of it's okay. Does *anyone* help you here?"

"I had an apprentice, but he is now a journeyman." He pulled a rueful face. "Which is a loss. I am getting another boy soon."

He took the horseshoe out of the fire and turned back to the anvil, hammering at the iron and making sparks fly. Then he walked over to the mare and stroked her flank, soothing her. He lifted her front left leg, clamping it between his thighs while he checked the shoe for fit. The metal was still hot, and smoke trickled up from the hoof.

"She's a beautiful horse," said Ellie.

"Aye. But she can kick like a mule when the mood is on her!"

The mood clearly wasn't on her today as she stood quietly and let Kit work without even a flared nostril in his direction. Finally satisfied with the fit, he cooled the shoe in a bucket of water, held some nails between his lips, then finished shoeing the horse. All the while, the mare stood patiently. Only when he'd finished and released her leg did she bunt him with her head, pushing him off balance. He scowled at her good-naturedly, patting her flank.

"Aye. I've finished!"

Ellie grinned at him. His gaze travelled to her shoes, and he sighed.

"I wish I could re-shod you as easily as I can a horse! Your

110

shoes are sewn together from scraps."

She peered down at her feet. Her trainers *did* look as if they had been put together from left-overs.

"Do you have cobblers in your time?" he said.

"Yes, but shoes are bought from a shop. And although these might look as if they're sewn together from scraps, they're actually very comfortable."

He blinked disdainfully, then joined her, wiping his hands on a rag.

She indicated his face. "You have a huge smudge on your brow."

He rubbed at it with the cloth, making it worse.

"Give it here!" she said, holding out her hand.

He passed her a cloth that was at least as grimy as he was, and she hunted in a pocket for a clean tissue. Finding one, she scrambled off the crate, dipped the tissue in the bucket of water by the anvil, and beckoned him to stand in front of her. He did, lowering his face to hers, and she wiped the sooty mark away.

"There. That's better."

He took the tissue from her and turned it over in his hands. "Paper is cheap enough to waste like this?"

"Mm, hm. Just throw it in the fire. Or keep it for the next smudge."

She expected him to step back now that she had finished cleaning his face, but he didn't. He stood close enough that his breath tickled her skin. She half closed her eyes, breathing deeply. He smelled of smoke and soot, cedar wood, and fresh sweat.

The air crackled between them. She looked up, straight into his eyes.

"You bewitch me," he murmured.

Before he could say anything else, a woman's voice sounded from the path at the front, making both of them freeze.

"Kit? Kit!"

"Hide at the back," he urged Ellie, grabbing her hand and dragging her to the far side of the forge. There, he pushed her behind a crate and threw a cloth over her. She crouched in the space, trying hard not to make a sound, wondering who had arrived. She could just see Kit around the edge of the cloth, if he stood close to the horse. If he moved back into the main part of the forge, he was out of her sight.

"Kit?" The woman's voice had a frantic edge to it.

"Janet? What is the matter?"

Janet?

Janet Shaw?

21

Ellie peeped around the cloth covering her hiding place, curiosity burning her. Janet flung herself at Kit and wrapped her arms around his neck.

"Oh, Kit! What do I do?"

"Janet, sit down. What is the matter?"

He led her towards the crate Ellie had so recently vacated, and they both disappeared from Ellie's view. Silently, she shifted position until she was comfortable, suspecting Janet's visit might not be brief.

Although she could no longer see them, their voices reached Ellie, loud and clear.

"It's Hugh Ellis." Janet's voice was tearful and broken. "Kit, he... he..."

Her tears prevented her from saying any more for a few moments. Kit made soft soothing sounds, reminding Ellie of how he had calmed the mare. Janet's hiccupy snuffles eased, and she sniffed loudly.

"He forced me," she whispered. "I was walking back home, and he came riding past, all hoity-toity. Oh, and I wish I had kept my mouth shut, but I can never forgive him for Edward!"

She dissolved into sobs, and Kit made more gentle sounds of comfort until she spoke again.

"And he said he would teach me to respect my betters, as if *he* was any better than a rat! And he got off his horse and shoved me against a tree, and..." Janet stopped again.

Ellie closed her eyes, desperate to return to her own time,

feeling horrible for eavesdropping. It would be taking all of Janet's courage to tell Kit about being assaulted. How would she feel if she knew a stranger was listening in?

"What did he do to you?" Kit's voice thrummed with anger.

"He… he… forced it into me. His… and it hurt, and made me bleed, and his…*mess*… it was all over my skirts." She wiped her nose on the back of her wrist. "And he just *laughed*!"

Ellie swallowed bile. Was the story right in one aspect, albeit so wrong in others? Was Hugh Ellis the father of Janet's child?

"You must tell your father," urged Kit.

Janet snorted. "Father would thrash me. And I will never marry if everyone knows I am not a maid!"

Was *this* why Kit asked her? To save her from shame? Jealousy stabbed her in the guts, surprising her, and she mentally scolded herself. She barely knew the man! She *certainly* had no claim on him.

There was an abrupt rustle of skirts.

"I am keeping you from your work. And Mother will wonder where I am."

"Janet, stay. You are still distressed."

"No, I must go. Kit, you must swear never to tell a soul about this. I should not have told you, but it would have burst out of me. I want to scream at the sky."

"At least tell your mother what happened."

"She would tell Father."

Kit sighed heavily. "Then stay out of Ellis's way and do not speak to him if you see him." Another rustle. "Janet, I am so sorry."

Ellie peeped out enough to see Kit release Janet from a hug. Janet smeared her hands over her cheeks, turned abruptly, and hurried away. When Ellie was sure she was far enough away, she came out from her hiding place.

"How much did you hear?" asked Kit, his face drawn.

"All of it. The poor girl. What will happen to her? Could she report him to someone else? A magistrate?"

Kit snorted. "Hugh Ellis *is* the magistrate." He tipped his head back, then stared at her. "May I ask something?"

"Of course."

"The story about me and Janet Shaw and Hugh Ellis that is in your time… what is it? It is more than you have told me."

Ellie swallowed. "I'm sure it's been corrupted over the years."

"Tell me."

She breathed shakily. How did you tell a man that he was going to murder a woman? Did she even believe he would? It seemed unlikely after what she'd just witnessed, but the story had been clear. She eyed the thick muscles on his arms and shoulders. What on earth would happen between him and Janet to change the kindness she'd just witnessed into a murderous rage?

"Lass, what is it?" His voice was low and gentle. "Why are you suddenly afraid of me? I will not hurt you. I swear."

She hesitated, collecting the right words. "The story can't be right. It says that you were angry about Janet." She ground to a halt, unwilling to say more.

"And that I killed Hugh Ellis?" he asked, uncertainty lacing his voice.

Her eyes widened. "No… Would you?"

He laughed hollowly. "No! Though I am almost angry enough to."

Maybe the story had got muddled and Kit killed Hugh Ellis and then the village turned on him? The thought of him being killed, whether by a baying mob or getting hanged for murder, made tears prickle her eyes. She blinked hard, and Kit reached across and brushed her cheek with the back of his fingers.

"Why are you crying?"

"I couldn't bear it if something happened to you. If you were hanged." Her voice caught on the final word and he drew her to him, resting his hands on her waist and touching his forehead to hers.

"Sh. I am not about to kill Hugh Ellis, however much he would deserve it."

She wound her arms around him and buried her face against his neck, holding him tight. Should she tell him? Would that stop him? She bit her lip hard, her breathing ragged.

"Sh. What is wrong? Come into the house?"

He led her to the kitchen, sat her down at the table there, and poured her a glass of wine. He sat opposite her, his hazel eyes locked on hers, and picked her hand up, smoothing his thumb over the back of it. A rough bit of skin on the ball of his thumb scraped her.

"Come on, lass. Tell me what you know. The story cannot be that I asked Janet to marry me and she preferred Ellis instead!"

Ellie scrubbed her fist over her face and drew in a long breath. "There is a *lot* more to the story. But Kit, I don't believe it's true."

He squeezed her hand. "Just tell me."

22

Ellie sat at the kitchen table and drew in a shuddery breath, trying to compose herself. Kit held her hand across the table.

"Okay," she said. "This is the story in my time, but I don't think it can be right. Not when you are such good friends with Janet." She swallowed, biting her lip. "The story claims that Janet's ghost haunts a building on the corner of the market square. That her spirit can't rest because she was murdered."

"By Hugh Ellis?"

She hesitated. "No. By you."

Kit's eyes widened. "Why would I murder Janet?"

Ellie studied her lap, unwilling to look at him. She fingered her brow with her free hand. "According to the story, you asked her to marry you, but before you were wed, you realised she was with child and that you were not the father. The rumour was that Hugh Ellis was the father, and that Janet had been trying to get *him* to marry her, instead of you." She paused briefly. "You were angry about that, and in a fit of rage, you hit her with a hammer and killed her."

She stopped, scared about how Kit might take the news. Her gaze crawled back up to his face. Shock filled his eyes, and he shook his head, breathing fast.

"I would never hurt Janet. She is like a sister to me. I would never hurt *anyone*." His face fell. "Please tell me you do not believe I could do that?"

"No. I think the story must be muddled. But there's more."

117

He trembled. "I am hanged. For something I did not do."

She shook her head. "No. The village turns on you and dispenses their own justice before you can be tried. They kill you."

The blood drained from his face, and his posture collapsed. "Janet is killed, and the village blames *me*? And kill *me* for it?"

"Mm."

He sat back heavily, making his chair groan. "I swear, I would *never* hurt Janet. Never. You must believe me!"

Ellie leaned forwards, squeezing his hand. "I do. I saw how kind you were to her just now. But *someone* kills her. At least, according to the folklore. And you are blamed."

Kit pulled his fingers free and rested his elbows on the table, his head in his hands. "We must stop this! Janet is just a lass! Who would kill her?"

"I don't know. Hugh Ellis?"

"I do not know. I think not." He lifted his head and blinked slowly. "Forcing a woman? Yes. *Killing* a woman? No, I do not think so."

Ellie chewed her bottom lip, then blurted out, "Your brother puts up a really strange stone for you. In the churchyard."

Kit raised wary eyes to her. "A stone? A gravestone?"

"No... Well, maybe. It's right at the back, by the wall. It just says that you disappeared. I assumed it was because..." she tailed off, swallowing. "Because there was nothing to bury."

A sob caught in her throat, and Kit held her hands again, ashen-faced.

"When? When do I disappear? Does the stone say?"

She scrunched her face up, sniffing hard. "Soon. September 6th, this year." She gazed at him, tears threatening. "Kit, how do we change all of this? I don't want Janet to be murdered. I don't want *you* to die." She hunched her shoulders. "I mean, I know that by my time you *will* have died, but I don't want you to die like that."

Kit chafed his thumb over the back of her hand, his eyes never leaving hers, saying nothing for several minutes. Finally, he spoke. "The story starts with Janet being killed—"

"No," Ellie interrupted. "The story starts with you asking her to marry you."

118

He huffed his breath through his nose. "I love her as a sister. I would not ask her, so that part is wrong. No, it starts with Janet being murdered. If we can work out who kills her, perhaps we can stop it all."

Ellie's head spun with the concepts. "But if the story is there in my time, it *must* happen. The stone is there. You disappear in September." She pulled a hand free to scrub a tear from her cheek. "Kit, we *can't* stop it, because for me it's already happened!"

He cradled her against his broad shoulder, shaking. "Then I had better make the most of my time, for I have less than three months." A sob erupted from her and he rocked her, holding her tight. "Perhaps there is another reason for why I disappear. One that does not involve something bad happening?"

"But you would still disappear." Realisation hit her hard. "Thomas won't erect a stone in your memory if you are still here. And this is the only place where I go back in time, so if you disappeared from here but still lived, we wouldn't see each other again after September."

He stroked her hair, tangling his fingers in it. "Then let us make every encounter the best it can be."

She moved back, needing to see his face. His eyes were full of warmth for her, and he smoothed the back of a finger over her cheek, brushing away a tear. *Man*, she wanted to kiss him! That surely wouldn't be the done thing, though.

He made the decision for them both. He pressed his palm against her cheek, drew her face closer, and brushed his lips over hers. They kissed softly, and Ellie melted into him. Slowly, he drew back, his face flushed and his breathing fast. Behind him, lights danced, and frustration ripped through her.

"No! I don't want to go back yet!"

Overlapping images of the two kitchens surrounded them.

"Come back soon?" urged Kit.

"I'll try!"

She kissed him, but then her lips touched nothing, and she found herself sprawled on the floor of her kitchen. Shadow stalked over and sat next to her head, bunting her shoulder.

"How is it you can come to my time and *he* can't," Ellie muttered, sitting up. "Because I hate to break it to you, cat, but if

I had to choose between you, I'd pick him." She rested her elbows on her knees and her cheek on her forearms. "Oh, Shadow. What am I going to do? How do I save him?"

She scraped herself up from the floor and made herself a mug of tea. Back in the study, she willed the room to shift and take her back to him, but it didn't.

She chewed at her thumbnail. If so much of the modern story was wrong, why had it persisted? Why had Kit got the blame? Ellis *must* be the one who killed her, too. But *why*? Without being mean to Janet, she was a nobody, and Ellis was a wealthy landowner and the magistrate. Did she threaten to tell? Ellie screwed up her nose. No. She'd sworn Kit to secrecy. *Her* honour was at stake, more than Ellis's, however unfair that was.

She closed her eyes, remembering their kiss. The light tickle of his beard, his fingers in her hair, his breath on her skin, the softness of his lips. She could have kissed him for hours.

Her heart cracked. If they couldn't work out how to change the past, he would be dead in less than three months.

23

Ellie chewed the end of a pen, one eye on the pot bubbling at her side where she was dyeing skeins of wool, the other on her laptop screen on the worktop next to her. She'd been thinking about Kit and the story since she'd overheard Janet talking to him. Kit *surely* couldn't be the one who had murdered Janet, so if it wasn't him, *was* it Hugh Ellis? Because she was absolutely certain that the poor lass *would* be murdered. Had been murdered. She shook herself, sighing at how confusing it was to think about it all.

Hugh Ellis had already raped Janet. Was it such a leap to think he could kill her and blame it on Kit? Although why? Poor Janet was barely a threat to him. A thought struck her. Was *Kit* a threat to him? He couldn't kill Kit directly; Kit would be too strong. She frowned. Why would Kit be any threat to Hugh Ellis? He wouldn't tell, any more than Janet would.

She typed Ellis's name into a search engine, then scrolled through the results. After a lot of false starts, she finally found the right Hugh Ellis. According to the online sources, Sir Hugh Ellis had been a wealthy landowner who'd made his money in the wool trade. He was the local magistrate in Kit's time with a reputation for being harsh, frequently sentencing people to be hanged, even for very minor offences such as poaching or the theft of small things. Kit had said that Ellis had condemned Janet's brother to hanging for poaching. The idea that she would have wanted to marry the man who had assaulted her and had her brother killed seemed utterly preposterous.

After some more digging, she found a picture of Ellis: an overweight man with a florid complexion and a contemptuous sneer. The portrait had been painted in 1786, and Sir Hugh appeared to be around sixty, making him in his late thirties, maybe forty, in Kit's time. He wasn't *Sir* Hugh in Kit's time, just plain Hugh Ellis. His knighthood had been for his wool merchant work. And probably donations to a political party, if the 18th century was anything like modern day.

She turned the heat off under her dye pot and replaced the lid on the pan, then turned back to her laptop. After more scrolling and more clicking, she'd found nothing else of significance. Nothing that might suggest he was a murderer or a rapist. But then, unless he'd been tried for either offence, nothing would appear in online searches over 250 years later.

What would drive someone to murder? Ellie had never been a fan of crime novels or cop shows on TV. What reasons did people have for killing someone? She chewed her pen again. If it *was* Sir Hugh who killed Janet, why had he done it? It couldn't be for money or power, as she had none and he had plenty. It seemed unlikely to be a crime of passion. The most obvious thing was that he would lose status if anyone knew what he'd done to her, but Janet had sworn Kit to secrecy and seemed determined not to tell anyone else herself. Did something else happen to Janet that made her change her mind over keeping quiet?

She checked the time, needing some fresh air. The yarn she'd dyed needed to cool in the pot, and she had a pile of orders packed and ready to post. The Post Office van would still be in the village if she hurried, and she could have a quick wander around the churchyard afterwards to see if she could glean anything from Sir Hugh's headstone. She closed the lid of the laptop and collected her parcels together.

The stroll down into the village lifted her spirits. Birds chirped noisily from the hedges and the verges overflowed with flowers and insects. Few cars passed her, allowing her to imagine what the walk would have been like in Kit's time. Their lives differed in so many ways, but this road couldn't have changed much, apart from the arrival of asphalt.

Her parcels dealt with at the mobile Post Office, she walked on to the churchyard. Ellis had died wealthy and powerful, so no doubt his gravestone would be one of the bigger, more ostentatious ones, close to the church.

It was. And if it represented the rest of his life, he had money but no taste. Most of the headstones were of local stone, but Sir Hugh's memorial was polished red marble, with columns and fancy shaping, gold lettering now a little worn in places, and a huge plinth. The whole thing stood almost as tall as Ellie. The other gravestones that size listed lots of family, rather than being for only one person, but Ellis's was all about him. Her research had told her he'd married and had seven children, but not one of them got a mention. She took a picture with her phone and was about to head back home when an urge to see Kit's stone came over her.

It was still there, hiding at the back next to a wall. The very opposite of the grandiose affair of Sir Hugh's stone, it was small and plain; the lettering picked out by algae and moss, not by gold. She kissed her fingertips and pressed them to the stone, then picked some daisies and left them in front of it.

"Hopefully see you soon," she breathed. "And let's see if we can stop Janet from getting murdered and you from being killed."

24

Bright sun poured in through the skylight over the stairs, highlighting dancing dust motes and bathing the hall in soft light. Ellie had just finished parcelling up several orders and strolled through to the kitchen to grab a coffee. On the wall of the kitchen hung a large railway clock, its second hand making a soft clunking sound as it marked off time. Ellie flicked the kettle on and stretched her arms above her head, idly looking at the clock. The second hand trembled but didn't tick on a second, and Ellie frowned. It happened again. She groaned.

"Oh, don't say the battery's gone. I don't think I have any others. And you look like you weigh a ton!"

If the battery was dud, she was either going to have to tackle the heavy clock on her own, with the risk of dropping it, or wait until Joe was back down, and get teased about needing him to do stuff for her.

The second hand quivered again. And then colourful lights swirled around her and she was in the kitchen in 1762. Which had a different layout to hers.

She found herself jammed up against Kit's back, pressing him into a table, where he was chopping meat. He jumped violently, and the knife bit deep into his finger. He swore loudly and turned, just as she stepped back. Her hand flew to her mouth.

"God, Kit, I am so sorry!"

He clasped his left hand, scarlet beginning to ooze between his fingers. "Please pardon my language!" He sighed. "I am delighted to see you, but why can you not walk in through the door, like

124

everyone else does?"

"I don't get to choose! And in my kitchen, the table is over there!" She cast around to find a cloth, spotted one, and retrieved it. "Here. Press hard. Do you have clean water?"

He nodded to a jug on the side, taking the cloth from her and wrapping it more tightly around his cut hand. She found another cloth and soaked it in the cool water, then went back over to him.

"Let me see?"

He eased the cloth back. The wound still bled, but not as badly as before. She bathed it carefully, found a clean area of the dry cloth, and pressed it tightly against it.

"I really am sorry. Maybe we need to coordinate our rooms."

He offered her a smile. "Maybe. If it will stop you from appearing in my house and startling me like that!" A blush spread from the neck of his shirt and stained his cheeks. He cleared his throat. "Which room do you sleep in? Thomas's room is directly above this one. Mine is on the other side. In each room, the bed lies against the outer wall, with the head-end towards the window. In case you need to coordinate."

She smiled. "Useful to know. As embarrassing as it might be to materialise in *your* bed, I certainly don't want to appear in Thomas's!"

His colour deepened, and she grinned at him. "My room is in the new part of my house and it doesn't shift, so we should manage to avoid scandals and embarrassments."

Although… the idea of materialising in his bed had a definite appeal.

She moved back, but he caught her hand with his uninjured one, drawing her to sit next to him. Just the touch of his hand made butterflies appear in her stomach.

"How are you?" she asked. "I've missed you. I've obviously not been in the house when our two times have bunched up. Though I think I might get a signal that it's about to happen."

"Oh?" He played with her fingers, making her pulse race.

"Mm. There's a large clock on the wall." She pointed to the equivalent space in his kitchen, trying to concentrate and not be distracted by him. "And just before everything shifted, and I ended up making you cut yourself, the second hand stopped moving."

"What happened to the pendulum?" he asked, his face full of curiosity.

"It doesn't have one." She glanced around. "Do you have a clock?"

He nodded, amused. "Yes. But not in the kitchen. It is in the room you call the study."

"Perhaps you should keep an eye on it, and if the pendulum stops or the hands stop moving for a few seconds, it might herald my arrival."

"I am mostly in my workshop or the kitchen during the day, and you do not appear in the evening. Or, not so far."

"Mm. Probably a good thing, otherwise Thomas would see me. Anyway, how are you?"

He shrugged. "I am well – apart from a cut hand – though I have missed you. I feared you could no longer visit."

It was over two weeks since she had last been transported to 1762. More than two weeks since he'd said she bewitched him and had kissed her.

"Mm. I was fearing the same thing. Now that I get a few seconds of warning, I'll try to bring you a gift from the future. Mind you, I only get the warning if I'm looking straight at the clock at the right time, so it's not all *that* helpful." She scanned the table. "What are you making? Or what *were* you making before I materialised so close to you that you almost cut your hand off?"

"Dinner for tonight. Stew."

"You don't have a cook or a housekeeper?"

His lips twitched. "Why would I be making dinner, if I had a cook or a housekeeper?"

She laughed. "Fair point. Let me help you. It's the least I could do after making you cut your hand. How's the cut now?"

He peeled the cloth back. The cut had stopped bleeding, but it wouldn't take much movement in his hand to make it open back up again. She re-tied the cloth binding it and took the knife from him.

"Dice this lot?" she said, waving her hand at the array of meat and vegetables.

"You do not have to make my dinner. You are a guest."

She ignored him and took over cutting the meat into chunks.

126

"What meat is this?"

"Rabbit."

Her head whipped up, her eyes wide. "Please tell me you didn't poach it! Given what happened to Janet's brother."

He chuckled, his eyes sparkling. "No. I bought it!" He paused, nibbling his lower lip.

"What?" said Ellie. "You look like you want to tell me something."

He sighed. "It is not my story to tell."

"Janet?"

"Yes."

Ellie's hand stilled over the vegetables. "Has Sir Hugh assaulted her again?"

Kit snorted. "*Sir* Hugh? He is plain Hugh Ellis."

"Oh. Yes. Well, he ends up Sir Hugh Ellis." She did the maths. "In about fifteen years, I think. Anyway, has he hurt Janet again?"

"No. She has stayed out of his way. But her courses have not come, she says."

It took Ellie a second to work out what he meant. "Oh. Oh! What will she do?"

Kit rested his back against the table. "She does not know."

Ellie swallowed. Being pregnant out of wedlock in 1762 would be a disaster.

"Will her family support her? Will she be able to marry?"

He bunched his lips. "Her family does not know. Yet. It will be hard for her to marry if she has the child. She is thinking of going to a woman who may have herbs that would help."

A lead lump settled in her guts. "Help? You mean abort the baby?"

Kit nodded unhappily.

"Oh, Kit, no! And that's so risky! They might poison her."

"I know," he said. "But what can she do? I do not think her family will support her."

Ellie hated the idea of Janet trying to kill the baby, though in 1762 there were precious few alternatives available. She finished dicing the last of the meat in silence and laid the knife down.

"The rabbit's chopped. Where do you want it?"

He took it from her and added it to a large pot while she got on with preparing the vegetables.

"Leave them," he said after a moment, standing next to her. "I want to show you something."

"In a minute. I've nearly finished."

He leaned against the table again. "What if you disappear before you see it?"

"Then show whatever it is to me the next time I come." She chopped the final carrot and put the knife to one side. "There. Done!"

Kit added the vegetables to the pot on the fire and replaced the lid, then beckoned to her to follow him out to the forge.

The sun warmed her neck as she picked her way across the cobbles, and raucous sparrows cheeped from the trees. Inside the forge, he ushered her to sit on a crate, then retrieved an intricate piece of metalwork from a bench and handed it to her with a flourish. She took it from him and turned it around in her hands. Fine filigree work entwined in a complex pattern to make a heart, and within it, she could trace her initials. As she looked, more details emerged, including his initials and the date 1762.

She raised her eyes to him. "Oh, Kit, this is *amazing*! Thank you!"

Relief flooded his face. "I do not just make nails and horseshoes," he said, adding ruefully, "Though no one would ever pay me to make this."

"It's fabulous. No one has ever made me a gift before. *I* would buy this from you, except my money would be useless here." She had a bit of change in a pocket and fished it out and laid it on the workbench. "This is what money in my time looks like."

He took the scattering of coins – a couple of twenty-pence pieces, a pound, and some coppers – and inspected them.

"Who is the woman on them? Another queen?"

"Mm. Queen Elizabeth. She's been The Queen for ages. It was her Platinum Jubilee in June."

"Platinum?"

"Seventy years on the throne."

His brows rose. "She must be very old. Or have become The Queen very young."

Ellie wrinkled her nose. "Bit of both. I suppose she wasn't *that*

128

young. She's in her nineties now." She frowned. "Which King George are you on at the moment?"

He laughed. "Third. How many are there in total?"

"Four in a row. Then another couple before my time. I can't quite remember the order of who comes between George IV and my time. Queen Elizabeth's father was George VI. How long has George III been reigning?"

"Just two years. Why?"

Should she tell him? He dipped his head, prompting her for an answer.

"Um. He goes mad, and his son has to be Regent, on and off. Not for a while though, as far as I remember."

"The King is mad?" Kit blinked a couple of times. "Oh."

"Mm. There are turbulent times ahead."

She almost told him about what would happen in France, and American Independence, but caught herself. She put the heart on the workbench. A mark on his forearm caught her attention, and she pointed. "Are you hurt?"

He turned his arm to look at it. "No. Not really. A bit of charcoal from the fire caught me."

Now she looked, she saw his arms were peppered with small scars. "Do you get burned a lot?"

He rolled his sleeves down self-consciously. "I'm a blacksmith." He studied his feet, tucking a couple of strands of hair behind his ear, then raking his nails through his light beard. "Yesterday, my hair was tidy, my beard combed... and today, I am untidy and my hair is being wilful, and you only see my scars."

"You look gorgeous to me."

He raised his eyes, unsmiling, crossing his arms tightly over his chest. "Do not mock me."

"I wasn't. I promised I never would, and I meant it. Trust me, I don't care about the scars, or your hair being 'wilful' as you put it. I care that the man underneath all of that is kind and warm and honourable. You can tame your hair. But you cannot change your nature. Don't be embarrassed about the scars, because that's not what I see when I look at you." She slid off the crate, picked her way across to him, and unpeeled his folded arms. "I see an amazing man that I want to spend time with."

He slipped his arms around her, his eyes soft. "That is truly what you see?"

"Yes." She pushed some of his hair behind his ear. It sprang free almost instantly. "Which is probably a good job, because I'm not sure you *can* tame your hair."

He laughed hard.

She stood on tiptoe and kissed him, taking her time, resting her palms against his broad chest. He tensed briefly, then relaxed, drawing her tighter to him.

"Ellie, you make me so happy in the times we have together," he breathed as they parted. "You make me laugh the way no one else does. I feel so at ease with you."

"Likewise. I don't know if I can explain it. I can be 'me' and it's enough. I don't have to try to be more than I am."

He fussed with her hair. "Why would you need to be more than you are? You are wonderful."

Her mind flicked to Simon and why their engagement had ended, and she twisted one side of her mouth up. "Not everyone has thought that."

He cocked his head, his brow twitching, but she didn't elaborate. She glanced around the forge. The fire wasn't lit, and all his tools were tidied away neatly. "Are you not working today?"

"It is the Sabbath."

"Oh. Where's Thomas?"

He smiled. "Seeing a young lady."

"He doesn't want to marry Janet?"

Kit shifted her in his arms. "No. Though I agree that if he did, it would be a better solution than her seeing the woman with the herbs."

Ellie fidgeted. She didn't want to ask the question, but it burned her, demanding to be voiced. "And what about you? Would you marry her? I mean, you're good friends. You don't *dislike* her. You would probably be happy together. She'd certainly be happier than being pregnant and unmarried."

Kit's eyes locked on hers, and his breathing became unsteady. He didn't speak for a moment, and Ellie's mouth dried.

"I see it would offer another solution," he said eventually. "But my heart lies elsewhere, and I could not marry her when I love

130

someone else."

Ellie's heart missed several beats. Did he really love her?

Kit brushed the end of his nose against hers. "Ellie, I love you. Do you think you will ever become stuck here?"

She raised one shoulder and let it drop. "I don't know. I don't know what determines when the house shifts for me. It never shifts for my brother. He's never even seen you. I don't know why it only shifts for us."

"Perhaps we were fated to meet," he whispered, his hazel eyes full of happiness.

"Perhaps we were. Though it would be a cruel fate if we were only ever able to meet like this."

And even crueller for you to be killed for something you haven't done.

"Would you choose to live here?" he asked. "If you could?"

She leaned into him, resting her forehead against his collarbone. "I think I would prefer that you came to my time. If I had the choice."

He lifted her chin and kissed her tenderly, drawing her closer, then groaned. "I do not want you to leave."

"That makes two of us. I wish I could take you back with me."

He rested his hips against the workbench, settling her in his arms. "And what would I do in your time?"

"What you do now? Shoe horses. Make things in metal. Make beautiful filigree hearts. People in my time *would* buy plenty of those. There would be enough for you to do." She rubbed her cheek on his shoulder, the rough fabric of his waistcoat tickling her skin. "I can't imagine anyone would value my skills as a knitter if I came here. I read and write and I know stuff, though. Maybe I could be a teacher."

He huffed. "You would not need to do anything. I make enough money for us to live well."

She tipped her head up and met his eye. "Hm. By 'not need to do anything' you mean I would cook and do laundry and housework. In my time there are machines to help with the laundry, and both men and women cook and do chores." She grinned. "Maybe the idea of having to do chores would make you choose to stay here, rather than come to my time."

He raised his brows, challengingly. "I have no cook or

housekeeper. I cook and do chores." He tilted his head. "Admittedly, there is a washer-woman who does laundry." His gaze rested on her again. "I think I would choose to come to your time. If I could."

She chafed her thumb over the small of his back. "It's a moot point, though, isn't it? I don't know if you can get to my time. You haven't so far. And you disappear. Soon." She swallowed. "Kit, the next time the world shifts, can I try to take you back to my time with me?"

"Do you think it will work?"

"Well, your cat strolls back and forth as if there's no barrier!"

He snorted. "Is Shadow with you in an evening? I have not seen him."

She leaned back, her hands locked at his waist. "Most evenings, he comes to me for his dinner, sleeps on my bed for a while and then at dusk he goes out. I don't know where he spends his nights."

"Mousing. Although if you keep on giving him dinner, he will not want to catch mice," he chided.

"True."

She drew in a deep breath, savouring the scent of leather and cedar wood from him. *Could* she take him back to her time? If she couldn't and he was killed... her heart cracked.

Shadow strolled into the workshop, stretched languidly, and sat down next to her. She drew back from Kit and reached over to fuss the cat, making Kit roll his eyes. As Ellie tickled Shadow under his chin, the workshop shifted. She grabbed Kit's hand, clenching it hard. "Don't let go!"

His eyes widened, and he gripped her hand firmly, wrapping his other arm around her waist. To no avail. A few moments later, Ellie found herself in her workshop. Alone.

"Damn it!" she yelled.

She flung her head back, frustration pouring through her. She *had* to find a way to get him to her time. She just had to.

25

The crunch of tyres on the gravel outside the windows had Ellie springing up from her seat and rushing to the front door. Joe parked in the space next to the garage, then clambered out, stretching his back and rolling his shoulders. He beamed at her, some of the stress melting off him.

"I made it!" he said, grabbing his bag and hurrying over to sweep her up into a bear-hug.

She leaned back in his arms. "Tough journey?"

"A *lot* of roadworks. *Please* tell me you have beer in the fridge."

"Bought especially for you. Come in. Is that the only bag you have? I thought you were going to be up for ages."

"I am. The other bag's in the boot. This is just my overnight stuff. You take this one and I'll grab the other." He released her and handed his bag to her.

Dumping the bag at the foot of the stairs as she passed, she made her way to the kitchen, Joe close behind her. As she handed him a bottle of beer from the fridge, he peered intently at her.

"Wow. I haven't seen you look so good in *years*! The country air must suit you." His face lit up with mischief. "Or have you found yourself a hunky bloke?" His mouth dropped open. "Oh, my god. You're blushing. You *have* found yourself a hunky bloke! Well, get yourself a drink and spill the beans."

"There are no beans to spill," she said. What on earth could she tell him? That she'd fallen for Kit Greenwood, who lived in 1762?

As she retrieved a glass from the cupboard, her gaze alighted on the one she'd brought back from Kit's. Joe opened the fridge and passed her a bottle of wine.

"Seriously, sis, have you met someone?"

She'd always talked to Joe, and she yearned to tell him everything now, but she could imagine the reception she'd get from her level-headed, scientific brother, if she told him she popped back and forth between now and 1762, and that the 'hunky bloke' was Kit Greenwood. In Joe's eyes, the *murderous* Kit Greenwood. She *did* have the glass as proof, though. And her filigree heart.

"Kind of," she said. "It's complicated."

"Then you'll need a bigger glass." He nodded at the one in her hands.

She laughed, poured herself some wine, and flicked her head towards the door. "Go through to the lounge."

He sat on one sofa and she took the other, tucking her feet up under her body. Joe sipped his beer straight from the bottle, waiting. Ellie tried to gather her thoughts. How on earth could she tell him what had been happening?

Joe cocked a brow. "Come on!"

She sighed. "Okay. I *have* met someone. It's just... complicated."

"Does he have a name?"

She took a large slug of her wine, steadying herself for his reaction. "Kit Greenwood."

Joe's bitter chocolate eyes settled on her for a moment. "Kit Greenwood? Isn't that the name of the blacksmith who murdered that lass?"

Ellie bit the inside of her lip. "Mm. It's the same guy. And he didn't murder her."

Joe's hand paused as he went to take another drink of beer. "What? You're not making sense."

She took a deep breath, wishing she could take it back and pretend she'd fallen for Mr What's-his-name, the chemistry teacher Liz had mentioned. But she hadn't, so, in for a penny...

"The house shifts. Sometimes it's now, and sometimes it's 1762. I keep stumbling into 1762 and Kit's there. And he's really lovely. And then I end up back here. I don't know why it happens or even *when* it's going to happen, but it does."

Joe's eyebrows were almost in his hairline. "What time did you start drinking today?"

She scowled. "With this glass! I swear, Joe. It's happened. I've been to 1762 and met Kit. He made me a beautiful heart in metalwork. And I ended up bringing one of his wineglasses back with me. I'll fetch them."

She jumped up and put her drink on the trunk between them. A minute later she was back in the lounge with the filigree heart in one hand and the wineglass in the other. She handed them both over to Joe. He turned the heart around in his hands.

"This is beautifully made. *Hand* made. Where did you get it? Honestly."

"*Honestly,* I got it from Kit."

Joe put it on the steamer trunk and turned to the glass. "Well, I know nothing about antique wineglasses, and even if it *was* from 1762, you could have picked it up in a flea-market or antique shop." He leaned back in his seat. "Are you being serious? The man you thought was a ghost is actually just in 1762, but you travel there and see him?"

"Yes!" She threw herself back on to the sofa. The analogy Kit had made on one of her first visits came back to her, and she pinched up a fold of her jumper. "It's like this is me now; this is 1762. Sometimes the space between lies flat and time is normal, but sometimes it wrinkles up and the space between our time and his disappears and I'm in 1762."

"Then why doesn't he keep popping into our time? Why don't I ever go back?"

She flung her hands up. "I don't know!"

Joe said nothing for a few moments, staring at her.

"Well, say something!" she said, his silence crushing her.

He pushed his bottom lip out. "I think you've finally lost the plot. You *can't* flit back and forth to 1762."

She glared. "Fine."

Joe sipped his beer. "Okay. Let's say it's true. Where do you see it all ending? Will you flit back and forth between his world and yours until he either murders you, or gets killed by a mob for murdering the girl?"

She folded her arms tightly across her chest. "You know what, Joe, just forget it. I don't want to fight."

He held his hands up, offering peace. "Okay. But as your big brother, it's my job to vet all the men you get involved with and see off the losers. And someone who murders a girl is *definitely* not one I would approve of."

She picked up her wine again. "Kit's *not* a murderer."

Joe opened his mouth, then closed it abruptly.

They lapsed into silence, each sipping their drinks. Joe's question whirled in her head. Where *did* she see it all ending? Where *could* it all end, except in tears?

Opposite her, Joe closed his eyes and rested his head against the back of the sofa. Soft shadows formed under his eyes.

"You just tired from the long drive? Or are you stressing?" she asked.

"Bit of both," he replied without opening his eyes. "The drive was hellish. Moving wouldn't be simple. *If* I move. I'm juggling a lot of things."

"Well, hopefully you can recharge your batteries up here."

Shadow strolled in, and Ellie reached down to fuss him. In typical cat style, he ignored the person happy to give him attention, and marched over to Joe, jumping up and clambering on to his lap. Joe started, then stroked Shadow, who turned around twice and settled down on Joe's lap, purring loudly.

"When did you get a cat?" he asked, tickling behind its ear.

"He's not really mine. He just comes and goes. He's called Shadow."

"Whose is he? He's beautiful."

Ellie didn't answer.

Joe raised his brows. "Is he a stray? He's a bit too shiny and well-kept for that. Mind you, your nearest neighbours are pretty far away, so he must be a bit of a wanderer."

She braced herself. "He's Kit's cat."

Joe eyed her, still fussing Shadow. "Right. And he just waltzes back and forth through time, too?"

"Dinner will be ready soon. It's casserole, because I didn't know quite when you would arrive."

"Nice change of topic. You're serious about all of this, aren't

136

you?"

"Shall I dish up? We'll eat in the kitchen."

Ellie got up before Joe could answer and stalked through to the kitchen. She hadn't expected Joe to believe her, but she hadn't expected to be so hurt at his dismissal, either. Shadow wandered in, nose in the air, no doubt hoping for some of the casserole. She spooned a bit of the meat and gravy into a dish for him and left it to cool on the worktop, then served up for her and Joe.

He joined her, throwing her a conciliatory look as he sat at the kitchen table.

"Okay. I don't buy that you're a time-traveller, but you're clearly keen on this guy, so tell me more about him?"

She slid a plate in front of him, poured him a glass of wine, gave Shadow his tidbit, then finally sat down.

"He's lovely," she said. "Kind. Generous – he made me the heart as a gift. He's smart. The girl who gets murdered is his friend, and far from cheating on him with Hugh Ellis, she hates the man, because he had her brother hanged for poaching, and he raped her."

Joe opened his mouth as if to argue, then closed it again. They ate in silence for a few moments.

"So, is there a special place where you go back in time?" asked Joe.

Ellie glared, stabbing her food with her fork.

"What?" he said. "I'm trying to understand it all."

She paused, then gave in. "The back half of the house. The kitchen, the study, the utility room. Part of the yard and workshop."

"And does it happen all the time? Or what?"

She breathed steadily. "I don't know if there's a pattern to it. I've tried to work out if there is, but I don't have the right kind of brain. It doesn't happen at the same time every day, and it's not for the same length of time every day. The first couple of times it happened, it was so short we barely spoke before I was back. The only warning I have is that the clocks stop – the second hand stops moving properly. That happens about five seconds before the room shifts. Kit doesn't have a clock in every room, so I don't get any warning that it's all about to shift back again when I'm with

137

him. I just come back and he's left staring at an empty room." She turned her wineglass on the spot. "I've made a note of all the times I've experienced it, and also when Shadow appears and disappears. Would you have a look at it? See if your science-head can spot a pattern that I can't?"

"Sure."

She gritted her teeth. She hadn't expected him to believe her, but now his humouring her was somehow worse. She needed to change the subject.

"Talk to me about why you're so stressed. Anything I can help with?"

He rubbed his left eye, scrunching his face up. "I know I have to move." He looked away. "I have to if I want to have kids, because to have kids, I need to be with someone, and I know I can't do that unless I move."

He tailed off and ate some of his dinner. Ellie waited.

"It feels like a betrayal." His voice gained a slightly gravelly edge, and he stopped.

"I know. I know exactly how hard it will be for you to sell your house. But letting go of the house wouldn't mean that you loved Hayley any less. She would never have wanted you to stay single forever."

He scraped his hand through his hair, leaving it in messy clumps. "I know. I'm sorry. It's hard."

"Hey, it's okay."

Her heart ached for him. She'd grasped the opportunity to move here with both hands, but she hadn't been risking anything, and had no ghosts tethering her to her old place.

"You know you're welcome to stay here as long as you want. It's your house as much as mine! Convert the dining room into your study if you like. I can't imagine either of us holding enormous dinner parties!"

He swirled the wine in his glass. "Thanks, Ellie."

She reached across and squeezed his hand. "Hey. I'm here for you. Always. You're on dishes, by the way."

She cleared their empty plates to the side of the sink, hugged her brother, and followed Shadow back through to the lounge. Joe joined her a few minutes later, the neck of a wine bottle in his hand. He flumped down opposite her and poured her another glass.

"Are you serious about Kit Greenwood?"

"Yes," she snapped.

"Hackles down! Granny Molly always said you'd been visiting your red-headed boy when you went missing when you were little. Do you think you were?"

"I do. Kit actually remembered it. He got thrashed for lying, apparently. And he's more chestnut than red."

"And he's a blacksmith? *The* blacksmith?"

"Mm. Except I don't think he killed Janet. I think Hugh Ellis probably did and blamed Kit."

Joe topped his glass up. "Do you think Kit got killed by the mob, the way the story says?"

"I don't know. I think so. His brother Thomas put up a strange stone in the churchyard." She fished out her phone and scrolled through the pictures until she found it, then passed her phone across to her brother.

He studied it for a few seconds, then handed the phone back. "Well, you've clearly fallen for him. How does he feel about you?"

"The same."

Joe stared at her, fiddling with his wineglass. "Are you going to get really hurt, sis? If this is for real, he either turns out to be a murderer, or he's innocent but still gets killed. How does the date in 1762 compare with now? Is it the same day of the year when you go there?"

Unease prickled in her belly. "Mm."

"Then if this stone *does* relate to him being killed by a mob, it's coming up soon."

"I know. I'm hoping he can come back here with me, but he hasn't yet. I tried to keep hold of his hand the last time I was there, but the room shifted for me but not him." She squared her shoulders. "Anyway, I can tell you don't really believe any of it, so you can quit humouring me."

Joe held his hands up. "Okay. No, in my heart of hearts, I don't really believe you waltz back and forth between now and 1762. I don't know *who* you think you've met, but I am worried you're going to get hurt."

139

Ellie sucked her teeth. "Who *do* you think I've met? What *is* your rational explanation?"

"Honestly? Some weird romance-scam guy. Some bloke who's found out you've inherited a house and live in it on your own. You fall in love, he needs rescuing, you need to give him money or marry him or something. And then he makes off with all your stuff and leaves you high and dry."

She said nothing. That absolutely *wasn't* what was happening. Maybe if she vanished in front of him, he'd *have* to believe her.

26

The following morning, Joe sat at Ellie's desk, put his glasses on, and looked at the list of times and dates Ellie had collected for him.

"Is this data complete?" he asked, grabbing a pencil and some scrap paper.

"Almost certainly not. I have a life, Joe. I haven't been in the study every minute of every day. I've been out to do shopping, and I've met up with Liz and stuff, so there could have been shifts when I wasn't here."

He rasped his palm with his chin. "Okay. That makes it trickier, but I'll have a look."

"Thanks. I know you don't really believe all of it, but can you analyse it all as if you do? Don't just pretend to look at it."

He held her gaze for a moment, then shooed her out of the room. "I'm not going to figure it out while you're standing peering over my shoulder. Go away."

"Shall I bring you a coffee?"

"Mm."

She retreated to the kitchen to make coffee, one eye on the clock, hoping the second hand would shudder and stop and she could see Kit, but it kept ticking on. Coffees made, she took one through to Joe. He pored over the times and dates, his brow furrowed.

"Are these the times when the cat comes and goes?" He pointed to a column of information.

"Yeah. They're probably even less accurate than the other

times, because he could be coming and going all night for all I know. Do you think you can see a pattern?"

"Not yet. Shoo! Leave me to it."

She ruffled his hair and did as she was told. She took her coffee through to the lounge, deciding to investigate 18th century costumes while she waited. A quick internet search brought up a heap of sites. More than half of the clothes were ridiculous and impractical. If she was going to get *anything*, she wanted something that at least looked like a normal woman would wear, not something made of silk or brocade. After more browsing, she found a drab coloured skirt and bodice. It was no doubt far from historically correct, but would surely look less bizarre than her jeans and a sweater. She sucked her teeth. It was also expensive. She sighed and saved the page. Maybe she could buy the material and just make it.

Reality kicked in and she shook herself. Was she really going to spend that much money on an outfit and wear it all day, just in case? What if people dropped by for coffee and found her wearing it? How on earth would she explain that? She closed down the window.

She was still humming and hawing over it when Joe joined her.

"I might, *might*, have found a pattern in it," he said, resting his shoulder against the door-frame. "But given that the data isn't complete, I also could be *way* off."

"For real? You're not just saying that to humour me?"

"No, for real. I promise."

"And when will the rift open again?"

He snorted. "If I'm right, you've missed it for today. It would have been about half an hour ago. Assuming there *is* a rift. And that I've spotted a pattern in it all."

Ellie plonked her laptop on the trunk. "Can you extrapolate out to more days? Predict when the window opens over the next week?"

"I'll put it as no more than I can give you a list of times, based on what you've given me." He paused. "Changing the subject entirely, how on earth do you find *any* of your wool in the back bedroom? It's been breeding!"

She laughed. "Yeah, I just did a huge batch of dyeing. I need

142

to get more storage for it all."

"There's bound to be somewhere in Ripon where you can buy storage. Fancy a run out there this afternoon?"

She brightened. "Yes, please. Much as I love the house and pottering about, I don't have any work to do and some retail-therapy would be good."

"Right. I'll try to give you an idea of when this mythical time-travel-window will open over the next week, and then do you want lunch here, or in Ripon?"

"Ripon."

***

By late afternoon, they were back at the house, laden with boxes of flat-pack furniture. Joe hefted them on to his shoulder, ready to take them upstairs.

"Still the one over the study, Ellie?" he called back over his shoulder. "Or are you expanding into the other bedroom as well?"

"The one over the study." If she was going to end up in a bedroom in 1762 after sorting out wool, she would rather it was Kit's than Thomas's.

She made a couple of coffees, then joined Joe in the back room. He'd already opened all the boxes and sat cross-legged on the floor, reading the instructions.

"Have you got a toolbox?" he asked, looking over the top of his glasses at her.

"Um. Yes. I think so. Well, it was Granny Molly's. Hang on."

She scurried downstairs and out to the log-store, sure that there was a plastic toolbox on a shelf in there at the garage-end. Grabbing the flashlight hanging by the door, she squeezed past her car to reach the area where various random tools, bottles of screws and nails, packets of sandpaper and so on had been left. She hauled the toolbox down and turned back towards the log-store area. In front of her, the building shifted and warped. At the end of the yard, Kit's forge shimmered in and out of view, but the world was solid and fixed where she stood. She checked her watch. The second hand quivered. She hung back, waiting until the images settled in front of her. Kit walked into the forge, and her heart skipped a beat. He glanced in her direction, then beamed at her and waved. She waved back, desperate to hurry through the rift to him, but it was already late and she had no idea when it would open again, so she stayed where she was. Kit frowned. Did he wonder why she hadn't joined him? She stepped forward, but as she did, the building changed again, reverting to the modern log-store. She breathed deeply, her pulse racing, then inched past the car again and took the toolbox up to Joe.

"The window to 1762 just opened again," she said. "While I was in the store. I could see Kit through it and he could see me." Shadow strolled into the room, winding past her legs. "And the cat's back."

Joe sat back on his haunches. "Then my calculations are rubbish, because I'd predicted that the next time it would appear would be tomorrow." He took the toolbox from her. "I'll look at them again in the morning." He studied her. "You didn't go through the window."

"No. Clearly." She sighed, half wishing she *had* gone through. "It's getting late, and I don't know when I could get back. And you would wonder where I was. Kit doesn't live alone. He lives with his brother, Thomas, who would be home soon, and he doesn't know about me, so that could have been tricky." She joined her brother on the floor. "The rift is the whole of the back half of the house. The bit that's here in 1762. You didn't see anything? The room looking all weird, and strange lights or anything?"

He shook his head. "No. Just what's here. You must be the only one with the time-traveller genes."

She pulled a face at him, but he'd bent his head to the instructions again and wouldn't have seen her.

"Do you think we'll get this built before dinner?" She surveyed the piles of parts doubtfully.

"Nope. I'm going to lay it all out and read the instructions and make it after we've eaten. I have *never* found making up flat-pack furniture on an empty stomach a good idea."

She finished helping him to sort the bits, deep in thought. If she hadn't gone down to the log-store to get the toolbox, she would have been shifted to 1762, right in front of Joe. Then he would have *had* to believe her. Had Kit wondered why she didn't go to him? Was he as disappointed as she was that she hadn't? If Joe could work out when the rift opened, she could plan her day around it better, and not end up missing it.

Getting a re-enactment costume didn't seem like such a mad idea, after all.

27

A few days later, Ellie laid her 18th century costume out on her bed. She'd never had clothes with instructions on how to wear them before. She picked up the page describing what went under what and how things fastened, and sighed. Was she completely mad to be doing this? What if Joe was wrong over when the wrinkle in time would manifest and she ended up walking around the house in this get-up all day?

She put the loose shirt-like garment on over her 21st century undies, peeked at the instructions again, then worked her way through the other bits and pieces until she was fully dressed in a 21st century version of an 18th century woman's clothes. She pulled on a pair of socks and boots and studied herself in the mirror.

"*Please* don't let anyone come over today. Not while I'm wearing all of this."

She squared her shoulders and checked the list of times Joe had scribbled on a sheet of paper that morning. At the last minute, Joe had remembered that British Summer Time had not been thought of in 1762, and that her time of return would be an hour earlier on Kit's clocks. According to Joe's new calculations, the wrinkle between her time and Kit's was likely to appear at about 3:45 p.m. BST and reappear for her to return at about 6:30. 5:30 in Kit's time. It was now half-past three.

She gathered up her skirts and trotted down the stairs to the kitchen. There, she secreted a couple of bananas in the large pockets in the skirt, along with a bag of toffees, and checked the clock again, waiting for the second hand to quiver. Joe joined her in the kitchen.

"Dear life, what do you look like?"

"Hopefully more like someone from 1762 than I usually do," she muttered.

He still hadn't bought into the idea she would go back in time, though he *had* conceded that there was a pattern to the data she'd given him.

She patted a hand over her costume, then checked the room. "Hang on, I need to be here, otherwise I'll be right where the table is." She took a step back. "Right. Watch the clock with me. A few seconds before the room shifts, the second hand stops moving."

Joe gave her a sceptical look but dutifully studied the large clock on the wall with her. Bang on cue, the second hand shimmered.

"See that!" cried Ellie. "Now, watch the room."

As she waited, the room morphed in and out of 1762.

She turned to Joe. "Please tell me you see this?"

He stuck his arms out to the sides and let them drop again. "I see nothing different. What's happening?"

"The room. It's 1762."

But Joe had vanished. She stood in Kit's kitchen on her own. She dashed out to the workshop.

"He was right! He *did* manage to work it out!"

The words died on her lips as she came face-to-face with not only Kit, but another man she hadn't met before. He seemed vaguely familiar to her. Kit's eyes widened at the sight of her, and she bobbed a small curtsy.

"Sorry, Mr Greenwood, I did not know you had company," she garbled.

She bobbed again and fled back to the house. Behind her, Kit explained to the man that she was Nelly, the new woman coming to cook and clean for him.

"Does she live in?" asked the man salaciously.

"No. She does not," Kit replied curtly.

"She looks like she works upstairs as well as downstairs."

Ellie's cheeks burned. How could she have been so stupid as to rush out like that? She grabbed a brush from the corner of the kitchen and busied herself sweeping the floor, half an ear on the chatter in the yard. What did 18th century domestic servants *do*? Should she peel some vegetables or something, in case the man came into the kitchen?

Outside, the man discussed an order with Kit, then bid him farewell. She propped the broom back in the corner, waiting for him to go. Instead, he came into the kitchen. His gaze travelled slowly over her body, making her flesh crawl.

"Ah, Nelly. Fetch my hat? There's a good girl. I left it by the main door."

Ellie hurried out into the hallway, her eyes searching for any sign of a hat. The man followed her, and she whirled, her senses prickling. He kept advancing, and she backed away until her shoulders collided with the wall.

"I cannot find a hat, sir," she said, her heart thumping hard.

"No." He laughed and pressed closer, his hand drifting over her breast and squeezing it firmly. "My, you *are* a pert little thing. Kit has a good eye."

He squeezed again. Ellie shrieked and brought her knee up into his crotch, and the man backhanded her viciously, knocking her to the floor.

"Little bitch!"

He raised his hand to her again, but Kit grabbed the collar of his coat and dragged him backwards.

"Out!" Kit barked.

He threw the man out through the main door, then rushed over to her. "Ellie! Are you alright?"

She nodded, shaking, and accepted his hand to help her back to her feet. He drew her close to him, wrapping his arms around her.

"Thank you for pulling him off me," she mumbled into his shoulder.

He kissed her forehead, then the end of her nose, then finally her lips. "What did he do to you? Why did you scream?"

She cuddled closer. "He groped me. Grabbed my breast. I kneed him in the crotch."

A smile tickled his lips, then faded swiftly. "I am not amused at him assaulting you. I am amused by your response."

148

She shuddered. "Who was he?"

"*That* was Hugh Ellis."

No wonder he had seemed familiar. She'd seen his portrait online, though it had been painted when he was a good twenty years older and much fatter. Nausea bubbled in her stomach at the thought of what he had done to Janet.

"Are you hurt?" Kit asked, his voice soft. His fingertip grazed her cheek where Hugh Ellis had hit her. "I think this will bruise."

"It's okay. A bit sore, but I'll live." She peered over his shoulder. "Is he gone? Are you expecting anyone else?"

"He is gone and no, I do not expect anyone else today." He drew back and looked her up and down. Her cheeks warmed.

"Are the clothes okay?" Maybe they were just as inappropriate as her usual attire of jeans and a sweater. "It isn't easy to get suitable things. *Are* they suitable?"

He smiled gently, slipping his arms around her again. "They are more conventional than your long breeches and a gansey. Most women would also wear a cap, but the bodice and skirt are what women wear here." His fingertips stroked the small of her back, and he frowned as they smoothed over the zip fastener in her skirt. "What is this?"

"Oh. That's a kind of fastener. I don't think they've been invented for you, yet."

She eased out of his arms and turned around. He leaned down to inspect the zip, lifting the zipper. "May I? Just a small amount to see how it works?"

"Yes. I trust you."

He unzipped her skirt a tiny amount, then re-fastened it. "Ingenious."

She turned back to face him. "I've brought you something."

She rummaged in the pockets of her skirts and pulled out the two bananas. He peered at them, his face crumpling, and she laughed.

"They're called bananas. They grow in hotter countries than this. You eat them. Shall I show you?"

He nodded, and she slipped one back into a pocket and peeled the other for him.

"You eat the inside bit, not the skin," she said as she handed it over.

He nibbled cautiously, then his face lit up. "It is sweet. Thank you. It is a most unusual plant. Do you want to share it?"

"No, it's a treat for you." She paused. "You should put the skin on the fire. I don't think bananas arrive in the country for more than a hundred years, and even then, they're not common."

"These are common in your time?"

"Mm, hm. I can bring you less common things if you like."

He finished the last part of the banana and led her to the kitchen, where he tossed the skin on the fire.

"Let me get a cold cloth for your face." He bustled around the kitchen and returned with a wet cloth. He touched it to her face, his hands gentle, his eyes full of concern. "Why did you not come last night when I saw you?"

She took the cold cloth from him and pressed it against her cheek.

"It was late, and my brother is staying with me at the moment. He would wonder where I'd gone. In fact, I've just disappeared in front of his eyes. Maybe now he'll believe me when I tell him I've been here. He's been utterly sceptical about it all so far!" She stood on tiptoe and pressed a kiss to his lips. "That said, I gave him a list of all the times I've ended up here, and all the times Shadow has been back and forth, and he worked out a pattern. He's a scientist." She withdrew a sheet of paper from her pocket and held it up. "Here. If Joe's right about all of it, I have three hours with you today! These are the times in the next week or so that I should be able to come here."

Kit took the piece of paper from her and studied it. "May I take a copy?"

"Of course!"

He drew back from her, but kept hold of her hand, leading her to the study. There, he sat at the desk and copied out the schedule, the pen making a soft scratching sound on the paper as he wrote. He blew on the wet ink before tucking the paper away in the desk and handing her copy back to her.

She perched on the window-seat, next to the desk. "If Joe's right about the times, maybe we can see if you can come to my time?"

He gave her a sad smile. "We have tried that, and all that happens is that you leave and I stay."

"But there *has* to be a way!"

He got up from the desk and sat on the window-seat next to her, holding her hand. "Ellie, I will never regret meeting you." He sighed. "I do not think that we can be together the way both of us want to be, and so I relish every minute that I have with you."

She rested her cheek against his shoulder, and he settled her against him more comfortably, winding his arm around her waist.

"Have you coordinated the furniture between my time and yours?" he murmured.

"Mostly. In my time, my desk is in the window."

He turned his head to make eye-contact. "You do not use the window-seat?"

She shook her head. "I prefer to see the view, and Joe has offered to build me a window-seat in the lounge, which would be warmer, since it gets the sun. No doubt as soon as he does, Shadow will take up residence. He appears to like the 21st century."

"Mm. Because you feed him and let him sleep in the sun, whereas I make him catch his dinner."

They sat in comfortable silence for a moment, then Kit asked, "Can I get you anything to eat or drink?"

Ellie leaned back. "Do you have tea? Or have I just asked for something really expensive and hard to get?"

He smiled. "I have tea."

They returned to the kitchen, and she sat at the table while he added water from a jug to a fire-blackened kettle suspended from a hook next to the fire. He swung the kettle over the heat, then disappeared into the small pantry off the kitchen, returning with a dark wooden box. He spooned tea-leaves from it into a metal teapot and set it on the table, then retrieved two porcelain bowls from the wooden dresser.

"Is tea expensive for you?" he asked as he worked.

"No. It's the national drink. I think the British drink gallons of tea per person per week and it's pretty cheap. Is it expensive now?"

"The import tax is very high. If it is paid."

He winked at her, making her laugh.

The water had boiled, and he grabbed a cloth, unhooked the kettle, and poured steaming water into the teapot. He returned the kettle to its hook beside the fire and brought the two bowls over to the table. He poured out the tea, straining out the tea-leaves with a metal strainer. She almost asked to have some milk in her drink, but given that he had no fridge and clearly had no cow, fresh milk would be impossible. The bowls surprised her. How did you drink from them? She watched to see what to do, trying to be surreptitious about it. Not surreptitious enough.

He caught her eye as he picked up his bowl and frowned. "What?"

"Nothing. Sorry! Our cups have handles and I wasn't sure how to hold this type, that's all."

He eyed her. "How are our worlds so similar and yet so different?"

"Mm. If you ever manage to come to my time, it will seem strange to you."

It would be less of a palaver to make a cup of tea for a start.

She sipped her drink. Without milk, it had a bitter edge. It smelled stronger too – almost leafy.

What was Masham like in 1762? She had the right clothes, and it was warm and sunny out. If Joe's calculations were correct, they had plenty of time to go and come back. *If* his calculations were correct. Did she risk it? He'd been correct to the second over when the anomaly would appear this afternoon.

Kit touched her hand, startling her.

"What are you so deep in thought about?"

She bit her lip. "Do you have a lot of work to do today?"

"No. Why?"

She put the bowl of tea down. "Well, since I have more appropriate clothes, I wondered if you would walk into the village with me? I want to know what it looks like in your time."

He nodded. "Tell me, in your time, how large is Masham?"

She considered the question for a moment. "Just over a thousand people live there, I think. About that."

His eyes widened. "It is not so large at the moment."

"Are you too busy for us to go there? It doesn't matter if you are. Now I have the clothes and we know when the window

152

between us opens, we could go another time."

"No, I am not too busy today. You are sure that your brother has calculated things correctly?"

She scrunched her face up. "I think so."

He peered at her feet. "What shoes do you have on? The roads are not well-kept in places."

She lifted the hem of her skirt to reveal leather boots.

"Perfect. Let us walk down to Masham together."

28

Kit banked the fires in the kitchen and the forge, and closed up his workshop, then offered her his arm. She slipped her palm against the crook of his elbow, and they strolled towards the road.

"I don't actually know if I will stay in your time if I leave the property," she murmured. "I hope I don't suddenly end up disappearing."

Her steps slowed as she approached the boundary, but they crossed into the road and she was still at his side. A light breeze cooled her face and clouds hurried across the sky. She peered up apprehensively. "Do you think it will rain?" How heavy would a woollen skirt get if it emptied down on them?

"No. Not today."

They sauntered down the road towards Masham. The surface of the track comprised compacted earth, rutted in places, muddy in others, and Ellie was glad of her sturdy boots. In the verges, plants frothed with flowers, and the hedges lining the track rang with birdsong.

"I have a friend who always says the countryside is noisier than the city, with all the birds cheeping," she said. "It's as nothing in my time as to how loud it is here!"

"It is louder in my time?" Kit's brow puckered. "How?"

"We have fewer birds in my time, I think. Farming is very different. A lot of hedges were taken up to make fields bigger, and the farmers also put things on the crops to stop insects from eating them. It means we get much more from an acre than you do."

"That might be helpful. The newspapers talk of the population increasing, and that there will be food shortages."

She dodged a muddy patch, and he steadied her. "Mm. But the downside of fewer insects is that the birds don't have as much to eat, and with the loss of the hedges, there's nowhere for them to live, either. If you ever came to my time, you would be surprised by how different it all is. This road is not made of earth, for a start! It has a hard surface that isn't affected by rain."

As they walked, she described the village in her time. Kit listened keenly, questioning her closely about the modern village, eager to learn more. They encountered few people, but those they did, acknowledged Kit respectfully, even if they threw curious glances to her. It was hard to believe that they would turn on him in less than five weeks.

They'd almost reached the marketplace when Ellie plucked up the courage to ask him something that had been burning a hole in her brain for some time.

"Kit? May I ask you something personal? You're clearly well-respected here. You have a good business. You're kind and funny. And handsome. But you have no wife?"

Kit's pace faltered, and he turned them down a side-street. "Shall we walk down to the riverbank?"

Ellie sensed he didn't want to talk in the village. They walked on in silence down a path until they reached a stone bridge over the river. Next to it lay an open area of grass. Kit took his jacket off and spread it out on the ground. Ellie sat, trying to negotiate her voluminous skirts. Eventually, she sat cross-legged, her skirt draped around her like a puffball. Kit smirked as he sat next to her.

"Yes. Your usual clothes are more practical."

She picked a blade of grass, twirling it in her fingers. "Talk to me? I get the feeling you aren't unmarried by choice."

Kit's gaze drifted away, and he brought his hand up, covering his birthmark. Ellie waited.

He let out a long breath through his nose. "After Father died, and Thomas and I inherited the forge, it was hard. I was 21. Thomas just 17." He paused. "I had learned the forge work, but not how to do bookkeeping. Manage money." He snorted. "That

155

is Thomas's realm. He has the head for that." He broke off again, picking at some hard skin on his hand. "We had a couple of lean years, but by the time I was 23, the forge was thriving. Thomas had found work as a clerk. We had a good living. I had been friendly with a young woman – Anne. She is the daughter of the butcher. She is a couple of years younger than me. We had known each other all of our life and I thought we were good friends. I thought she was kind."

He trailed off, tipping his face up to the clouds.

"I was walking her home after church. I had been doing this for more than a month. She was always laughing with me. I thought she enjoyed my company. I thought she liked me. I was wrong."

He stopped again and stared at his knuckles. Ellie leaned over and slipped her hand over his.

"What happened?" she asked softly.

He chewed at his lower lip, blinking.

"I tried to kiss her. I thought we were more than friends. I hoped she would be my wife."

His shoulders tightened and his breathing hitched. Ellie gently squeezed his fingers, but he turned his head away.

"Tell me?" she coaxed.

He gave a short bark of a laugh, devoid of humour, full of pain. "She laughed. She stepped away from me, and she laughed. Asked me why I thought she would ever have felt that way about me. How I could ever have imagined she would want to be with someone so *marked*."

The word had spines.

Ellie frowned, perplexed. "She turned you down because of your *birthmark*?"

She moved to duck into his field of view, and his eyes met hers, brimming with old pain.

"What a completely stupid thing for her to have done!" she said. "You're wonderful. You are so kind, so loving, so caring, so gentle. The woman was a complete *idiot*."

A wan smile lifted his lips, then he shook his head. "That is kind of you, Ellie. But who would choose to look at this—" he waved his hand over his face "—every day?"

She blinked, astounded. "I would. Every single day. Because I look at you, and I see the kindest man I have ever met. A man who lifts my spirits and makes every day that I see him a special day."

He levelled his gaze at her. "You teased me once. Said that I had a strawberry for a face."

Her heart lurched. "I know. I'm sorry. I was a child. I always regretted saying it. That's not what I see now. I see *you*. An incredible man. I would happily look at you every day of my life."

He snorted. "Then it is a great shame that you never stay here and that I cannot go with you to your time."

She kissed the tips of his fingers. "Maybe you will, one day."

"I would love that."

Ellie played with his fingers. "She is a total fool, but in some ways I'm glad, because if I'd met you and you'd been a married man, I would have been heartbroken."

He smiled. "Thank you. I was very hurt for a long time, but since I met you, I have almost forgotten her."

They sat in a comfortable silence before he spoke again. "And you, Ellie? You are intelligent and witty. And beautiful. And unmarried. What is your story?"

She sucked in a deep breath and blew her cheeks out. "Oh. I was engaged. But then…" She fiddled with the blade of grass she held. "It was a Sunday evening. I had been away at a fair, selling my wool. I'd thought I would be away until the Monday, but I decided to go home early." She grimaced. "I'd missed him. I went home early, full of joy because I'd sold a lot of wool at the fair. I wanted to see him and share my happiness over how well the fair had gone." She closed her eyes, and the scene played out on the back of her eyelids. "I went in, and there was no sign of him. But it wasn't *that* late, and there were lights on, so he was at home. I went through the house, trying to find him, bursting to tell him about the fair." She opened her eyes again. "I wanted to celebrate with him."

Her words died, and Kit held both of her hands, his thumbs caressing her skin.

"He was in the bedroom," Ellie said eventually. "In bed. With one of my friends."

Kit's mouth fell open. "He was…?" He didn't finish the

sentence.

"Mm. Well, he *had* been. They'd stopped when I opened the door." She dipped her head. "So, I cancelled the wedding, I had to find somewhere to live, and money was difficult… I really struggled. And I'd done nothing wrong." She pulled a hand free to rub her nose. "Anyway, he married *her*. I don't think he's very happy with her, but somehow, I can't muster any sympathy for him."

Kit crooked his finger under her chin, raising her face to his. "He, too, is a fool."

He leaned in and kissed her softly, his beard tickling her cheek. She tangled her fingers in his hair, releasing it from its ribbon and letting the thick waves fall around his face. He laughed lightly, then kissed her again. She drew him down until they both lay half on, half off his jacket. Cool grass pressed against her neck.

"You will get grass stains on you," he murmured between kisses.

"I don't care," she whispered back. "We have good soap in my time that will get them out."

His breath dusted her skin as he chuckled.

After many more minutes, she eased away a fraction, groaning. "Mmmm. Fabulous as this is, and much as I want to just stay here with you forever, the window will re-open soon. We should walk back."

He pulled a face, but got up and helped her up. He shook his jacket out, brushing off dry grass and leaves, then put it back on. She picked up the ribbon, combed his hair with her fingers, and tied it at the nape of his neck again. He held out his arm, and she slipped her hand into the crook of his elbow.

"I do not want you to leave," he said, his eyes sad.

"Nor do I, but I don't get to choose. If I'm in the house when the shift happens, I go. If it's not today, it would be the next time the rift opened."

They wandered back along the road. As they re-entered the village, they passed some houses being built, and Ellie recognised them.

"These are still standing in my time." She indicated another house that stood unfinished. "That one is too, but maybe not for long. It's in a dilapidated state."

They walked on, and Ellie drew the packet of toffees out of her pocket and offered the paper bag to him.

He peered at it. "What is this?"

"Toffee. It's incredibly sweet, and very chewy."

He took a lump and popped it in his mouth. His eyes widened and his brows shot up. "That *is* sweet! What is it made of?"

"Sugar, treacle, and butter, I think. I didn't make it. I bought it."

They skirted the edge of the square and turned into the churchyard, sharing more of the toffees. Kit glanced down at her.

"Where is the stone that you told me about? In your time? The one that says I disappear."

"Oh. Over that way." She led him through the grounds to the boundary wall and pointed. "Just there, tucked against the wall. There's another tree near here in my time." She turned and indicated an empty area of ground. "Thomas's gravestone is over there. Will be over there. He marries someone called Esther and they have three children."

"When does he die?" Kit asked softly.

Ellie smiled reassuringly. "When he's an old man. Is the woman he's seeing now called Esther?"

He nodded, amused. "And they will have three children?"

"Mm. They named the oldest boy after you."

Kit's eyes shone, but he said nothing.

They finished walking around the churchyard and headed back towards the forge.

"When does the window open and you have to leave?" asked Kit.

"About half-past five."

He stared at her, his colour fading. "The window re-opens at half-past five?"

His expression alarmed her. "What time is it, Kit?"

"We need to hurry!"

They dashed back along the road as quickly as they could, but the muddy, rutted surface forced them to slow down to a brisk walk. Ellie berated herself internally. What would she do if she missed the rift opening?

"Will Thomas be home tonight?" she asked, jumping over a large pot-hole.

"Yes."

So much for her remaining a secret if she missed the window.

They reached the house and hurried towards the workshop. As they rounded the end of the house, the workshop and yard flickered between 1762 and her time. Ellie hitched up her skirt and ran towards the mirage.

"Please don't fade. Please don't fade," she whispered.

Just as she was about to step through the boundary and return to the 21st century, the building solidified as Kit's forge, with no trace of her workshop or the modern log-store. She turned to Kit, stricken.

"Now what do I do?"

29

Kit stared at her. "When does the window open again?"

Ellie's heart raced. "In the middle of the night. And then again in a few days. Kit, I'm stuck here until then. When will Thomas be home?"

"Soon."

Ellie scanned the workshop. There were few places where she could hide for hours out there. She could curl up in the study overnight, but she needed to be invisible before then. Of course, she could camp out in Kit's room, but this wouldn't be as acceptable in the 18th century as it was in the 21st. The window re-opened between their times at about three in the morning. She eyed the workshop again. It was dry, and although the day hadn't been hot, she would hardly freeze out here in August.

"I suppose I can stay out here. Thomas won't see me, and I'll go back to my time when the window re-opens."

Kit shook his head rapidly. "You cannot stay outside all night."

A low whistle floated in the air to them. Kit took her arm and tugged her towards the house. "Thomas."

Inside, they stood at the foot of the narrow stairs.

"Hide upstairs in my room. I will sleep in the study tonight. Thomas cannot see you. Go!"

She scrambled upstairs, reaching the upper landing seconds before Thomas entered the house. She tiptoed to Kit's room and eased the door open. His bed sat exactly as he'd described it – the long edge against the outer wall, the head-end pointing towards the window. A soft quilt covered the bed, along with some

161

scratchy blankets, and dark curtains hung around the three open sides, suspended from a wooden rail. When drawn, they would entirely enclose the bed. The walls of the room were white-washed plaster. She stepped softly towards the bed, the thin woollen rug covering the wooden floor deadening her footsteps.

Next to the bed stood a small cupboard, and she eased the door open to find a prayer book and two candles. She left them where they were. A wooden chest sat under the window and she lifted the lid, curious. A waft of the scent of cedar wood emerged. The chest must be made of it. Cedar *was* a moth-repellent and many of Kit's clothes were made of wool, so it made sense. She closed the lid again and sat on the edge of the bed, glad to feel that the mattress was stuffed with something other than straw or hay. Under the bed was a chamberpot with a cloth over it. She *really* didn't want to have to use that. The idea of Kit having to empty it after she'd used it made her cheeks burn.

She flopped back on the bed and pinched the space between her brows.

You idiot, Ellie. You knew when the window would close. Joe will be frantic. He didn't even see the room shift earlier. He'll worry that you're never going to get back.

She tried to imagine him waiting for her return and what he would do when she didn't appear. Hopefully, he would assume she had just missed the rift or that his calculations were off and wait until the next window. She sighed. However unintentionally, she'd caused him several hours of anxiety.

She made herself more comfortable, and closed the curtains around the bed, in case Thomas came up and peered in. Closing her eyes, she breathed deeply.

Stupid, stupid girl! You've fallen head over heels for someone you can't be with. It's all very well, dressing up and popping in and out of this time, but he's going to disappear and there's nothing you can do to stop it. You've tried getting him back to your time, and it doesn't work. Stop hoping there's a happy ever after for the two of you, because there isn't.

Tears nipped her eyes. Now she knew when the rift opened, should she stop coming? The fateful day when Kit disappeared was rapidly approaching. If something bad happened to him, would she ever get over it? However much Joe said that he would always choose to have the few years he'd had with Hayley and the heartbreak that followed, rather than never to have known her, Ellie had already had her heart broken once. She stared at the fabric canopy of the bed, her mind ticking things over. Her heart would still be shattered if he died, even if she stopped coming and never saw him again. The thought of him being beaten to death... or hanged... She bit her lip hard to stop herself from sobbing.

If she couldn't get Kit to her time, was there *any* way to keep him safe? She rubbed her forehead. There *was* a potential solution that might prevent Janet from getting murdered and Kit blamed for it, but it wasn't one that resulted in her being happy. She scrubbed the heel of her hand over her face, smearing her tears, then burrowed down in the covers, drinking in the scent of him.

She woke to voices outside the door and froze, holding her breath.

"You would sit up all night with a book, given the chance, brother. Goodnight."

Thomas, speaking to Kit. The door to the room eased open. Ellie peeked through a chink in the curtains around the bed. Kit held a lamp, and the soft light gilded his face and threw long shadows over the room. He tiptoed over to the bed and set the lamp down on the small cupboard.

She drew the curtains open to show him she was both awake and fully dressed, wondering what time it was.

Kit crouched next to the bed to speak, barely even whispering. "Sorry. Thomas insisted on me retiring to bed. I will sleep on the floor."

She pushed the rest of the curtain back. "What time is it?" She kept her voice as low as he had.

"Nearly midnight."

She tugged at his waistcoat, miming to him to lie next to her. He shook his head vigorously, indicating the floor. She sighed and yanked hard at his waistcoat. "Just lie down next to me. I'll be gone soon."

He hesitated, unlacing his boots, then shook his head again. She glared, then pointed at the space next to her. He chewed his bottom lip. "You are sure?"

She shuffled backwards to make more space for him. He blew

the lamp out and set it back on the cupboard, then lay down next to her, making the bed creak and the covers rustle. The narrow bed barely had space for the two of them and Ellie tucked under his arm, curling on her side against him. He slipped his other arm around her waist, and she tilted her face up and kissed him. His muscles tensed and he drew back.

"We are not married." He swallowed. "Though I wish we were."

She rested her head against his neck, her body thrumming with disappointed passion.

"Is the bed in your room in the same place?" he whispered.

"No. When I return, I'll end up on the floor. I didn't expect to have to line them up over the centuries."

He snorted. The light touch of his fingertips on her shoulder sent squiggles of electricity through her, and she yearned to kiss him.

"You are the first woman to share my bed," he said, his voice no more than a breath. "I wish you did not have to leave. Ever."

She rubbed her cheek against the wool of his waistcoat, saying nothing, desperate for there to be a better outcome than the future held for them.

He kissed her hair. "I love you, Ellie. Come again soon?"

She swallowed. "Yeah," she croaked. "I'll come back soon. Now go to sleep."

She pressed a swift kiss to his lips, then snuggled back down, her heart aching.

***

She must have drifted off to sleep in Kit's arms, because she woke with a jolt as she landed in a heap on the floor. She sat for a moment, getting her bearings. A light came on in the hallway outside, and Joe poked his head around the door, clad in pyjama bottoms and a t-shirt, his hair a mess.

"Is that you, Ellie?"

"Yeah. Sorry to wake you."

"What happened? I was worried sick. I thought you were never coming back! I thought you were lost in the ether or something, trapped between two worlds."

164

She raked a hand through her hair. "Sorry. I went to 1762 okay, and we walked down to the village and were late back. I missed the window by seconds, so had to stay until this one opened. I'm really sorry I worried you, but I didn't have any way of letting you know." She tilted her head. "So, do you believe me *now*? The house *does* shift. Kit's *not* a ghost."

"I think I have to." He rested his back against the door-frame, smirking. "Am I allowed to ask why you've reappeared in the wrong bedroom?"

Ellie clambered to her feet. "Thomas came home, and I had to hide. So, I hid upstairs in Kit's room."

"With Kit?" He grinned cheekily.

"For some of it." She gave her brother a firm stare. "All perfectly innocently, I'll have you know! As you see, I'm still fully dressed, including boots."

He held his hands up. "None of my business. Was he impressed with the outfit? Was it historically correct?"

"Well, I blended in enough for us to go for a walk."

"And no boundary issues. You obviously weren't confined to the property. Interesting."

Ellie rolled her eyes. "Joe, it's the middle of the night. I want to get out of these clothes and go to sleep. Can we do all the scientific analysis in the morning?"

He laughed. "Sorry! I'm glad you're back safe."

***

The next morning, she stumbled downstairs in her pyjamas, the aroma of coffee enticing her to the kitchen. There, Joe had a full pot of coffee on the go and was making toast.

"Morning!" he said breezily. "Jeez, you look like you had a rough night! Not sleep when you got back?"

She sat at the table, grunting an affirmation. After arriving back in a heap on the floor, and then tossing and turning the rest of the night, 'a rough night' barely covered it. Joe slid a large mug of coffee in front of her, along with a plate of toast. She glanced up at a whiteboard propped against the wall above the worktop. On it, Joe had written out all the times the rift would appear. The next time was a few days away. The final date was September 6th. She

165

buttered her toast, her mind churning. Joe sat opposite her, taking the butter from her to spread on his toast.

"So, what's up, little sis? You look terrible. I'd have thought a long day with Kit that finished with you in his bed would have left you looking happier than this."

She sipped her coffee, her emotions in turmoil. "I don't think I can do it any more."

"What? See Kit?" Joe took a bite of his toast and chewed slowly. "Why not? What happened last night?"

"Nothing happened last night. He was a perfect gentleman." She nibbled the corner of her toast. "I can't do it any more because he disappears. I keep hoping that he will come here, but it never happens. He was in *exactly* the same place as me last night when the rift opened, and I came through and he didn't. He never does. It's only ever me." She peered across the table at Joe. "I've been thinking. If Janet doesn't die, Kit can't be blamed, and then he won't get hanged or ripped apart by a mob."

Joe sat up straighter. "Have you figured out who *does* murder her?"

She flapped a hand. That wasn't where she was going with this. "Hugh Ellis, probably. Oh, and he's a *real* creep. I met him yesterday, briefly, and he groped me!"

"What?" Joe's expression hardened.

"He was with Kit when I arrived. I pretended to be a new maid. As he was leaving, he shoved me against a wall and groped me."

"And what did Kit do?"

"He wasn't there. I kneed Hugh in the balls, then Kit came in and threw him out." She shook her head. "Anyway, that's by the by."

"Have you thought of a way to stop Hugh Ellis from killing Janet?"

"Not directly." She took a gulp of coffee, flinching at the temperature. "I think that if Kit married Janet, she would be safe."

Joe stared. "You want the man you love, who you just spent the night with, to marry someone else?"

She scraped her hands through her hair. "No. I don't *want* him to, but it might save both of them." She pointed to the whiteboard. "It all stops on September 6th, whether or not he marries Janet.

The rift never opens again, according to your calculations. We get to that date and then either Kit gets killed, or he doesn't, but either way, I never see him again. If he marries Janet, then maybe they're both safe." She slumped in her chair.

Joe rubbed his nose, his eyes piercing. "Do you love him?"

She nodded, miserable to her core. "Yeah, I do. More than anyone I've ever met. The way you loved Hayley."

"Let me keep trying to work out why *you* can shift in time, but no one else can. Maybe I'll have found a way to get him here before September."

She rubbed her eyes, needing to change the subject.

"What did it look like from this side, when I went back in time?"

Joe laid his toast down. "It looked like one second you were there, standing right next to me, the next moment you were gone."

"You didn't see any of Kit's kitchen, superimposed over ours?"

"Nope."

"What did the second hand on the clock do?"

He let out a long breath. "It stopped moving properly for a few seconds. Then you vanished, and the second hand jumped to where it should have been. What did you see?"

She thought for a moment. "You remember the kaleidoscope we had when we were kids? Imagine that, but one image is the current day, and another image is the house in 1762. The two twist around each other. One moment now is clearer; the next moment 1762 is clearer. And then it settles into 1762 and the image of the modern house disappears. The same when I come back. The house shifts and morphs, and then I'm back here."

Joe slurped his coffee. "The other night, you said you saw Kit through the rift, but you didn't end up in his time. You chose not to go. Could you have chosen not to go yesterday and stayed in the kitchen with me?"

"No. I was standing inside the rift. The other night, I was outside it. Kit and I could see each other, but because I was outside the boundary of the rift, I could stay here."

Joe scratched his neck, thoughtful. "What does the boundary look like?"

She conjured a picture in her mind, trying to find the words to describe it. "It's a bit like a wall of coloured lights. You can see through it, and behind the lights it's like looking at those 3-D films, but you're not wearing the special glasses. The screen has the double image, but the rest of the cinema is normal. Looking through the boundary is like that screen, but the two images are the two times. Everywhere outside the boundary is normal. If I'd crossed the wall of lights, I would have been with Kit."

"So, if you're inside the house, you get no choice? The lights appear, the clock stops, the room gets all funky, and bam! You're in 1762. Right?"

"Yeah, recently. When I first moved here, I just saw 1762, but didn't time-travel."

"At least it's not happened when you've had a visitor! Can you imagine if you and Liz were having a coffee in the kitchen and you suddenly disappeared?"

Ellie acknowledged the point with a flick of her head. "Have you caught up with her since you arrived?"

Joe's cheeks coloured. "Mm. I rang her yesterday and asked if she wanted to do something. Go out for a day; have lunch. We're going to York tomorrow. I haven't been in years. I'm looking forward to walking the walls again."

Ellie leaned back in her seat. "It's fabulous to see you so happy. Maybe Granny Molly was right. You *have* found someone here."

Joe held her gaze for a moment. "How would you feel if I had?"

"You and Liz? I'd be delighted. She's lovely. She won't rush you, either."

His shoulders softened, and he breathed deeply. "Let's hope Granny Molly was also right about you, and that you *do* find happiness with your tawny-haired boy."

Sadness settled over her joy. "It's so hard knowing what's coming." She took a shaky breath. "I mean, it's wonderful being with him, but it's difficult. I wish you could meet him. You'd like him."

"I'll keep working on getting him here. I mean, his cat swans in and out!"

"Thank you." She gave him a wan smile. "I'm going to get dressed."

Upstairs, she flopped back on her bed and stared at the ceiling, thinking about Kit.

Please let Joe be able to work something out.

September 6th was less than five weeks away.

30

Three days had passed since Ellie had been trapped in 1762 overnight. She'd installed a loudly ticking clock on her desk in the study, in case Joe's calculations were off and the house shifted outside of his predictions while she was in there. The three days had given her time to think, and the more she did, the more she became convinced that Kit should marry Janet, to stop her from being murdered and therefore him from being blamed for it and killed by a mob. The next time the window between their times opened, she would tell him she couldn't come any more; suggest he marry Janet. And then never see him again. It made logical sense, but it broke her heart. Only the hope that it would save his life and Janet's made it even remotely bearable.

Joe had set himself up in the dining room, and most days she could hear him on the phone, sorting out work. To her delight, he'd also made several arrangements to meet up with Liz: a coffee here, a walk there, the trip to York. Small steps, but steps nonetheless. She'd talked to Liz and asked her to be patient with him. Liz had been fabulous, understanding how much time he might need.

In case Joe's calculations had been wrong, Ellie had worked in the lounge rather than the study for some of the time, recognising that earning money and maintaining a professional reputation had to take priority over being catapulted back in time, at least occasionally.

Now, she stood in the kitchen, clad in her 18th century costume, repackaging the last of the gifts she was taking to Kit.

On the table in front of her was a roll of brown paper and a ball of string, next to the packages she had finished. She'd contemplated putting a sticky label on each of them, but it was too historically inaccurate, so she'd written the contents on the packets instead. No doubt her handwriting was also historically inaccurate, but it would have to do.

She finished creating a small parcel of loose tea and added it to two others. Already packed and ready to go were a parcel of sugar and a small stack of individually re-wrapped bars of chocolate. Ellie had one of the posh paper bags from one of the shops in the village – the kind made of strong brown paper with stiff string handles – and she transferred the gifts to it, one eye on the clock. The rift would open in roughly two minutes.

The doorbell rang, and Liz called out a hello. Ellie's heart sank. She couldn't answer the door dressed like this, but if she didn't, Liz would come around to the back of the house to look for her, see her dressed peculiarly, and Ellie would then vanish before her eyes. Ellie couldn't call out to Joe to get the door, either, because Liz would hear and then wonder where she had gone.

Liz called again, making Ellie's palms sweat. She stared at the clock, willing the rift to open.

"Come on… come *on*!"

"Hi, Liz! Just coming!" called Joe in the hallway.

She turned to say a soft thank you, and he gave her a quick nod and pulled the kitchen door shut. Not that it helped hugely to block any view of her, because the top half of the door was glass.

Joe opened the front door and Ellie kept her eyes fixed on the clock.

"Hey, Liz. Just me here today. Come in!"

"No Ellie? Isn't that her in the kitchen?"

Ellie clutched the bag, praying that Joe would whisk Liz away into the lounge.

"Huh? No, Ellie's out shopping," said Joe.

Around her, the room splintered. Just as Liz was arguing with Joe that there *was* someone in the kitchen, Ellie shifted to 1762. She breathed a deep sigh of relief, letting her head sink down while her heart-rate settled.

"I wondered where you would appear."

171

Kit leaned in the doorway at the back, his arms folded loosely over his broad chest, his head on one side, a fond expression on his face. Her spirits soared at the sight of him, banishing all thoughts of telling him to marry Janet.

"Are we alone? No one is going to come in and wonder who I am?" she asked, remembering her last visit.

Kit shook his head, his eyes never leaving hers. "All alone. Well, there is a horse to be shod outside, but I do not think that counts." He jutted his chin at the bag in her hands. "What is that?"

"Gifts for you."

He smiled, pushed his shoulder away from the door-frame, and crossed the kitchen to her. She put the bag on his table and he drew her into an embrace. She tucked her arms around him, relishing the feel of his firm, warm body under her hands.

"Gifts?" He brushed his lips over hers. "As sweet as the last ones you brought?"

"Some of them are." She rubbed his nose with hers, making him laugh.

"I have missed you," he murmured. "I went to sleep in your arms and woke alone."

"Did Thomas suspect anything?"

"No. Although he keeps asking me why I am so happy suddenly."

She pressed another kiss to his lips, then drew out of his arms, remembering why she had come. She cleared her throat. "Gifts."

She picked up the paper bag and withdrew the packets from it.

"I re-wrapped everything, because the packaging they came in would have been hard to explain here. I've written on them what they are. So. Tea." She laid the parcels out on the table as she described them. "Three lots, because you said it was expensive here, and it's cheap for me. Sugar, because I suspected that was also expensive for you. And these are bars of chocolate." She stacked the wrapped bars on the table at the side of the other parcels.

His brow puckered. "*Bars* of chocolate? It is a drink here. Do I need to carve it from the bar, like with a sugarloaf? I have never had it."

"Oh. I guess chocolate bars haven't been invented yet. No,

172

they're not to drink. You eat them. They're made from cocoa and cocoa butter and sugar. And probably other things, too. You'd better hide them from Thomas if they don't exist now."

"I think I will hide all of it from him."

She grinned. "Well, they are gifts for *you*. Though you might share the tea."

He prodded at the packet of sugar, making a small dimple in it. "You have already cut it?"

"Er, no. It comes like that in my time."

He studied her for a moment, his eyes soft. "Thank you. These are very fine gifts."

"Hm. Don't eat all the chocolate at once. It's quite rich."

He caught her hands, drawing her towards him. He smelled of soap, overlaid with a hint of smoke. "Do you wish to walk to the village again today?"

Ellie shook her head. "The rift re-opens too soon for that, and then doesn't open again for a couple of days. If I miss it this time, we would have much more of a job hiding me!"

"Was your brother worried when you did not return the other night?"

His proximity sent tingles through her. She tried to focus. "Mm. I vanished in front of his eyes, then didn't reappear when he'd calculated I should. He thought I was gone for good until I landed with a thump on the floor in the small hours."

He nuzzled her temple, kissing her hair, then her nose, and finally touching his lips to hers. "Does he think I have ruined your honour?" He kissed her again.

She laughed. "No."

She pushed him away, and he collected up the packets and disappeared out to the pantry off the kitchen. He returned, still carrying the sugar and the chocolate.

"Are you going to hide them in your desk?" asked Ellie.

"I will put them in the cupboard under the window. Thomas never looks in it."

Ellie pulled up a mental image of the room in her time. Her desk lay in front of the window, but she couldn't recall there being a cupboard there when she'd been crawling on the floor to plug in her laptop.

173

"What is wrong?" asked Kit.

"Nothing. I don't think that cupboard lasts until my time. The window-seat is there, and the window recess is still that deep, but I don't remember there being a cupboard under the seat. Mind you, my desk is there, and it weighs a ton, so I haven't looked that closely."

He put the sugar and chocolate back on the table. "Can I make you some tea?"

She smiled. "Yes, please. Can I help?"

He shook his head. "Sit. You are a guest."

She sat at the table as bidden, while he busied about making tea, then piled the bowls and teapot on to a tray, and added the chocolate and sugar. He nodded towards the door. "Let us sit more comfortably?"

They went through to the sitting room – the study in Ellie's time – and he placed the tray on his desk. He squirrelled the sugar and chocolate bars away in the cupboard beneath the window, then poured the tea.

"What have you been doing since I was last here?" Ellie asked, taking the bowl of tea from him.

"Mostly shoeing horses, though I have also been repairing some parts for the mill." He sat in the chair on the other side of the fireplace from her, clasping his hands around his tea. "What have you been doing?"

"Mostly designing. Lots of inspiration coming here!"

She stalled, but Kit leaned forwards, encouraging her to talk. She described the collection of garments she was planning, talking to him about colour combinations and which plants produced which colours, and how pre-treating the wool with different things could lead to a different result. He asked lots of questions, genuinely interested in the range of colours possible from a single plant, depending on the dyeing process.

"I had no notion it was so complicated," he said. "That the same plant could give blue or red. Do you keep records?"

She grinned. "Yes! I have these enormous scrapbooks, where I have small samples of each result and notes on what I did to get it. Plus, silk dyes differently from linen, which is different from wool, and different again to cotton."

174

"Huh! I will never look at clothes the same again. I see now why my waistcoat fascinated you so much."

She bit her lips together. "Am I right in thinking that the colour of the fire tells you how hot it is?"

He sat back, his lips twitching. "Yes. And the colour of the iron. I am surprised you know that. It is something you need to learn from experience. It cannot be taught."

"It's an amazing skill. I'm in awe of how you can bend iron to your will the way you do."

He blushed.

A question that had been eating at Ellie grew so big that she had to spit it out. "How's Janet?"

Kit turned his tea in his hands, his expression serious. "Her mother knows she is with child and told her father, who beat her."

"Why? It's hardly Janet's fault!"

Kit lifted one shoulder. "That is not how her father sees it."

"Is she still going to see the woman with the herbs?"

"She has already been. The woman gave her a drink which made her very sick, but she is still with child."

"What will happen to her?"

Kit's posture sagged. "Her father has said that he will throw her out of the house as soon as it is clear that she is having a baby."

The injustice stung at Ellie like hornets. "Can she not go to a relative? Have the baby away from the village? Maybe someone would adopt it."

Kit shook his head. "There is no one she could go to. Her mother is hoping to persuade her father, but…"

He tailed off. Time to say what she'd come to say. Ellie's heart-rate climbed and her armpits became sticky from stress. The words wouldn't come. They were in her head, but her throat refused to say them.

"You should marry her," she managed at last, her voice coming out in a croak.

Kit stared at her, his mouth slightly open. His breathing turned shallow and rapid, and pain and confusion filled his eyes. "I do not love her. I love you. It would not be fair."

Ellie swallowed. She truly didn't want him to marry Janet, but this was the only way to change history and save them both.

"What's not fair is that she is being blamed for something Hugh Ellis did to her! What's not fair is that she will end up murdered." She caught her breath. "What's *not fair* is that you will get blamed and killed for something you haven't done!"

She stopped, breathing hard, tears wetting her cheeks. Kit put his tea down on the hearth, stepped over to her and drew her out of her seat. He held her against his chest, stroking her hair.

"Sh. Perhaps none of that will happen."

"Kit, it *does*! The story is *there* in my time!" She gripped fistfuls of his waistcoat, her knuckles straining. "We have to *try* to stop Janet from being murdered. If you marry her, she wouldn't be thrown out and she would be safe with you. And if she's safe, then you're safe."

Kit tensed. "I thought you loved me," he whispered, his voice hitching.

She screwed her eyes shut, holding him tight. "I do! Which is why I don't want you to be killed!"

"Ellie, from the first day that I met you, I have yearned to see you again. You are dressed so strangely; you speak so differently… but you make me laugh in a way no other woman has. When you are with me, my spirits soar. When you leave, it is as if a light has gone out. I *cannot* marry another woman when I feel this way about you."

His words only deepened her pain. There was no man in the world she wanted to be with more than him.

"Kit, the date on the stone that Thomas puts up is a month away! Unless we manage to change the story, you'll…"

A sob stopped her from finishing the sentence, and he held her close.

"You want me to marry someone else?" he asked, his voice gruff.

"No. I want you to live," she whispered, her tears soaking into his linen shirt.

There was a long silence from him before he spoke.

"If I marry Janet, I could not be with you. It would not be fair to either of you."

"I don't think in *any* version of this story we get to be together." Ellie leaned back and rubbed the tears off her face. "If you marry

Janet, I can never see you, but both you and Janet would be safe. If you don't marry Janet, she'll be murdered and you'll be blamed, and be killed for it. There's no version where both you and Janet are safe and you and I are together. I never stay here and you never come to my time."

Kit fell silent again, his hands caressing her back.

"Do you *know* that Hugh Ellis will kill Janet?" he said at last. "Perhaps we can prevent that from happening? Save Janet another way."

She shrugged. "I don't know if it *is* him, but I can't think who else it might be. If people knew what he'd done to her, his position and reputation would be in jeopardy. All I can think is that he kills her to stop her from talking. She hasn't said that she'll tell anyone else, has she?"

Kit eased away from her a fraction and rubbed his palm over his chin, his beard making a rasping sound against his hand. "No. But perhaps with her father threatening to throw her out, she will."

"Can you convince her not to? If Ellis thinks he's got away with it, Janet would be safe." That might keep her alive without Kit needing to marry her.

They were grasping at straws.

Kit glanced away. "I can try. But she's a wilful lass. If she decides she will speak out, I do not think me counselling caution would change her mind."

"If she felt she had nothing to lose, she may as well tell everyone what happened." Ellie sighed. "You can hardly tell her *why* she shouldn't say anything."

Kit gazed at her, his hazel eyes almost green. He blinked. "If she has the child, there will always be questions over who the father is."

"Not if you were married. Everyone would assume it was yours."

He scrunched his face up. "Ellie, I cannot! I love you!"

"Not even to save her life? To save yours?"

He didn't answer.

Her gaze caught the clock on the mantelpiece, and her heart sank. "According to Joe's calculations, my time is almost up." She gripped Kit's hand. "Kit, I love you. So much, I think I could burst. Which is why it is *killing* me to say this, but please, think about it. I couldn't bear it if something bad happened to you." She almost choked on the last words.

Kit ran his hand through her hair and pulled her into a kiss. "Ellie, I cannot. I love you."

"I know. But there isn't a future for us, is there? I don't stay and you don't leave. Kiss me again? I don't think I will be back."

She reached up and drew his face to hers, before he could plead with her any more. As they kissed, she sneaked a peek at the clock, half of her hoping Joe was wrong and that she had more time. This would be her last visit. Their last few minutes together. Their last kiss.

The pendulum quivered. Kit held her tightly, as if doing so could keep her with him.

She stood in the study, her arms empty, her heart full of sorrow.

Joe stuck his head around the door. "Ah. You're back."

"Yep. Thank you for distracting Liz."

"Well, she could hardly see you vanish. And it wasn't exactly a hardship."

Ellie peered towards the door. "Is she still here?" How was she going to sneak past to get changed if she was?

"No." He tilted his head to one side, studying her. "Why are you so upset? Did you tell him to marry Janet?"

She sucked in a long breath. "Mm."

"How did he react?"

Her shoulders sagged. "He said he wouldn't. That he couldn't because he loves me. It wouldn't be fair to either me or Janet."

Joe stuck a lip out. "He has a point."

Ellie closed her eyes, letting her head drop. "If I could see another way, I would never have suggested it. How sure of the rift timetable are you?"

"So that you can work out when you can see him?"

She shook her head, biting her lip. "No. So I can work out how *not* to see him. He needs to forget about me and marry Janet, and then they can all live happily ever after."

"And what about you? Don't you get a happily ever after?"

Pain crept into every cell of her body. "Not with Kit, no."

178

31

Ellie checked the whiteboard propped in the dining room. After telling Kit to marry Janet, she had been determined not to cross back into 1762, and had made Joe calculate the times the rift would open as accurately as he could. He'd listed the results on the board. So far, she had avoided travelling through time, though she had seen the lights dance along the border twice. She'd stayed resolutely in the more modern half of the house until they'd gone. According to the board, she had three days before the window to Kit's time opened again.

She had skeins drying in the workshop that needed checking and packaging. Collecting together a box of labels and a tin of string, she made her way to the workshop.

Although the workshop still needed plumbing for Ellie to dye her yarns there easily, it had proved to be an invaluable space for drying dyed skeins, at least in the summer. She'd installed two rolling clothing rails, and she clipped her dyed yarns to rings and then attached them to plastic coat-hangers, and hung them on the rails to dry. If the weather was fair, she could wheel the rails out on to the gravel area and let the sun and the wind dry the wool. If it threatened rain, she could swiftly wheel them back in again.

Her task for the day was to label all the dyed yarn, and twist the hanks into neat skeins. She checked the yarn hanging from the first coat-hanger was fully dry, then threaded half a dozen labels on to lengths of string. As she tied a label to the third skein, the workshop flickered. Her head shot up, and her breathing quickened. Her rails of yarn shifted in and out of reality. Beyond

179

them, Kit stood in his forge, his head turned towards her, his face etched with pain.

"I love you," he mouthed. He'd probably actually said it, but sound never crossed the rift.

Ellie waited to be catapulted into his time, but although the lights danced around the boundary like an extra-colourful version of the Northern Lights, she stayed resolutely in her time and he in his.

He pleaded silently with her across the rift, beckoning her to come to him, but nothing happened. So much of her yearned to cross and fling herself into his arms, but the room never fully resolved into 1762. Instead, the lights died away, the images of 1762 faded, and she was left alone in her workshop, her heart full of pain.

Shadow strolled across the room, then sat down to wash his back vigorously.

"How come you crossed?" Ellie demanded

Shadow blinked at her and went back to his ablutions.

Ellie tidied the string and labels away to a basket on the workbench and returned to the house. She peered around the dining room door. Joe tapped away at his laptop at the table, glancing up at her as he did. "Hey. You okay?"

"No. I nearly went to 1762."

He stopped typing, took his glasses off, and pushed his hair back. "What? It's not due to open for a few days. How come you didn't go? Did you get out of the area?"

"I was within the boundary, in the workshop. I could see Kit in his forge and he could see me. But I didn't get shifted back in time and the lights all just died away. Shadow crossed."

Joe put his glasses back on and scribbled a note on the pad at his side. "Interesting. I know the cat comes and goes a lot more than you ever have. I wonder if the rift has another variable in it that I've not figured out."

She twisted her fingers together. "Can you re-do your calculations? I don't want to go back in time again. I need to know when I can use the workshop. *If* I can use the workshop."

Joe stared at her over the top of his glasses. "I can look at them again, but I'm not making any promises. I thought I'd worked it all out already."

If she couldn't trust his calculations, she didn't want to work in the old part of the house.

"Can we swap rooms? Can you move to the study and me work from here?"

Joe's gaze swept the mass of notes and papers strewn across the large dining room table, but he nodded. "Sure. But not today? Let me get what I'm working on finished, and I'll move everything over this evening."

"Okay. Thanks." She pulled her hair out of its ponytail and re-fastened it. "I'm going for a walk."

"Take a brolly. It's due to bucket down."

Wrapped in a waterproof jacket and clutching a large umbrella, Ellie walked down to the village. Her feet found their way to the churchyard, and she meandered around, eventually wending her way past Thomas Greenwood's headstone, and on to the back wall where Kit's stone lay. As she reached it, the heavens opened, and fat drops of rain bounced on the ground. She stayed where she was, sheltering under her umbrella as the rain drummed on it, reading and re-reading the inscription.

"Just marry her," she muttered, tears prickling her eyes.

Did she really want that? She hunched into the collar of her coat. She couldn't be with him, whatever happened, so he might as well marry someone else, especially if it would save both his life and Janet's. The thought of him being with anyone else made her guts knot with jealousy.

She turned away. Why was life so unfair? Why did she finally meet someone so wonderful, only for it all to be snatched away from her?

32

That evening, Ellie chewed her lip, studying the window in the study. There was definitely a cupboard there under the window-seat in 1762.

"Joe? You busy?" she called through to the dining room, where Joe was packing up his work.

A moment later, he stuck his head around the door. "Not especially. What's up?"

"Could you give me a hand moving the desk? I want to see if the cupboard *is* still there."

"What cupboard? Where?"

"Under the window. In Kit's time there's a deep cupboard there. Before you get settled in here, I want to see if it's still here."

"Sure. I didn't see any signs of one when I was setting up your office, though."

They took all the drawers out of the desk and stacked them in the hall.

"Where are we moving this to?" asked Joe, eyeing the room. "Just along a bit, to the left of the window?"

"Yeah."

That was where it was in Kit's time.

"God, that thing weighs a ton," gasped Joe as he picked up one side.

Ellie didn't care. They shuffled the few steps needed to put the desk in the space next to the window recess, both of them blowing out their cheeks with the effort. The desk moved, Ellie's gaze fixed on the space under the window, searching for any sign of a cupboard there. First inspection wasn't promising. The wall was painted the same as the rest of the room, and there were clear signs of wallpaper underneath the paint. She crouched down, tapping the surface and listening carefully. The space definitely sounded hollow, and her excitement picked up. She ran her fingertips over the surface, probing for hinges or indentations where the cupboard would open. Nothing obvious emerged. Undaunted, she scrambled up and retrieved a tape measure and a Stanley knife from the toolbox in the pantry, then sat cross-legged on the floor in front of the window.

"What are you doing?" asked Joe.

"It's hollow behind here. I think the cupboard has been papered over at some point, then painted over that. I'm going to take the paper off. Worst-case scenario: I'm wrong, I make a mess of the wall, and we put the desk back in front of it to hide it."

She poked and prodded again, then measured the space, marking the centre. Gingerly, she pressed the Stanley knife into the surface. In the first couple of stabs, the blade met significant resistance, but on the third, it went in a little further. She kept going and found the groove where the two doors of the cupboard met. She cut a line through the small gap and picked at the painted paper. Most of it was stuck fast, making progress slow.

Joe came over and sat next to her. "You work on that side. I'll work on this."

Between them, they peeled away the wallpaper, revealing a scarred set of cupboard doors. Ellie grinned up at her brother. "Told you!"

The edges of the doors free, the next difficulty was actually opening them, as any handles had disappeared a long time ago. Joe used the blade of the knife to prise one door open. After a bit more tugging, it swung free, and they peered into the space.

The cupboard was empty.

Disappointment washed through Ellie. She didn't know what she had hoped to find there, and there was no earthly reason why someone would cover up a cupboard that still held something, but she'd been sure there would be something in the cupboard.

Something flickered in her memory. "Granny Molly *said* to look in the cupboard."

"This has been covered up for longer than Granny Molly lived here," Joe objected. "That paper looks like it's Victorian, and there's goodness knows how many layers of paint over it."

Ellie leaned in, scouring the space. A single shelf divided it into two halves, but held nothing except dust. She knocked on the sides and the back. It all sounded depressingly solid.

When she tapped the base of the cupboard, it rang hollow.

She pulled her phone out and used the flashlight on it to illuminate the base. How did you access the space? Would they have to prise the base out with the knife? In the back right corner was a darker bit of wood, almost as if there was a fingerprint over it. She pressed it experimentally. A soft click sounded, and the base of the cupboard sprang up a few millimetres. Enough that she could get her fingertips underneath and lift the base out.

A musty smell emerged from the space, and she thrust her head right into the cupboard, shining the light in from her phone. Tucked right at the back was a small book, and she reached in and drew it out. A rich brown leather cover surrounded thick, creamy-white pages, but this wasn't a printed book. This was a journal.

Ellie opened the cover, her heart fluttering anxiously. "Kit Greenwood. 1762"

Her hands trembling, she leafed through the first few pages. The book started in June 1762. The last entry was dated 4 September 1762. Two days before he disappeared. She skim-read the first entry. It described how he had encountered the ghostly figure of a strangely dressed woman. Ellie stopped reading abruptly and held the book up to Joe. "This is Kit's. He's describing seeing me."

Joe's brows arched, his face full of disbelief. Ellie ignored him. Was this why Granny Molly had told her to look in the cupboard? Should she read it?

Her instinct was to leave it unread. It was too much of an invasion of his privacy. Yes, technically, Kit had died a long time ago, whether or not that was in 1762. But she knew him; she'd talked to him, laughed with him, kissed him… reading his private thoughts felt wrong. Curiosity made her itch.

Joe cocked a brow at her. "Are you going to read it?"

She closed the cover. "I don't know."

Joe pointed into the cupboard. "What's that?"

Ellie reached in and retrieved three pieces of brown paper. She turned them over, but she already knew what she would find written on them as labels. Tea. Sugar. Chocolate bars.

Her hands shook.

"I took these to him. The last time I went. I took him some tea, some sugar, and a few chocolate bars."

She passed the papers to Joe. He stared at them, his brow crumpling.

"That looks like modern brown paper. And your writing. But they must have been in here since before it was papered up."

"He must have kept them. He said he was going to hide all of it in this cupboard so that Thomas didn't find it. I thought he just meant on the shelf, but he must have meant this space."

She checked all the nooks and crannies in the cupboard, but there was nothing else in there other than dust and a few dead spiders, their legs curled up like a clawed hand. She pushed the door closed and stood up.

"What are we doing with the desk?" asked Joe. "Is it staying where it is, or are we moving it back into the window?"

"It's up to you. I quite enjoyed being able to look out of the window when I was working, but a window-seat would be nice too. And it's your office now."

"A window-seat in the lounge would be better. At least that side of the house gets the sun. I promised to build you one." He glanced around the room. "Let's move the desk back. The corner there is gloomy and I don't want to work with the wall right in front of me. It's claustrophobic."

Ellie put the book and wrappers to one side, and she and Joe moved the carcass of the desk back into place. As Ellie slotted the drawers back in, Joe picked up Kit's journal. He flipped through a few pages, skim-reading it, resting his backside on the edge of the desk.

"This *is* a description of you, and the journal ends two days before he disappears," he said. "Maybe if we read it, we can work out *why* he disappears and prevent it. Let's go sit in the lounge. At least then, if the house shifts, you won't vanish."

In the lounge, they took a sofa each, the journal lying on the steamer trunk between them.

"Did you want *me* to read the journal? Let you know what it says?" offered Joe.

She shook her head. That felt as wrong as her reading it.

"No. I think I might read the dates that have passed." She caught Joe's raised brows. "Yeah, I know. *All* the dates have passed. But if it's August 18th *now* and I go back, it's August 18th in 1762. I'll read the dates that have passed. I don't want to read the dates yet to come. That would be too freaky."

In just a few weeks, Kit would disappear unless he asked Janet to marry him and that prevented her from being murdered. If he didn't ask her, it was highly likely both of them would be killed. Either way, she would never see him again. She closed her eyes, breathing deeply.

"I don't want to lose him, Joe. When I'm with him, I'm so *happy*. So relaxed. Like I was meant to be with him. But I can *never* have him, can I? I'm never allowed to have something good."

Joe changed sofas, sitting next to her and draping an arm around her shoulders. "Hey. Hey. Maybe you *don't* lose him? And even if you do, there will be someone else."

She faced him squarely. "Have *you* felt the same about anyone else, after you lost Hayley?"

He pressed his lips together. "I never thought I would, but yes. I'm beginning to feel like that about Liz. So, if even an old fool like me can find someone else, you can."

She tilted her head. "You really feel that way about Liz?"

"Getting that way." He sighed and kissed the top of her head. "Read the journal. Maybe it will explain what happens, and you can prevent it."

33

Ellie settled down on her bed, her feet tucked up and a mug of coffee next to her, Kit's leather journal on her lap. She'd taken it up to her room to read in private, though Shadow had tailed her upstairs. He lay curled up next to her with his paws over his pink nose, and she stroked him gently. A low rumbling purr emerged from his chest, and he stretched, blinked sleepily, and curled up again. Her fingers toyed with the cover of the journal, her mind filled with images of the man she loved. Him soothing the mare; the light catching in his hair and spinning some threads into copper and some into gold; his broad forearms with their scars; his easy smile. The feel of his lips on hers, his beard tickling her skin.

She hauled herself back from 1762, blinking away tears, and opened the cover of the journal. Kit had neat, angular writing, but the style made it difficult to read, not helped by occasional blobs of ink obscuring his letters. She took a long, deep breath.

25 June

The most extraordinary thing happened today. I met the ghost. Actually met her. She was walking through the house, as bold as brass. She is English, from her accent, and well-bred, though we barely spoke. She did not know what year it was. I told her, and she fainted in my arms and then disappeared. I searched the house for her, but there was no trace to be found. She was dressed in blue breeches that went right down to her ankles and what looked like a fisherman's gansey.

Ellie cast her mind back to that first encounter. To Kit, she must have been dressed as peculiarly as he had been to her. She

187

read on, but there was no further mention of her, just a description of the work he'd done in the forge.

Three horses shod today

Mr Archer's nails finished

She took a slurp of coffee and turned the page, curious to read about their encounters from his perspective. Their second meeting, when she'd asked about Janet, had puzzled him.

How can the ghost know about Janet?

He'd gone back and forth over whether she was a witch, a demon, or a spirit. Their third meeting had convinced him she *was* from the future, and he'd marvelled at the idea.

If she really has visited me from the future, how wondrous that is. I do not understand how it can be, but I believe she speaks the truth to me.

His feelings towards her had swiftly shifted from apprehension to delight, and his curiosity had been piqued over some of the things she'd said. He was disappointed that she had disappeared while he fetched her a glass of wine, wanting to talk more with her, and he was eager to see her again.

Kit wrote warmly of the day when they had strolled down to the village together. He mentioned the banana, though didn't name it.

She brought me the most wondrous fruit. Yellow and brown. The peel is inedible, but the fruit inside is sweet and soft. She also gave me something called toffy – small brown, chewy squares that were the sweetest food I have ever tasted.

He didn't mention that she had stayed half of the night in his bed, though he said that he had lain in his bed, thinking of her and wishing that they had a future together.

"You and me both, Kit, but it's not to be."

She reached the date where she had suggested that he ask Janet to marry him and stopped reading. She marked the page and closed the book, unwilling to hear his side of that particular day. Clearly, he never asked Janet, as the pamphlet about the cafe being haunted lay on the desk in the study and his 'disappeared' stone still stood in the churchyard. She ran her fingertip along the edge of the cover. *Should* she read it? What if she could glean some kind of clue that could help avert both his and Janet's deaths?

She re-opened the book and read, amused to read about the

second lot of gifts – the tea, the sugar, and the chocolate. He'd eaten one of the bars of chocolate in the evening after she had gone and found it rich and luxurious.

And then he wrote about her suggestion, and Ellie's breath caught in her throat.

I told Ellie that I loved her. She said that she loves me, but she also told me to ask Janet to marry me. I cannot. I cannot ask Janet to be my wife when I love Ellie with all of my heart. Ellie says that it will save Janet's life. And mine. I do not understand how that can be. The only woman I wish to marry is Ellie, but this is impossible.

Pain wormed its way through her, cracking her heart and forcing tears from her eyes. She put the journal down and buried her face in her hands as fat tears landed on her lap. Next to her, Shadow got up, turned around, and lay back down in exactly the same place he'd just been. She stroked his head, eliciting a loud purring from him, and sniffed hard.

"How do *you* wander in and out of the times, huh? If I don't figure out a way to get Kit, he's going to be killed, isn't he?"

She dried her eyes and turned to the last page of the journal. Less than a month after the visit where she'd taken him tea and told him to marry Janet, the journal ran out. Somewhere in those intervening days there *had* to be a clue that could help her save Janet, and, in turn, Kit.

She finished her coffee and turned back to the day after she had told him to marry Janet. She breathed in deeply, searching for something… *anything* that could help. Try as she might, she couldn't find anything. Kit talked about how much he missed her. How he had kept the list of dates she had given him and gone to the rift every time it had opened and she had never come through. That he was heartbroken at not seeing her again. And then, two days before he was due to disappear, this:

Janet's sister Mary came to tell me that Janet is dead. Her body was found on the road between the forge and the village. She had been hit in the head, violently, with a hammer.

One of my hammers is missing.

Ellie's hand flew up to cover her mouth. "Oh, Kit!"

The very last words in the journal were: *I should have asked her. Oh, may God forgive me. I should have asked her.*

34

For the third time in a row, Ellie stood at the edge of the rift, ensuring every part of her lay outside the perimeter of the time fault. She stared into 1762, the whiteboard from the kitchen clasped in her hands. On the other side, Kit stood silently pleading with her to join him.

She shook her head and held out the whiteboard so that he could read what she'd written.

"Please Kit. Ask her."

Kit mouthed back, *"No. I love you."*

Tears burned Ellie's eyes. She turned the whiteboard around, rubbed out what she'd written, wrote some more, then turned it back to him.

"Please. You must ask her before September 4th, or she will be murdered."

He twisted his fingers together, his hazel eyes fixed on her, and shook his head.

She turned the board back, wiped at it furiously, and scribbled some more.

"Kit, someone steals one of your hammers and kills her with it. You will be blamed. ASK HER!"

His mouth formed another "no" and he breathed erratically. She almost crossed the rift. Almost. But she held her nerve. They only had a few more seconds before the window would disappear.

She cleaned the board for a final time and wrote in capital letters: *"THEN JANET WILL DIE."*

His gaze dropped to the board, and he screwed his face up, his head hanging. Ellie turned on her heel and fled to the lounge, tears pouring down her cheeks. Joe scrambled up from his seat and wrapped her up in a hug.

"Are you crying because he's finally agreed he *will* ask her, or crying because he won't?"

"He won't."

She drew back, and Joe peered around her to read the whiteboard, wincing as he did so. "Ouch. Blunt."

Ellie blinked an acknowledgement. It *was* blunt, but she was running out of options.

"The date he disappears is two and a half weeks away. I've run out of time for subtlety." She scrubbed a hand over her face. "Any more joy with the rift calculations?"

Joe wrinkled his nose. "No. The main calculations when you can cross are right, but I haven't spotted any pattern in the times when the rift opens but you *don't* cross, or when Shadow comes and goes. I must be missing something. I'll have another look at it all."

Ellie blew her nose. "Is there *any* chance he can cross?"

She clung to the hope that he could, but the expression on Joe's face confirmed her fears. He hadn't crossed so far, and the fateful day crept inexorably closer. If he was determined not to ask Janet, then in two and a half weeks he would be killed by the villagers in revenge for something he hadn't done. She corrected herself. In two and a half weeks, 260 years ago.

She scraped a hand through her hair, deflated. "Okay. I'm going to pack some skeins. Or do some designing. Or some knitting."

Anything to take her mind off things.

She left Joe and headed out to the workshop. Several hangers of dry skeins needed to be labelled, twisted, and moved to the store in the back bedroom, and the rift wouldn't re-open for a while, so there was no chance of her ending up in 1762. She tied labels to the first batch and unclipped a skein, ready to twist it. Memories of times with Kit in his forge bombarded her, and she bowed her head. She wound two skeins, then hung the plastic coat-hanger back on the rail, her heart somewhere else.

Back in the house, she grabbed some bags from the kitchen, then poked her head around the door to the study.

"Joe, I'm heading out to see if the winds the other night have brought down any useful sticks."

Several birch trees lined the route into Masham. They might have shed some small branches she could harvest bark from. Even if there was nothing, it got her out of the house and gave her mind something else to focus on.

"I thought you were packing wool today."

"I can't concentrate."

Joe bunched his lips sympathetically. "Okay. See you later."

As she picked her way along the lane, Ellie fought her emotions.

"Oh, you amazing, wonderful, *stubborn* man."

She bent to pick up some fallen sticks and jammed them into her bag. How could she be glad that he wouldn't ask Janet when that meant he would die horribly? And yet… the thought of him with anyone else ripped her apart a hundred times more than finding out Simon was cheating on her had.

She stomped on up the lane, filling her bags with sticks and churning over everything. The bags full, she had no more excuses to be avoiding the house, and turned to trudge back.

At Rose Cottage, she skirted the house to go straight to the workshop to store the sticks. Her feet skidded to a halt as she rounded the corner and she checked her watch. So preoccupied with everything, she'd forgotten to keep an eye on the time, and coloured lights rippled along the edge of the rift. Through them, she could see Kit hammering furiously at something on his anvil. He turned his head enough to catch sight of her and shuddered to a halt, then flung his hammer down and rushed towards his bench.

His turn to hold a sign up for her.

"Will you forget me and marry another so easily?"

Hurt and pain filled his face. She dropped the bag, a sob catching in her chest. Tears rolled down his cheeks, and he thrust the sign towards her again, his eyes demanding an answer. She blinked, spilling tears. His workshop was so close. She could cross in a heartbeat. Hold him. Tell him how much she loved him. Hurting him like this was killing her.

"I love you," she said.

Kit shook his head, scrubbing at his face with the back of his

192

wrist. "No. You do not," he mouthed back.

The two stared at each other across time. Ellie still hadn't answered his question when the lights stopped dancing, and 1762 faded from sight.

She crumpled to the ground, sobbing.

35

Two days later, Joe and Ellie had arranged to meet Liz in the cafe in the corner of the market square. The siblings arrived first and found a table in the corner. Joe fiddled with the menu and a small container of sugar packets.

"The ghost story sheet isn't out today," he commented.

Ellie's heart missed a beat. Could this mean...? She hardly dared hope. She turned to Jill behind the counter. "Not got the ghost story out today?"

Jill's brow dipped. "What? Sorry, I don't know what you're talking about."

"The ghost story. About the lass who was murdered by the blacksmith."

Jill shook her head slowly, her bottom lip protruding. "Nope. No idea. Never heard of it."

Ellie turned back to Joe, trembling. "Do you think he's asked her? And that's why the story is gone?"

Joe frowned. "How can *we* know about the story if it never happened?"

Ellie flapped a hand. "No idea. I've never understood it. Nodes? Or ley lines?"

Before they could discuss it any more, Liz arrived in a flurry and Joe stood to kiss her cheek, his face wreathed in smiles.

"Hi, hi. Sorry I'm late. Have you been waiting long?"

"No, no. We just got here," Joe reassured her.

Liz unwound a printed scarf from around her neck and shucked out of her light jacket. "I've no idea what the weather is

194

doing today. I'm over-dressed in this, but it threatened rain when I set off!"

Her chair scraped the floor, then she sat, beaming at Joe.

"Liz, have you ever heard of a ghost story with a young lass murdered by a blacksmith?" Ellie tried to keep the tremor of excitement out of her voice.

Liz turned to her, puzzled. "No… I don't think so. What's the story?"

"A blacksmith from the 1700s killed a young lass from Masham, and then the village turned on him and killed him."

Liz rested her cheek on her knuckles. "Not ringing any bells."

"Okay. Thanks." Ellie struggled to contain her emotions. Had he asked her? Had that saved her? "Um. I think I might leave you two to it. Sorry. A shed-load of orders came in, and I really ought to get them sorted."

Neither Joe nor Liz seemed especially disappointed that she was going. Joe winked at her as she pulled her jacket off the back of the chair, clearly understanding that she was *not* going home to pack orders.

As soon as she left the cafe, Ellie turned on to the lane leading to the churchyard, her feet crunching on the gravel path. She hurried to the corner where Kit's 'disappeared stone' lay, quivering with anticipation. What she found when she reached it both filled her with relief and broke her heart.

In memory of Christopher Greenwood died 14 August 1810 aged 75 and his wife Janet died 1 February 1812 aged 71

The stone next to it read:

Eleanor Greenwood died 9 July 1822 aged 59

Ellie took a picture of each with her phone, then traced her finger over the names and dates. No 'disappeared stone' any longer. No ghost story because there *was* no story. Janet lived to be old; so did Kit. No one murdered her. He wasn't killed by an angry mob.

She found a bench in a quiet part of the churchyard and sat, her emotions roiling. Relief that Kit had lived to a ripe old age overlaid a deep, stabbing jealousy that he married Janet, and had the life with her that she craved to have with him. It had saved them both, but it left her bereft.

A couple walking a dog passed her, shooting her concerned, sympathetic looks, but they said nothing. It wasn't entirely unexpected that someone would cry on a bench in a churchyard.

She leaned back on the bench, taking long, deep breaths. How could she stay in Rose Cottage with all the memories and lost possibilities? A thought flashed cold through her. What if the rift was related to Kit? Joe had calculated that the last day the window to 1762 would open was the last day Kit was alive in the original story. If he didn't die, did that mean the rift would keep on opening after the 6th? Was she going to have to avoid half of the house forever? What if she forgot and got catapulted back to 1762, to Kit living happily with Janet? She wrapped her arms around her middle, crumpling.

"Oh, Granny Molly, *why* did you think I would end up with him? It was *always* impossible."

She dried her eyes and blew her nose, at a loss what to do or where to go. Her phone ringing distracted her.

"Hi, Joe."

"Hey. You okay? Where are you?"

"Sitting on a bench in the churchyard."

"Has the stone gone?"

She wiped her nose with a tissue. "Mm. It's been replaced by a joint headstone for him and Janet. And there's one for Janet's daughter. They called her Eleanor."

"Oh."

"Where are you?"

"Just leaving the cafe."

"Is Liz with you?"

"No, she had to get back. I'll come and find you."

He rang off. Ellie scrolled through the pictures on her phone, trying to find the one she had taken of Kit's 'disappeared stone' but there was no trace of it. She slid her phone back into her pocket.

Joe strolled into view and waved at her. She stayed on the bench, waiting for him to join her. He sat next to her, draped his arm around her shoulders, and kissed the top of her head. "Hey."

"Hey. I don't know if I'm happy or sad."

"Understandable. Shall we go to York for the afternoon?"

She leaned into him. "Mm. York would be fabulous. Thank you."

He squeezed her hard. "Come on then. Shall we check out the button shop there?"

She smiled through her tears. "Sure. I mean, you can never have too many buttons, right?"

36

Later that evening, after a fun day in York, Ellie poured herself a large glass of wine, picked up Kit's journal, and took both of them through to the lounge. Would his journal have changed? Did it now keep going after the last entry? Would it cover his married life? Her stomach knotted at the thought.

She curled herself into the corner of one of the sofas. Joe sat on the other, knitting. He slid his glasses down his nose to peer at her.

"Is that a good idea?" he said, lifting his chin towards her.

"The wine or the book?"

"Either, I suppose, but I meant the book."

"Not sure I can do the book without the alcohol."

"What are you looking for?"

She sighed, putting her glass on the trunk between them. "I don't know. That he's happy. That he's *not* happy?"

"Want me to read it?"

Did she? He could read it far more dispassionately than she could. She passed it across to him.

"Does it continue after the 4th? It stopped two days before he disappeared before. Has it changed?"

Joe flipped to the back of the journal. "Mm, hm. The entire book is now filled."

"What does today's date say? That's when the story disappeared."

Joe read, squinting at the writing a little. "Well, to give you the gist of it, your last whiteboard message, where you said Janet would die, devastated him. He couldn't bear to have it on his conscience, so he asked her to marry him. She said yes. Neither of them appears to be all that happy about it. She knows he's in love with someone else, although all he has told her is that you are not able to marry him." He read a little further. "Janet thinks you're a married woman that he's fallen for, and he's not disabusing her of the idea."

He flipped through to the end. "The last entry is from later in the year. November."

"When do they marry?" Ellie half whispered.

Joe flicked back and forth through the journal. "Um. October 2nd."

Ellie did the maths. Janet would be about three months pregnant by then. Starting to show? The baby would certainly arrive much sooner than nine months after the wedding.

Joe handed the journal back to her. "You might as well read it. All he does is talk about you."

She traced the ridges along the spine. Would reading it be like picking at a scab?

"He loves you," Joe said softly.

She exhaled deeply. "I don't know if that makes things better or worse."

Joe picked up his knitting again. "Just read it. You *know* you're going to eventually, and you're raw enough today. You might as well get all the hurt over with at once."

He was right. As ever. Ellie took a large gulp of wine and opened the cover.

The journal read identically to how it had before, up to the equivalent of two days earlier. From that point on, everything had changed. He'd clearly written the entry in the evening, after she'd seen him through the rift.

I saw her through the tear. She held up signs urging me to marry Janet and said that if I did not, Janet would be killed. What if she is right? What if Janet dies? It would be my fault, even if it is not me who kills her. Why should I disbelieve Ellie? She says she loves me. Surely she would not urge me to marry another unless she was certain it was the right thing to do. Unless she does not love me. Perhaps then, too, she would urge me to marry another.

She said that someone steals one of my hammers to blame me. That Janet will die on the 4th of September. So soon.

I do not love Janet the way I love Ellie, but I cannot bear to think of her being killed. I will ask her tomorrow.

I held up a paper, the way Ellie has for me, and asked her if she would forget me and marry another so easily. From her face, I think she could not. I do not know if this comforts me or not. I am betraying both women.

Ellie took a breath, then turned to the entry for the following day.

I asked her. Janet said I should not marry her for pity. I did not know what to say, for I would be marrying her for pity. I said that we had been friends for many years – since she was a girl – and that I could not bear to see her thrown out and abused. She asked me bluntly if I loved her and I could not answer. She said that she knows I have lost my heart to someone else. She has seen it in my face these last few weeks. I could not deny it and she asked me why I was not marrying the woman I loved, but asking her.

I told her that the woman was unattainable. She understood me to mean that she is married, and I did not correct her. Eventually she said: What a pretty situation. You do not love me and I do not love you. Not as a man and wife should. But we will be married. For the child's sake, if for no one else's.

Ellie bit her lips. In all the turmoil, she had half forgotten that the pregnancy would lead to a baby if Janet survived. One that did not deserve the stain of illegitimacy. Kit might be taking pity on Janet, but he was also taking on the responsibility of another man's child and giving it a loving home.

"Oh, Kit. You were a wonderful man," she murmured.

She turned the pages, skim-reading. Most of the entries were short, with him questioning his decision and lamenting never seeing Ellie again. The one for September 4th merely said: *The fateful day has passed and Janet is alive.*

The one for the 6th was equally brief: *I have not disappeared. Ellie was right.*

She steeled herself to read the entry for the day of the wedding. It was mercifully low on detail.

I married Janet today. Perhaps we will learn to love one another. She is a good woman. She did not deserve any of this. I will try to make her happy.

Ellie closed her eyes, swallowing. According to the joint headstone, they had been married for almost fifty years, though the only child they had hadn't been his. She wanted that to give her comfort, but it didn't. Had they muddled along as married friends for almost fifty years? Not much of a marriage, if so. Not much of a life.

She flicked through the rest of the journal, but he did not mention her name again. The journal became a summary of orders and trivia, eventually petering out when the pages did. She closed the cover and slid the book on to the trunk. Opposite her, Joe glanced up, his hands stilling over his knitting.

"You okay?"

"Yeah. I'll live. So will Janet and Kit."

"I'm sorry it didn't work out the way you wanted. From the bits I read and from what you've said, he seemed like a decent guy."

She blinked hard and drained her glass of wine. "He was. I'm going to bed. It's been a really shit day."

37

Ellie sat at the dining room table, drafting out a new design for a fitted bodice-style top. Pages of graph paper, along with the myriad of coloured pencils she'd been using to plan out the pattern on the bodice, littered the table. Next to her lay her scrapbook of dye samples, plus a shade-card of natural colour yarns from a local seller. Ellie hoped to work with him to produce kits of her designs, as the yarn from his sheep was amazing. *If* she could get the design right. At the moment, she was struggling to figure out the colourwork pattern across the different sizes.

She sketched a little more, then scribbled numbers, trying to get the maths of the knitting to work. It still didn't. Not helped by her looking at the numbers, but thinking of lying on the riverbank with Kit, the sun catching his hair and the two of them joking about her getting grass stains on her top. Ten days had passed since the story had changed, and Ellie hadn't stopped thinking about him.

She rubbed her eyes and laid her pencil down. Maybe a strong coffee would help her focus. She rolled her shoulders and eased out her neck, then headed to the kitchen. She filled the kettle and leaned against the table, her gaze idly settling on the clock.

The second hand wasn't moving.

Ellie scanned the room, straightening, her heart plummeting. Around her, the room settled into 1762.

"Shit!"

She didn't want to be here. She had sworn never to come again.

Her brain hunted for an image of the whiteboard with the dates and times of the time-rifts. When would the rift open again? How long would she be trapped in 1762? She couldn't remember.

What should she do? Hide? That would work if the window was a short one, but not if it wasn't.

"Oh, you *idiot*, Ellie. Set your watch to give you alerts!"

She stood in the centre of Kit's kitchen, unsure what to do. Outside, the banging of a hammer on metal stopped, and a lump formed in her throat. Was Kit coming into the house? The banging started up again a few moments later, and some of the tension in her shoulders dissipated.

What on earth was she going to do until the window re-opened? Read a book? Her eye alighted on a jacket in a basket at one side of the kitchen, and she went over to investigate. It was the same jacket Kit had worn when they had walked down to the river. A button was missing, and there was a small hole in the elbow. The missing button lay on the top of the folded jacket, and Ellie picked it up. Next to the basket sat a wooden box. She lifted the lid to find a small collection of sewing things: some buttons, thread, needles, a small pair of scissors, some spools of wool, and a darning mushroom.

"Well, if nothing else, I can do your mending while I wait to go back to my time."

She sat at the kitchen table and reattached the button, then rummaged through the sewing box to find a spool of wool in roughly the right colour to darn the elbow. One was close enough, and she poked the wooden darning mushroom into the sleeve of his jacket. A puff of air escaped from the jacket, the familiar mix of wool, cedar wood, and smoke bringing a lump to her throat.

Just as she was finishing the mending, Kit walked in through the back door. He stumbled to a halt.

"Ellie."

Ellie tied off the thread and replaced all the items she'd used back in his sewing box. Kit remained rooted to the spot on the threshold, his eyes wide.

"Why did you come? What has happened?"

She closed the lid of the wooden box. "I didn't mean to. I forgot the time, and I was in the kitchen when the shift happened."

Still Kit kept his distance. "I asked her. She said yes. Reluctantly. She knows I do not love her."

"I know. The story changed. In my time." She swallowed, trying not to cry. "You did the right thing. She isn't killed. No one comes for you."

He nodded miserably.

"I don't know when the window back to my time opens again. Do you?"

From the hallway came the sound of the clock in his study chiming the quarter hour. Kit's attention lifted to the doorway, then his gaze dropped back to her.

"A few minutes." He jutted his chin at the table. "You did not need to do my mending."

She shrugged. "I didn't know what else to do to fill the time."

The air crackled with pain and tension. Ellie yearned to go over to him, be held by him, kiss him. She stayed where she was.

"I never answered your question," she said at last, her voice hitching. "No. I will not forget you. I will not marry another easily."

His eyes brightened, but he stayed silent. Were they going to stare at each other across the room until she returned to her time?

"Kit…"

His face crumpled with pain and his chin lowered. Ellie scrambled up and hurried across to him. Kit folded his arms, taking a step back.

"I am not yours," he said, his voice gravelly. "You told me to marry another."

Ellie stood in front of him, her heart breaking. "I know. It was the hardest thing I have ever had to do."

"As it was for me. You cannot now ask me to go back on it."

"I'm not. I…" Ellie moved away from him. "I'm sorry. You just looked so upset."

His breathing was ragged, and he chewed at the inside of his bottom lip.

"I'm sorry," Ellie whispered.

Faint images of her kitchen appeared, superimposed over his. She swallowed, tears burning her eyes, determined to drink in every last image of him. They stood only about a metre apart, but the gulf between them was infinite and filled with pain.

"I love you," he whispered as the room fractured around them.

A sob caught in her throat. "I love you too. With all my heart."

But she was back in 2022, and he would not have heard her.

38

That Friday, Liz blew in to the cafe, a whirl of energy as ever, and dashed over to the table where Ellie sat.

"Sorry! Sorry!" she said, pulling out a chair. "Have you been waiting long?"

"No. I've only just got here. Your mum's made carrot cake today, by the way."

Liz's favourite. "Ooh, great! No Joe today?"

Ellie hid her smile. "No. He's got too much work on, but he sends his love."

Liz's face lit up.

As the two women studied the menu, Liz's mum, Jill, came over with a tray of items for the table. Ellie could take or leave the plastic flowers in a vase, but had to concede that they made the place cheerful. Jill added salt and pepper pots, flashing them both a smile. Ellie grinned back, then froze. Next to the vase, Jill placed a plastic stand holding a printed sheet. Ellie's mouth turned to sand as she saw the story about the cafe being haunted by the ghost of a young woman called Janet Shaw.

Her hands shaking, she picked up the plastic stand and read. Janet Shaw was bludgeoned to death by the local blacksmith, Christopher Greenwood, after he found out she was pregnant by another man. In retribution, the village had turned on him, killing him at his forge.

"Why are you reading that?" asked Liz, looking up from the menu. "You've read it a hundred times. You live in the murderer's house!"

No! No, no, no, no, no!

The world tilted on its axis, and an iron band tightened around her chest.

"Ellie? Are you okay? What's wrong?" Liz reached across to put a hand on her arm.

Ellie hauled air, tears welling. How on earth could she explain this to Liz?

"I'm sorry," she stammered out. "I don't feel well. I need air."

Her clothes prickled her skin, and sweat broke out on her brow. She scrambled up from the table, knocking into a chair and ricocheting out of the cafe. Liz followed her.

"Ellie? What on earth is wrong?"

"Sorry. I just don't feel very well suddenly."

What else could she say? That the tale of the blacksmith and the murdered girl was the cause of her distress? To Liz, the story was old news. It had *always* been that story.

What had Kit done?

Ellie leaned on her knees, trying not to vomit, her eyes locking on the gate to the churchyard.

"Can I run you home?" Liz rested her hand on Ellie's shoulder. "You can't walk back like this."

"Thanks."

She needed to check when the window next opened, and warn Kit what was coming; find out what he had done to change things.

Liz had parked in the market square and she helped Ellie over to the car, then drove them to Rose Cottage. By the time they arrived, Ellie's breathing had settled, although her heart still pounded, and nausea bubbled at the back of her throat.

"Joe?" Liz called out as she supported Ellie into the house. "Ellie's not well."

Joe shot out of the study. "Ellie? What's up?"

"I just came over all peculiar in the cafe," said Ellie. "We hadn't even had time to order."

Joe hustled over to her, taking her from Liz.

"The story's back," she whispered, too softly for Liz to hear.

Joe tensed, but said nothing. He half carried her to the lounge, and she sank down on the sofa, Liz perching next to her.

"I'll get you some water," he said. "Liz? Coffee?"

"Please. Need a hand?"

"No, I'll be fine, thanks."

He hurried out, returning quickly with a glass of water, then retreated again to make the coffees. Liz fussed over Ellie, still concerned at what might have caused her to take ill.

"I think I may have eaten something that disagreed with me," lied Ellie. "I'll be fine."

Joe returned with the coffees and put them on the steamer trunk. Ellie leaned her elbows on her knees, forcing herself to breathe more slowly.

What had he *done*? Why was the story back?

"Can I do anything?" asked Liz.

Ellie raised her head, smiling wanly. "Honestly, I'm fine now. I just had a funny turn."

"Are you sure?"

"Yeah, yeah. Thanks for bringing me back."

She sipped her water, desperate for Liz to finish her coffee and leave so that she could talk to Joe. The moment Liz put her empty mug back on the trunk, Ellie sat up straight.

"I think I'm going to go and have a lie down."

"You take it easy," said Liz.

Joe stood up, prompting Liz to get up, too. He showed her out, and as soon as she'd gone, he dashed back.

"Ellie, what did you mean, 'The story's back'? The story about Kit? I thought that was fixed?"

"I know. It *was* fixed. But the sheet in the plastic thing in the cafe, about Janet's ghost... it's back! It says Kit killed her and then the village killed him." She clasped her head with her hands. "I should have known we couldn't cheat fate."

Joe sat next to her, rubbing her back.

"What have you *done*, Kit?" she moaned. "It was fixed. You and Janet lived happily ever after. You had a gravestone saying you lived to be 75. What have you *done*?"

Her hands shaking, she dragged her phone out of her pocket and scrolled through the pictures. The photo of the joint gravestone for Kit and Janet had disappeared. She scrolled a little further, then caught a sob in her throat.

Erected by Thomas Greenwood in memory of his brother Christopher who was killed on the 6th day of September 1762

Killed. Not 'disappeared'.

It had been almost unbearable to give him up, but at least she'd been able to console herself with the knowledge that Janet wasn't murdered and he was saved. She showed Joe the phone, her heart breaking.

"When does the rift next appear?" she managed, between sobs. It was already September 2nd. If she was going to see Kit, it would have to be soon.

Joe fished his phone out of his pocket and pulled the times up. "The day after tomorrow."

He showed her his screen. The window opened at 7:12 in the evening and closed again a couple of minutes later. Nowhere near long enough to find out what Kit had done and work out whether things could be changed.

"What are you going to do?" asked Joe.

"When does it open again? If I go and stay there, when do I get back?"

Joe checked the dates and times. "The following morning, about half-past seven."

"I have to see him. I have to find out why it's changed again and warn him. It's four days, Joe. He's killed in four days. The day the window next opens is the day Janet is killed."

"Let me look at the data again. Maybe he could get through."

Ellie blinked back tears. She couldn't let her mind consider the alternative. Had she given up seeing him for *nothing*?

"What does his journal say?" asked Joe. "Maybe it's changed?"

"It's upstairs, next to my bed."

He hurried away, returning a few moments later. He went to press the book into her hands, but she clenched her fists so that he couldn't. "You read it."

She chewed at her thumbnail while he turned the pages, the colour draining from his face. "What happened when you went back by accident?"

Ellie's mind ran back over the awful visit. "Nothing. I didn't know what to do when I first got there, so I sewed a button back

209

on his jacket and darned a hole in the sleeve. Then he came in, and it was all horrible and awkward, and then I came back. Why?"

He flipped through the book, summarising for her. "Janet knew you had been there. She knew Kit couldn't sew that well. Plus, he was miserable. Said she couldn't marry him if he loved someone else and intended to keep on seeing them. They argued about it all. Janet went outside. Hugh Ellis had brought one of his horses to be shod, and Janet saw him. Ellis said something to her, but Kit didn't hear what. Kit came out to find Janet with her hands on her hips, saying it was his – Ellis's – reputation that would be the one in ruins, not hers. Hugh Ellis was white with fury and struck her. Kit told him to find another blacksmith as he would not accept work from a man who had assaulted his wife to be." Joe looked up from the book. "It looks horribly like Janet threatened to tell."

"What date is that?" Ellie whispered.

"Yesterday. The 1st."

She held out a trembling hand and Joe passed the book over. The entries ran out on the 4th again; the day Janet died.

Janet's sister Mary came to tell me that Janet is dead. Her body was found on the road between the forge and the village. She had been hit in the head, violently, with a hammer.

One of my hammers is missing.

Ellie's throat ached. "How do I fix this? How do I save him? How do I save *her*?"

Joe shook his head, his face pale. "I don't know if you can. By the time you get there, Janet will probably be dead."

She slumped, her chin on her chest. Joe sat next to her, resting his shoulder against hers.

"Let me look at it all again. And you go and see him and warn him. Maybe she's still okay. If Janet stays in the house when Hugh Ellis is scheduled to murder her, that might fix it."

She nodded miserably, but in her heart of hearts, she knew this wouldn't be enough. If Janet wasn't killed on the 4th, the story and the journal would just shift and say she was killed on the 5th. Or the 6th. Or some other date. Janet had threatened to tell. If Hugh Ellis didn't kill her on one particular day, he would do it another.

They had tried to cheat history and lost.

39

"How much does the cat weigh?" asked Joe, late in the afternoon of the day the rift opened.

Ellie looked up, perplexed by the question. The two of them sat in the study, Joe scribbling away on a notepad, a calculator up on the laptop in front of him. He'd been working on the data since the story had changed back, two days earlier.

"What?"

"How much do you reckon the cat weighs? And a question one should never ask a woman, I know, but how much do you weigh?"

"I have no idea about the cat. What's an average weight of one? I mean, he's a pretty normal-sized cat, isn't he?"

Joe tapped away at the laptop. "Okay. Somewhere between 3.5 and 5 kilos, apparently." He glanced up, brows raised. "You?"

"Um. 62 kg. Roughly."

He scribbled some more, then punched numbers in to the calculator.

"Do you think you've worked something out?" She moved to stand behind him.

"Maybe. How much do you think Kit weighs?"

"I haven't a scoobies! How much do you weigh? He's about your height, but heavier. Stand up."

Joe obliged and Ellie scrutinised him. "He's pretty much exactly the same height as you." She prodded him, then slipped her arms around him. "More solid than you. Whatever you weigh, I'd say he weighs more. Why?"

"Make me another coffee while I think a bit more about this."

He pulled free and sat down again.

Ellie wandered through to the kitchen, filled the kettle, and flicked the switch. Her gaze settled on the whiteboard propped on the side, and she read over the times the rift would open. As far as Joe could calculate, after the 6th, the rift never opened again. That was the day Kit would be killed. If she and Kit *couldn't* change history, would Joe work out a way to get Kit here in time? Is that why he was asking about her weight?

The kettle switched off, and she made two mugs of coffee and took them back to the study.

"Have you figured something out?" she asked, putting a mug down in front of Joe.

"I think so."

"And is there a way to get Kit through the rift?"

Joe breathed deeply. "Maybe. It depends how much more than me he weighs."

Ellie perched on the chair, clasping her mug. "Go on."

"You know how we've always been puzzled about how Shadow comes and goes so easily? And why sometimes you've been inside the bit of the house that shifts when the rift opens, but you didn't time-travel? I think that the individual rifts have a mass aspect. Shadow can slip through much smaller rifts because he's a cat and only weighs a few kilos. You don't always cross because you weigh more than the rift can transport. I'd wondered about it before, but I thought it was tied in with the time between the rifts appearing – that the bigger the mass factor, the longer the time between rifts, but there's absolutely no link whatsoever. They're each following their own patterns."

He pointed to a graph he'd sketched out on some paper. The bottom line indicated time, and the vertical was labelled 'kg'. The graph rose and fell, resembling a simple rollercoaster.

"The mass aspect has been oscillating." His finger traced over the peaks and troughs. "But the top value has been increasing. The time between rifts is following a completely different rhythm."

He drew out another piece of paper with a complicated equation on it. Even reading it made Ellie's head hurt.

"Can you cut to the chase and remember that I'm a designer and not a scientist?"

"Okay. In simple terms, Kit hasn't been able to cross before because the mass part of each anomaly has been too small. Sometimes, you have used some of it up or the cat has; sometimes, it just wasn't ever big enough. The times when you have been inside the anomaly but not crossed was for the same reason." He fiddled with the page of calculations. "The good news is that on the 6th, the rift has a bigger mass aspect than it's had so far. The bad news is that the window for anyone crossing from here to 1762 and back again is *really* short."

Ellie rubbed the back of her neck, processing the information. "Are you saying more than my 62 kilos can cross? Is the rift big enough for Kit to cross?"

Joe twisted one side of his mouth up. "Yes, I think so."

"How many kilos can cross?"

"In total, 147. Kit needs to be 85 kilos or less, if you cross too."

"And how much do you weigh?" she asked, her heart in her mouth.

Joe bit his lip. "79. Thereabouts."

She stared at him. Both Joe and Kit were just over six feet tall. Her brother was pretty lean. Was Kit *that* much beefier? He was pretty solid over his shoulders and back, with muscled arms. Muscle weighed more than fat.

She dashed out of the kitchen, sprinting for the bathroom and the scales there. She stepped on them, almost too afraid to see what they said. Joe had followed her and stood in the doorway.

"How much?" he asked, sounding as nervous as she felt.

"60.7 kilos. So, Kit can be 86.3 and we'll both get back?"

"*If* my calculations are right."

She considered what she was wearing and did a mental scan of her wardrobe. Floaty shorts had to weigh less than jeans, and she had a silk top that weighed almost nothing.

"I need to weigh clothes," she said, stepping off the scales.

She hurried to her bedroom and raked through her clothes, gathering up the lightest. She put the tops to one side, and the shorts and skirts to the other. Picking through them, she selected an outfit, changed into it, and stood on the scales again. Her chosen outfit – a silk top, some skimpy shorts, and flip-flops – trimmed over half a kilo off the total. Joe studied her.

"Kit is going to have a heart attack if you turn up with that much flesh on show."

"I don't care. It gives him another half-kilo."

She changed back into her jeans and t-shirt in her bedroom and tidied away her clothes, her mind racing. Could this work? If she told Kit what was about to happen, could she keep him safe until the large rift on the 6th?

Joe tapped on the door. "Come and grab something to eat before you need to get ready."

In the kitchen, Ellie threw together a sandwich, her eye on the graph Joe had sketched.

"Joe? Am I reading this right? Was the rift big enough for Kit to come through when I accidentally went back that day? If I hadn't gone."

Joe leaned over and traced the tip of the line over to the vertical axis. "If he weighed less than 83 kilos and if the cat hadn't crossed. Maybe."

She rubbed her eyes, gutted. "He could have come? And I ruined it."

"Was Kit avoiding you as much as you were avoiding him?" asked Joe, his head cocked.

"Mm."

"Then he would have made sure he wasn't inside the rift. You didn't ruin his chance of crossing. He didn't know he could."

She sucked her teeth. "He'd asked her by then. Even if he'd known he could cross, I don't think he would have. He told me he wasn't mine any longer." She took a bite of her sandwich. If only Joe had fathomed out all the mechanics sooner, Kit could be here already. Once he'd crossed, they'd just have had to ensure he didn't accidentally cross back.

She sighed. That might have saved Kit, but it wouldn't have saved Janet. She would have been left to fend for herself, and Hugh Ellis might still have killed her.

She chewed slowly. "If Kit crosses, Janet gets left behind, right? Either because she's been killed, or because he leaves. If she isn't killed, she will have no one to protect her and a child on the way."

Would Kit even agree to leave if that was the case?

Joe bit his lip. "I'm not sure you can save Janet. The date that

214

she argues with Hugh Ellis has passed. You can't change that. According to the journal, she dies today. I think you will arrive too late to help her."

A lump lodged in Ellie's throat.

"It's so *unfair*. She did nothing wrong. She was raped. She was *never* at fault."

"I know. She got an absolutely hellish deal. But she knew that at least one person cared enough about her to try to save her."

"He would have made it work, too."

Joe checked the clock. "Watch your time. Unless you're going to see him dressed like that."

She wolfed down the remnants of her sandwich and hurried upstairs to change into her 18th century costume.

"You tried," she told herself as she shook out her skirt. "You really tried to help her."

It hadn't been enough.

40

At just after seven, Ellie stood in the kitchen in her 18th century costume, waiting for the rift to open. A sick feeling lodged in the pit of her stomach. Could they change things? Was she too late to save Janet? Could she save Kit?

Bang on schedule, Kit's kitchen superimposed over hers. She gave Joe a quick hug and waited for the room to settle into 1762. As soon as it did, she scurried out of the back door to make sure she would be outside the rift when it flipped again. Given the hour, both brothers would be home, and she tiptoed to the edge of the property line, trying to work out where anyone was. The forge lay quiet and empty; presumably both men were in the house.

Next to her, colourful lights flickered. The rift re-opening. She took another few steps back, just in case. The lights died away, leaving her staring at the back of the house, trapped in 1762 until the following morning.

Should she find them? How did she explain to Thomas who she was?

"Who are you?"

She turned. A man who could only be Thomas, given how similar he was to Kit, stood at the back door, glaring at her.

She bit her lip. "Is Kit here?"

Before Thomas could answer, Kit appeared in the doorway behind his brother.

"Ellie!" He stared at her, wringing his hands. "I did not think that I would ever see you again. Why have you come today?"

"Kit, who *is* this woman?" snapped Thomas.

Kit squared his shoulders. "This is Mistress Eleanor Stewart." He hesitated. "A friend of mine."

The word 'friend' cut Ellie to the quick.

Thomas studied her, his face clearing. "*You. You're* the woman he's in love with. I have never seen you in Masham. Where are you from?"

Kit coloured, his eyes still fixed on her. "Ellie, may I present my brother, Thomas."

She bobbed a neat curtsy. "Pleased to meet you."

"How long will the window be open?" Kit asked.

She swallowed. "It's closed. It was only open for a couple of minutes. It re-opens tomorrow morning."

"You're trapped here until the morning?" He folded his arms and looked down at his feet.

The last time she'd been trapped in 1762 overnight, Kit had held her until she fell asleep. Now, she wondered if he would make her sleep in the forge.

"Mm. I need to talk to you about something, and it will take longer than the window was open for. It's okay. I'll sleep in the chair downstairs."

"What are you two talking about?" asked Thomas, interrupting. "What window?" He looked from Ellie to Kit, arching a brow. "And have you stayed before? No wonder Janet was so angry!"

Ellie eyed Thomas nervously. "It's a long story. I think we need to sit down."

Kit finally raised his head. "Are we telling him?"

"We have to. Kit, the story is back."

Kit blanched. "You had better come in."

Both men stepped back, allowing Ellie into the house. Kit nodded to Thomas to grab a bottle of wine, drew three glasses from the dresser in the kitchen, and the three of them decamped to the study-cum-sitting room. There, Kit seated Ellie in one of the chairs, Thomas took the other easy chair, and Kit moved his desk chair next to her.

"Tell me?" he asked, his voice strained. "The story is back? Janet...?"

Should she make one of them run and check that Janet was okay? Thomas wouldn't believe her, though. Why should he? She was a stranger who had just appeared. Kit would go, but what if he found Janet after she'd been killed? What if *that* was the reason he got blamed?

"We need to tell Thomas everything. Start at the beginning."

Thomas's brows rose, making her smile. "You look so alike."

They did, sharing the same light reddish-brown hair colour, creamy skin, and hazel eyes, though Thomas was clean-shaven. He was also an inch shorter than his brother, and a had more serious air, but there could be no mistaking the family connection.

Ellie settled herself in the seat, knotting her fingers and composing her thoughts. "Thomas, what I'm about to tell you will seem fantastical. Please let me finish? Let me tell you all of it and listen with an open mind. I have proof of what I'm saying."

She took a long drink of wine and started at the beginning – how she had visited the house in her youth and seen what she'd believed to be a ghost; how she and Kit had 'haunted' each other for several days before finally meeting. Several times, Thomas opened his mouth as if to protest, but each time he closed it again without saying anything.

Ellie finally reached the point where she needed to tell Thomas about the story.

"In my time, there is a story. It isn't true, but it has persisted down the ages. It says that Kit asked Janet to marry him, but that she was pregnant by another man."

Thomas turned to his brother. "Is she?"

Kit didn't answer. Ellie hurried on.

"It also said that Kit killed Janet in anger over this, and as a consequence, the villagers turned on him and killed him. You erect a stone to commemorate him."

Thomas's brow creased, but before he could speak, Kit butted in. "I asked her. You said that it saved us both."

"I know. I know. And it did. But then things changed." She peered at Kit, eyes wide. "Kit, where's Janet right now?"

He turned the colour of milk. "At her house."

Ellie shook her head. "I don't think so. I think Hugh Ellis has already killed her. I hope I'm wrong."

Thomas leapt to his feet. "What are you talking about?"

Kit motioned with his hand for Thomas to sit down again. Ellie

218

leaned on her knees.

"Kit. I've read your journal."

He blinked. "It survives?"

"It was in the cupboard under the window in here. In the false base. Along with the wrappers from the tea and sugar and chocolate."

"That is where it is now. Where all of those things are."

Ellie pinched the bridge of her nose. "It kept changing. What was written in it. When I first read it, it stopped on the 4th because you wouldn't ask her to marry you. Then when you did, it changed and went on to much later in the year. The stone Thomas put up disappeared. It was replaced with a joint headstone for you and Janet. You both died when you were old."

"What stone that I put up?" asked Thomas. "I have put up no stone."

She ignored him for a moment. "Two days ago, it all changed back." She met Kit's eye. "You and Janet argued about me. Hugh Ellis arrived. Janet then argued with Hugh Ellis. He struck her. You refused to shoe his horse."

"How do you know all this?" demanded Thomas, his colour rising.

Ellie ploughed on. "Janet said to Ellis that it would be *his* reputation that was in tatters, not hers. I'm guessing that she threatened to tell someone what he'd done to her."

Thomas opened his mouth, but Kit held his hand up to silence him.

"Yes. Janet saw the mending you did when you last came. She knew I had not done it. We had cross words and then she argued with Hugh Ellis. We talked after he had gone, and she agreed to stay silent."

"Ellis doesn't know that, though. He still thinks she's going to tell people what he did. And he's going to stop her. It's today, Kit. Go and check your hammers if you need to. But it's today."

The last vestiges of blood drained from his face. "And when does the mob come?"

"The day after tomorrow."

Thomas could stay silent no longer. "What are you both talking about? What has Hugh Ellis done? What is this stone that you keep

219

mentioning?"

Ellie pulled a sheet of paper out of her pocket – a printout of the picture she'd taken of his 'killed stone'. She passed it over and Thomas studied it.

"This is a painting?" He fingered the paper, his brow creased.

"No. I can't explain how it's made, but it's an exact image of the stone in my time – 260 years hence."

Kit took the printout from his brother and smoothed it out on his broad thigh. "You did not read the date, brother." His voice shook as he spoke.

Thomas took the page back. "The 6th. That is the day after tomorrow."

"I know." Ellie's eyes locked on Kit.

"Where is this stone?" asked Thomas, scrutinising the picture.

"Right now, the stone doesn't exist. In my time, it's in the churchyard, near to the far wall."

Disbelief filled Thomas's face. "You cannot be from the future!"

Ellie closed her eyes, breathing steadily. She needed Thomas to believe her, otherwise the next part would be even trickier to explain. She reached into the pocket of her skirt again and drew out her phone. Next to her, Kit leaned in. "What is that?"

"A machine from my time. It's used to send messages to people and to speak to them when they are far away. It can also access information and store pictures." She held it up and took a picture of Kit, then turned the phone around to show him the screen.

His mouth dropped open. "How? How?" he stammered.

Thomas leaned over to see what he was looking at, then sat back sharply. "Are you a witch? A magician?"

"Neither. I swear to you, I am from the future, and the picture on that paper is an image of a stone that you erect for Kit."

Thomas sat back, his posture tight. "Why does Kit die in two days? If you're from the future, you must know."

She put her phone back in her pocket, her hands shaking. "I'm *really* hoping he doesn't die. I'm hoping he *disappears* in two days, and that we can change the story again."

Kit tilted his head. "What do you mean?"

"Joe thinks he's figured out the rifts. Not only when they open, but why so far only I've crossed."

Hope bloomed in his face. "You think I will be able to cross?"

"Yes. Maybe. Joe thinks the rifts each have a particular size and that until now, they've not been big enough for both of us to cross. And because *I* have crossed, you've not been able to. But the one in two days might be big enough. It *will* be big enough for just you. But in order to cross, you *have* to be in the house when the rift opens, and not being torn apart by a baying mob, blaming you for Janet's death."

Kit studied his knuckles. "There is no way we can save Janet, too?"

Ellie reached across and held his hands. "I don't think so. In your journal, Mary comes to tell you that Janet's body has been found. If Ellis hasn't already killed her, I think he will before you have a chance to warn her."

"But we must try!" He turned to Thomas. "Tom, you are faster than me. Run to her house! Tell her not to speak about Hugh."

"What has Hugh Ellis *done*? Why would he kill Janet?"

Kit shook his head. "I cannot tell you. It is Janet's secret. Please, Tom. Go!"

As Thomas scrambled to his feet, a commotion sprang up outside the house.

"Kit? Kit!" yelled a woman, panic in her voice.

Ellie shot a glance at Kit. "Is that Janet?"

He paled. "No. That is her sister, Mary."

41

E llie shot to her feet. "I need to hide!"

The last thing anyone needed was to have to explain who Ellie was or why she was in the house.

She grabbed her glass and the printout, and Kit hurried her to the kitchen while Thomas went to the door. Ellie hid in the pantry, but left the door ajar, hoping to hear everything Mary said.

"Oh, Kit! It's Janet!"

"Mary? What has happened?" Pain laced Kit's soft voice, making it hitch.

"She is dead! Mr Burrell found her body in a ditch, on the road between here and the village. Oh, Kit!"

Their voices faded. Ellie presumed Kit had taken Mary into the sitting room. From her position in the pantry, she couldn't hear anything beyond soft murmuring and the occasional wail, but she didn't dare get closer in case she was discovered. To have to explain her presence at all would be one thing. To explain why she had been hiding in the pantry would be something else entirely.

A few minutes after Mary had arrived, Thomas came to the pantry door.

"Mistress Stewart?" he whispered. "Are you still here?"

"Yes. Is it as we feared?"

"She has been hit in the head with something. A hammer probably."

"Was her body still soft when it was found?"

"What?"

She exhaled shakily. "If it was still soft, she would have been

222

killed only a short time ago and Kit would have an alibi. If it was not, he could be blamed."

"Ah."

Thomas withdrew, collecting a drink from the kitchen for Mary. In the darkness of the pantry, Ellie hugged herself, praying that the village wouldn't turn on Kit before he could cross the rift. Her legs ached from standing, so she sat behind the door, waiting for the coast to clear.

After some time, voices trickled through to her again. Kit saying goodbye to Mary. Ellie squinted through a chink in the frame. Thomas left with Mary. Kit remained in the doorway for a few minutes after Mary had left, before finally closing the door and hurrying to the kitchen.

"Ellie?"

She got to her feet as he opened the door. He stood, silhouetted against the light of the hallway, stricken. She pulled him into her arms, cradling him against her.

"Oh, Kit. I am so sorry." She stroked his hair and his back.

"She was my friend."

"I know. And I am so, so sorry." She leaned back and kissed his tears away, standing on tiptoe to do so.

"I told her not to say anything. Oh, Ellie, our last words were cross."

Her hand rubbed circles over his back. "You were a good friend to her. You did everything you could to protect her."

He turned tear-bright eyes to her. "It was not enough."

She smoothed her fingertips over his face. "You did your best. It is *not* your fault."

"They will blame me," he whispered. "She was cold when they found her. She died this morning when I was here on my own. Thomas was at work."

Her stomach lurched. "Go check your hammers. I expect one will be missing."

He pulled away and ducked out through the back door. Ellie waited, absolutely certain Kit would find one missing. His expression told her she was right. He took her hand and led her back to the sitting room, ushering her to a chair, then he sat in the easy chair opposite, his shoulders slumped.

"When do they come for me?"

Ellie moved to stand next to him and rubbed his shoulder. "According to the story, the day after tomorrow. What day is it today?"

"Saturday."

"Yeah. I don't think anyone's going to come for you on the Sabbath. Has Thomas gone with Mary?"

"He is walking her home. He will be back soon. What happens now?" he asked in a low voice.

She caressed his neck with gentle fingers. "I think that Hugh Ellis will blame you for Janet's death, and then either he will send men for you, or some of the villagers will rise against you."

"Do you know when the rift opens on the 6th?" Kit tipped his face up to her, blinking hard, his whole body trembling.

"Yes. In the morning, for two minutes only."

Thomas hurried back in, breathless, and threw himself into the seat Ellie had just vacated.

"Her father is breathing fire," he gasped. "He wants whoever killed Janet to be torn apart. I do not think even hanging would suffice for him."

Kit blanched, and Ellie squeezed his hand.

"Thomas, if we are to save Kit, he *must* be in the house on Monday morning. A window will open between your world and mine, and it will be big enough for him to cross. He will be safe in my time."

Thomas studied her, pressing his lips together. "Say that I believe this. That it is true that Kit can be taken to the future. When does he return?"

Ellie cleared her throat. "He doesn't. He can't. The 6th is the last day that the rift is big enough for anyone to cross from one time to the other. As far as I can tell, Kit either disappears because he's with me in the future, or he's killed by the mob."

A violent tremor wracked her body, and Kit slipped his arm around her hips.

"You genuinely think that I will manage to cross to your time?" he asked.

"I think so. I *hope* so. But you need to be here. The rift never opens again."

Thomas stared at the two of them for a long time before speaking. "Kit, if you could leave with Mistress Stewart, would you?"

"Yes," said Kit, without hesitation.

"Even though you would never return?"

Kit swallowed. "Yes. I love her, Thomas. I do not want to be without her. Nor do I wish to be blamed for Janet's murder and killed for it."

"If you go to her, I would never see you again."

"If I am blamed for Janet's death, you would not see me again. I would be killed by a mob, or hanged for murder. I expect my hammer will be found, covered in blood. All of my tools have my initials on them. There are few other KG with hammers."

Ellie shivered again, and Kit drew her down to sit on his lap, settling his hands together at her waist.

"Kit, you need to tell Janet's story," she said suddenly. "Only you know it now. And Hugh Ellis, and *he* won't tell it. It's not fair that he can get away with all of it."

"What did Ellis do?" asked Thomas.

Ellie faced him squarely. However much Kit might say it was Janet's secret, it was time it was known. "He violated her. She was with child. His child."

Thomas looked from her to Kit, his face clearing. "Is *that* why you asked her to marry you?"

Kit nodded. Thomas leaned back, letting out a deep breath. "I *knew* you did not love her. Not like that. I knew you were in love with someone else. Janet said to me that you were in love with a married woman, but you are far too honourable for that." He pushed back tousled auburn hair. "You are in love with Mistress Stewart, but you asked Janet to be your wife, to protect her honour?"

Kit breathed heavily. "Partly. I asked her because Ellie told me it would save her life. And mine."

"And it worked for a while," Ellie said. "The story changed."

Kit pulled her closer, shaking his head. "Janet was hot-headed and quick-tongued. I doubt that we could have cheated fate forever." He searched her face. "You think I should tell her secret? Shame her in death?"

"There should be no shame on *her*. She did nothing wrong. Bring the shame on Hugh Ellis!"

Doubt still clouded his face. She didn't push it.

Thomas leaned his forearms on his thighs. "Will you leave, Kit? Will you go to the future with Mistress Stewart? Leave your life here?"

Kit paused, then said, "Yes."

"Then you should get your affairs in order."

Kit laughed hollowly. "I have little to leave, Thomas. What I have is yours, although what you will do with a forge is a mystery to me."

"And Mistress Stewart. When do you return to your time?"

"Um. Tomorrow morning. And please call me Ellie."

Thomas smirked at his brother. "Tomorrow morning?"

A deep blush crept up from the neck of Kit's shirt, staining his cheeks scarlet. "I will sleep in the chair down here."

Ellie almost blurted out, *"You will do no such thing!"* but caught herself in time.

Thomas clapped his hands on his knees. "Well. I think you two have much to speak of, so I will leave you alone. Goodnight. I will see you in the morning."

Ellie flashed a glance at the clock, smiling internally. It wasn't even nine. "Goodnight."

Thomas clumped upstairs, and the air thickened with awkwardness. Kit turned to her. "I will sleep down here."

"I would vastly prefer for you to sleep upstairs with me."

His eyes widened. "We are not married. We are not even betrothed. Your reputation…"

"I don't live here, Kit. I have no reputation to protect. In my time, spending the night with the person you love doesn't ruin a reputation, even if the two people are not married. I've already stayed before!" She sighed. "Kit, this might be the only night I have with you if I can't get you back to my time on Monday."

He nibbled his lip. Even in the low light in the room, his cheeks showed crimson. She slipped off his lap and caught his hand.

"Come on. You're *not* sleeping down here in the chair."

She led him upstairs, then closed the door behind him, suddenly nervous. He turned to her, fiddling with his fingers, his

226

shoulders taut. Was he as anxious as she was?

"I need to get out of this bodice," she said. "And preferably my skirt and boots. The bed isn't big enough for both of us and the amount of space my skirt will take up!"

"You have a chemise on?" he asked, his words catching in his throat.

She laughed softly. "Yes, I have a chemise on."

She removed her bodice and laid it on the wooden chest, then unzipped her skirt and stepped out of it. Kit swiftly turned his back, amusing her. She took off the roll that made the skirt puff out, leaving her in modern underwear and a cotton shift, socks, and boots. She kicked the boots and socks off.

"I'm decent," she said, humour rippling through her voice.

He turned, snatching his gaze down to the floor. She stepped past him to the bed and slipped under the covers. He stripped down until he wore just a long shirt, and sat on the edge of the bed.

"You are sure about us sharing the bed tonight?"

"I stayed half of the other night."

"We were both dressed then."

"Just get in," she muttered, shuffling back to make space for him.

He climbed in next to her and drew the curtains closed. She curled against him in the narrow space.

"You made me choose another," he said, his voice thick.

"I know. Because I wanted to save your life. And hers."

"And now she is dead anyway." He sniffed.

Ellie propped herself on her elbow to peer at him in the dark. Tears tracked over his temples, and he swatted at them.

"She knew I did not love her. She knew I loved someone else."

Ellie stroked his face. "She knew you cared enough about her to marry her and protect her."

"But I did not protect her."

"You tried your best." She breathed in deeply and let it go slowly. "If I had not come and mended your coat… She was angry because of that. Maybe she wouldn't have argued with Hugh Ellis if she hadn't been."

Kit huffed. "I think she would have. Eventually."

Ellie cuddled back down next to him. "Will you really come to my time with me? If it's possible?"

"Yes." He brushed his fingertips over her hair. "I want to be with you more than anyone. I always did."

"You're going to find it strange in my time." She couldn't even begin to think how many things would be utterly alien to him if she got him through the rift.

"Perhaps. The only thing that matters is being with you."

She rubbed her fingertips over his chest. Please let Joe be right. *Please* let the rift be big enough for him to cross. Kit wasn't carrying any fat, but his job made him toned. Maybe it would have been better if he had a less physical job.

He tucked her hair behind her ear. "You seem far away suddenly."

"I'm thinking about Monday." She chewed the inside of her lip. "How much do you weigh, Kit?" She hoped the answer wouldn't come back in a unit she couldn't convert at least roughly in her head.

He turned his head, making the pillow rustle. "Do you think I will weigh too much?"

"I don't know. It might be close." She fiddled with the neckline of his shirt, then traced the hollow behind his collarbone. "I won't cross. I'll stay on the edge of the rift. If I look as if I'm only in undergarments, don't have a heart attack. I'm going to be wearing as little as possible to give you some leeway, in case I have to cross, too."

He brushed a kiss over the top of her head. "You are only in your undergarments at the moment."

She smiled. "Then don't have a heart attack tonight, either!"

She cuddled closer, her fingertips exploring his chest through his shirt. If he wasn't there, would she cross so that she could be with him? The rift never opened again. She'd be trapped in his time. Would she be able to leave behind her modern life?

"What time does the window open on Monday?" he said, pulling her attention back to him.

"Eleven minutes past ten. You absolutely must not miss it."

"And if I am in the house, I will be moved to your time? I do not need to do anything special?"

"Well, that's how it's always worked for me. You just need to be inside the house."

He tensed steadily, and she wriggled to see him better in the gloaming. "What is it?"

"What will I do in your time?"

"You could be a blacksmith. The forge is long gone, I'm afraid, but we could build another."

Getting any kind of paperwork for him would be tricky, but they could cross that bridge when they came to it.

"There is work for a blacksmith?"

"Yes. I think so. A lot of people have horses in the area, although more for racing or leisure than for work. And there would be other work."

He lay in silence for a few minutes, his muscles tight.

"I know. It's a lot to think about," murmured Ellie.

"I do not want you to regret me coming to your time. I do not want to become a burden to you."

She ran her fingertips down the groove in the centre of his chest. "That's not going to happen. I've never met anyone like you. I couldn't bear to be without you, whatever you end up doing. I just want to share my life with you. I love you."

"I love you too," he whispered back. "With all of my heart and my soul. You bewitched me on the very first day that we spoke."

She tilted her face up to him, and he kissed her gently, taking his time. Eventually, he drew back. In the darkness, she could only just make out his features.

"We should sleep," he murmured.

"Only if we must."

He made a soft choking sound, and she laughed. She propped herself up on one elbow. "Kit, if you don't manage to cross the rift on Monday, this will be our only night together. Shall we try to make the most of it?"

His heart thumped against her palm, and he swallowed, his eyes locked on hers. She waited.

Finally, he nodded.

42

Her watch buzzed. She blinked sleepily and peered at the screen. Six in the morning. She snuggled closer to Kit, waking him. The tight confines of his bed meant their legs were knotted together, and she lay half on him, half jammed up against the wall.

"Morning," she murmured.

"Good morning."

Their clothes lay in a heap next to the bed. He'd taken a little persuading that it was okay for him to lose his, and even more that she was perfectly happy to take hers off. After that… she'd convinced him that a few other things were okay, too.

Kit shifted next to her and cleared his throat. "Shall I pass you your chemise?"

"Not until after you've kissed me."

He laughed. They kissed tenderly, his beard tickling her skin, his lips soft against hers. She wished that moment could go on forever.

"I have never shared my bed with any other before," he murmured, drawing back, his hazel eyes bright. "Only you."

She ran her hand over his chest. "I'm really hoping this isn't the last time you share it with me."

"You think it will work? That I will come to your time?"

"I hope so."

Thomas clattered past their door. Ellie checked her watch again, calculating how long it would take her to get back into her costume and therefore how long she could stay in bed with Kit.

She cuddled closer, but Kit tensed up.

"No. It is Sunday." He stroked her hair back from her face. "And we should join Thomas."

She pouted, disappointed. "Okay."

He chuckled at her, and tweaked her nose, before pushing the curtains back and retrieving her top from the floor. He passed it to her, along with her underwear, his eyes sparkling. As soon as she got out of the bed, he turned his back, amusing her.

"Kit, you saw it all last night. You kissed most of it."

He dressed swiftly, saying nothing, and keeping his back to her. When he finally looked at her, his cheeks were crimson, and he cleared his throat again. She pressed her palm to his cheek and kissed him.

"Come on then. Let's join Thomas."

In the kitchen, Thomas poked his tongue into his cheek, smirking at the two of them.

"Tea? Something to eat?" Kit offered, pointedly ignoring his brother. "Bacon? Eggs?"

Ellie sat at the table while Kit fixed a plate of bacon and eggs for her and Thomas made a pot of tea. Her mind drifted. What if the mob arrived sooner than Monday? His 'stone' had always had Monday's date, whether it said he'd disappeared or been killed, but she couldn't rely on that. Not when the story had changed so radically before.

"Can you be somewhere else today?" she asked. "Not here."

Kit raised scared eyes to her. "I will be at church this morning."

"No! Hide today. In case Ellis's men come for you sooner than tomorrow."

"That will make him seem guilty," argued Thomas, putting a bowl of tea beside her. "Innocent men go to church. Guilty men run away."

Ellie averted her gaze. "I'm only trying to keep him safe."

Kit reached across and gripped her hand. "I will be safe at church."

"And afterwards? At least hide afterwards." She winced at the note of hysteria in her voice.

He didn't reply.

All three of them picked at their breakfast. Ellie's nerves

jangled. Everything rested on Kit being safe from the mob until the following morning.

Eventually, Thomas cleared their empty plates, and Ellie caught Kit's eye.

"Thomas, I don't mean to be rude, but I only have a few minutes before I will go back to my time, and I would like to spend them alone with your brother."

Thomas grinned and withdrew. Ellie turned back to Kit. "I know you don't think it's honourable, but *please,* will you hide today? You *have* to be here tomorrow morning."

"I will do everything I can to be here, but I will not hide. I will face anyone accusing me head on. It is hard enough that Thomas will end up tarnished as the brother of a murderer. I will *not* give them more reason to shun him."

Shame made her cringe. She hadn't even considered the effect on Thomas.

"Promise me you or Thomas will tell Janet's story? That Hugh Ellis won't get away with everything?"

Kit rested his cheek on his knuckles. "With Janet dead, there is no one to disprove Ellis's claim that *I* killed Janet. All the evidence points to me. If Thomas declares Ellis guilty, people will think he says it all merely to defend me. Or to protect *his* reputation."

Ellie's head dropped. It was so *unfair.*

"I won't come through the rift tomorrow, in case my weight means you're unable to cross. But you must be here! Promise me?"

"I promise. I love you."

"I love you too."

Her watch buzzed, reminding her that the window back to her time would open imminently. She leaned forwards and rested her forehead against Kit's neck. "These might be our last few minutes if you don't manage to cross. Kiss me properly?"

He kissed her tenderly, tangling his hands in her hair. All too soon, the room warped and shifted around them.

She shoved him away from her suddenly. "Kit, you try to go to my time! I'll stay!"

"No. I cannot leave you here."

The intensity of the double images increased, and panic flashed through her. "Kit, *please!* If you go there now, then the mob *can't*

232

get you! I can cross tomorrow."

Her heart thumped wildly. They didn't have much time. She pushed at him again, but deep down, she knew the rift wasn't strong enough to let him cross. The room around her dissolved, and she tumbled to the floor in her modern kitchen.

Joe sat at the table, but he leapt up as soon as she returned. "How did it go? What happened?"

Ellie leaned over her knees, drawing them towards her chin. "I didn't manage to save Janet. She was already dead. Her sister came to tell Kit." She rubbed a tired hand over her face. "One of his hammers is missing. It's just like the story."

Joe joined her on the floor, stretching out long legs and leaning back on his hands. "The next window opens tomorrow. Will he be safe today?"

"I don't know. It's Sunday there today. I told him to hide, but he said he was going to go to church; that if he hid, he would appear guilty." She rubbed her face. "I'm hoping that it isn't the done thing to exact mob-vengeance on the Sabbath."

Joe bunched his lips. "Here's hoping."

She rested her forehead on her arms. "I don't know if I'll ever see him again." Tears clotted in her voice.

Joe shuffled over and slipped his arm around her shoulders. "There's no point in being upset until you know for certain. What's the point of wasting tears, then tomorrow morning it turns out he's here with you?"

"I should have stayed. I *tried* to stay, but Kit wouldn't let me."

"Was Thomas there?"

She nodded, smearing tears down her face with the heel of her hand.

"He'll keep him safe. Sh. Come on. Don't cry."

But the tears flowed. She had come so close. So *close*. She wrapped her hands around the back of her head, her elbows on her knees. Joe rubbed her shoulder.

"Sh. Sh. Ellie, all the tears in the world won't change things. Don't give up yet."

"What if the mob comes today, after all? What if he's not there tomorrow? I said I wouldn't go, so that there would be no problem over the weight limit. But what if I wait outside the boundary and he doesn't come? I'll have missed my chance to go back and stay with him!"

A long silence stretched between them.

"You would do that?" said Joe, his voice wavering. "Leave here to stay with him?"

She scraped her hands over her face and raised her head. "I love him, Joe. He loves me. Yes, I would go to be with him."

He nodded, his expression serious. "I understand. But Mum and Dad would be devastated, as would I. Do you love him more than us?"

Ellie crumpled, tears pouring over her cheeks. "I don't know! I love *all* of you! I just want to be with him."

She blew her nose and straightened up, unwilling to talk more. "I need to get out of these clothes."

She stood abruptly and hurried upstairs.

Out of the costume and in 21st century jeans and a t-shirt, she lay on the bed, her brain spinning. If he didn't cross the rift tomorrow, *would* she go to 1762? Could she really leave her family behind for him? What if he didn't come through the rift because he was dead? She'd be trapped in 1762 with no chance of return, and no Kit. What would happen to her?

She picked up Kit's journal and turned to the back, wondering if he'd written any more. He hadn't. The last entry remained the same: Mary had come to say Janet was dead; one of his hammers was missing. She closed the cover and laid the book down on the bedside cupboard.

Shadow strolled in and jumped up on to the bed to nestle down beside her. She scratched behind his ear.

"*You* are getting shut in the new part of the house tomorrow! I'm not having your podgy little body being the reason Kit can't get here!"

Shadow merely purred and rolled on his back for her to tickle his tummy. She fussed him, trying to take her mind off everything.

Joe tapped on the door. "You can't wallow in here all day. And you know as well as I do that there's nothing you can do until tomorrow. He'll either get to the rift, or he won't." He stopped, and when he spoke again, his voice caught. "Ellie, if he doesn't, I don't want you to go through."

"I know. And I don't know if I could do it. The idea of not being with him devastates me, but then, so does the idea of never seeing you, or Mum or Dad, or modern life."

"Shall we go out? Do something. Take your mind off things?"

She swung her legs off the bed and sat up, eliciting indignant chirruping from Shadow.

"Sure. Let's go and do something."

43

On Monday, at eleven minutes past ten, Ellie stood in the front hall of the house, wearing her skimpy shorts, floaty silk top, and flip-flops, her eyes locked on the edge of the rift. Through it, she could see into the back hall and study. The rooms shifted and twisted, one moment in their present-day conformation, the next in 1762. However hard she looked, the space was empty. She'd propped the large clock from her study on the floor next to her. The second hand quivered but didn't tick off seconds. Nausea flooded her stomach, and her pulse raced.

"Come on, Kit," she muttered.

Next to her stood Joe.

"Can you see him?" he asked. Again.

"No. He's not there. The mob must have got to him already."

Her voice cracked as she spoke, and a sob billowed in her chest. Did she cross to 1762? Try to find him? The rift was open for such a short period of time, if he wasn't actually in the house, it would be pointless. And what if the weight limit *wasn't* big enough for her *and* Kit to traverse the rift if she found him? They could both end up trapped in 1762, or she might be returned to her time, but he would be left in his.

The mob could have come already. If she crossed, she could end up getting trapped in a 1762 in which Kit might already be dead. She checked the time. The rift would only stay open for another few moments, then re-open two minutes later. She blinked away tears. He hadn't made it.

A fresh movement through the rift caught her eye. Light

reddish-brown hair? She gasped, then held her breath.

"Is he there?" asked Joe.

"I don't know. Maybe. Kit, hurry!"

Her voice wouldn't carry through time. She peered again, trying to work out where he was. Her heart lurched when she realised he was just *outside* the boundary of the rift, and limping badly. What should she do? Go and help him, and pray that the rift was big enough to let both of them cross? If she got trapped there, at least he was alive.

"Joe, he's hurt. I need to help him." She hugged him hard and kissed his cheek. "If I don't get back, the house is yours." She gripped him tightly. "I love you."

He held on to her. "Ellie?"

"Joe, please, I have to help him."

She ripped free and ran to the edge of the rift. Behind her, Joe yelled, "No! Ellie!" and then she was in 1762. Almost instantly, the coloured lights died away. She was trapped.

She sprinted for the back door, praying that she had enough time. "Kit!"

He raised his head, blood running down the side of his face, barely able to walk. "Ellie!"

Five men brandishing sticks appeared in the yard, yelling. "Greenwood!"

They had almost reached Kit. He struggled to get to his feet, but the first of the men reached him, bringing his stick down hard across Kit's back. Kit yowled with pain and sprawled on to his hands and knees. A second blow struck his head.

Panic rippled through her. She *had* to get him into the house by the time the rift opened again. With her heart pounding, she stepped out into the yard and held her arms out wide to the sides, her floaty silk top hanging down like wings.

"Leave him be!" she bellowed, taking another step forwards, terrified in case the men turned on her.

The men stumbled, gaping at her, their arms hanging by their sides. She stood over Kit, desperate to protect him. She was absolutely sure that angels didn't wear flip-flops and skimpy shorts, but it was all she could try. At her feet, Kit let out a low moan.

"This is an innocent man!" she cried. "May God rain down vengeance on you for your crimes against him!" She strode forwards, relieved that the men staggered away from her. "Begone!"

She reached down to Kit, grabbing his arm and draping it over her shoulder to help him up, her glare scouring the thugs.

One of them came to his senses. "He is a murderer! He is to stand trial. We are to take him to the magistrate! Hugh Ellis will see him hanged for what he did to that lass!"

Ellie had got Kit to his feet, though barely. His eyes had glazed, and his knees sagged, his weight pulling on her, dragging her down. She lurched towards the house, walking crabwise so that she could keep the men in her sights. The men surged forwards, sticks raised, barely two metres away from her.

She held her hand out, her palm flat. "He is an innocent man, and God will punish you for what you have done!"

The angel trick had stopped working. The men rushed towards her, galvanising her. She heaved at Kit's body, wrapping an arm around his waist and hanging on to his wrist at her shoulder for dear life. Around them, coloured lights flickered into life. Ellie floundered towards the door of the house, Kit heavy in her arms and barely conscious.

"Please hold. Please be big enough for both of us."

Kit was a dead weight, and she almost lost her footing on the slippery cobbles. Six more steps and they would be inside the boundary.

Before her eyes, the edge of the time-window started to collapse inwards, moving away from them at the same pace that she could help Kit.

"No!" she shrieked.

The nearest man lunged at them.

"Greenwood!" he roared, brandishing his stick.

With one last haul on his arm, Ellie dragged Kit towards the back door, reeling from the effort. A club smashed down on Kit's shoulder and he slumped, slipping out of her grasp, and crashing to the ground. The sudden loss of weight made Ellie lose her footing, and she crashed to the floor, just inside the kitchen door.

The rift disappeared.

44

Ellie hauled herself to her knees, her heart in her mouth. She scoured the surrounding space, desperate to see Kit, but he wasn't there. A long, heart-rending keening escaped from her lips.

"No! I let go of him! They hit him, and he was too heavy for me, and I let go of him!"

She crumpled back to the floor, despair shredding her. Joe dashed to her side and clasped her. She wailed, inconsolable.

"I had him, Joe. I had him."

Tears poured down her face, and sobs wracked her body. Joe rocked her gently, but his comfort couldn't come close to easing her desolation. She wrapped her arms around her torso, her anguish tearing her apart.

"Maybe the rift wasn't big enough," murmured Joe.

Had she lost him for the sake of a few grams? The idea was unbearable.

"Oh, Joe, the men were there. They had sticks! They will beat him to death!"

Joe gripped her, but images of Kit being killed flooded her brain and she howled, heartbroken.

"Ellie?"

Her head shot up, her eyes wide. The faint croak had come from outside. Her heart rattled against her ribs, hope blooming in her chest.

"Kit?"

She heaved herself up and rushed to the back door. The

modern back door. Where Ellie had crashed back through the rift was now a wall and at the base of it lay Kit, clutching his shoulder, bleeding heavily.

"Oh, god, Kit! You're here. You're here!"

She wrapped herself around him, covering his face with kisses.

"Ellie," he wheezed, his eyes meeting hers, his face shining with joy.

"They hit you, and you fell, and you were too heavy for me. I thought I had lost you."

"Sh. I am here." He groaned deeply as he tried to move. "You did not tell me the door had moved."

She laughed, despite herself, then her brain registered how much blood covered him, along with all the bruises, and her mirth evaporated.

"You're hurt. Let me see?"

Blood poured from a scalp wound, staining his jacket red at the shoulder. She gingerly moved his hair to one side, her breath catching at the amount of blood.

Joe gently elbowed her out of the way, the first aid box from the kitchen in his hands. "Kit? I'm Joe, Ellie's brother. You made it."

Kit held a shaky hand out, and Joe shook it, grinning.

"Let's have a look at you," he said, easing Kit's jacket away from his shirt. "Ellie? Get some water and a cloth?"

Ellie scraped the tears from her face and hurried to the sink in the kitchen. She ran a bowl of water and tossed in a clean tea towel, then grabbed two more clean cloths. She dashed back outside and put it all down next to Joe, before scooting back to the doorway, her eyes never leaving Kit.

Joe finished removing Kit's jacket, then unbuttoned his waistcoat. He moved Kit's shirt back from his shoulder to reveal a huge purple-red welt – the result of the blow that had made him stumble. Kit's breath hissed between his teeth as Joe peeled his shirt away from the wound, and he screwed his face up. Ellie could bear it no longer and crouched next to them, desperate to take over. Joe ignored her, continuing his inspection of Kit's injuries.

He sat back, his expression serious. "I don't think anything is broken, but you are going to be black and blue for a few days. I'm more worried about your head."

Ellie wrung the cloth out and bathed the wound on Kit's head as gently as she could. He flinched, holding his breath. Where he'd been struck, the skin had split open, leaving a nasty gash over an egg-like bump.

"I'm sorry, this is going to hurt," she whispered. She finished cleaning the injury and pressed a fresh cloth to it.

Joe moved her out of the way and took over applying pressure to the wound.

"Ellie, there are some steristrips in the first aid box. Pass me a pack?"

Ellie rummaged through the box and handed a strip over. Joe carefully closed the wound on Kit's head with them, then found a dressing and a bandage.

"I knew my first aid course would come in handy one day. Where else are you hurt?" he said as he finished dressing the wound.

"Just bruising." His focus locked on Ellie. "I thought I had lost you. I thought the rift had closed, and you had crossed, and I had not. I thought the mob would reach me."

She sat beside him, desperate to be closer to him. "Why were you running back to the house? Why weren't you already there? What had happened?"

He closed his eyes, his face crumpling. "Hugh Ellis accused me of killing Janet. He stood outside church after the service yesterday, saying that he had found my hammer covered in blood. I made the priest get the Bible from the church and I swore on it that it had not been me. I came home, and I thought I was safe. And then this morning, Ellis sent men to drag me to the village. I was to be sent for trial." He paused, shifting position and wincing. "Before we reached the edge of the village, I escaped. Ran back to the forge. I thought I would be too late. I thought all was lost."

Joe crouched next to him. "Let's get you inside."

He lifted Kit's arm over his shoulder and helped him to his feet. Kit stared at the back of the house.

"Did you run into the wall?" asked Ellie, conjuring the 1762 layout to the front of her mind.

A slow smile crept across Kit's face. "Yes." He dragged his eyes away from her and turned to Joe. "Thank you for attending to my injuries."

"Come on," said Joe. "Let's run you a bath. You're pretty much the same size as me, so I can lend you some fresh clothes."

Between them, Joe and Ellie helped Kit into the house. In the kitchen, he gaped at his surroundings.

"Where is the fire? Where do you cook?"

"Oh. The fire would have been there, where it is in your kitchen, but we cook on that." She indicated the electric cooker. "Would you like a bath? Though you'll need to keep the bandage dry."

"That is too much work for you," Kit said. "I do not want you to fetch and carry for me."

She grinned. "Not in this time. The water is already hot. I can run you a bath in just a few minutes, and I won't need to carry any water."

He relented, and they helped him up the stairs to the bathroom at the front of the house. Again, his eyes widened as he stared at the room, but he said nothing. Joe helped Kit into a chair, then disappeared briefly, returning clutching an armful of clothes and a clean bath towel. A mischievous glint showed in his eye. "Erm, I'll leave you two to it. Kit, have you eaten today?"

Kit shook his head, and Joe offered to make him some food and put a pot of coffee on. Ellie turned the taps on, sticking her hand into the water to check the temperature.

"So, what happened?" She swirled some of Joe's shower gel into the water. "How did you escape?"

He unlaced his boots, taking his time. "Ellis's men came to take me to be held in Masham, but before we had reached the village, they set about me. I think they would have beaten me to death. Dispensed with justice." He paused, taking off his boots. "I am a strong man, and I got free from them near to the end of the lane. I tried to run back, but one of them struck me and knocked me to the ground."

Ellie's breath caught in her chest. She reached over to help him take his shirt off. "Go on."

Purple bruises stained Kit's torso, and he blanched as he undressed. "I had no way of knowing the time." He stopped and

242

steadied his breathing. "I was sure that I would not make it back to the house in time. I twisted my ankle and fell." He opened his hands out, revealing skinned palms. "The men gave chase, but I was determined to get to the house. I reached the forge, and the lights showed. And through them I could see you." He raised his head. "I did not know how long the lights had been there. I did not know if you would come through. You said you would not, in case that might prevent me from being able to cross, but I knew I could not get into the house without help. I feared that if you came to help me, I would not be able to cross, and you would return home and I would never see you again." He scrubbed at his face. "Or that you would *not* cross to help, and the window would close forever and I would have been left there."

"I would never have left you." She smoothed his hair back. "I would have come to you, even if it meant I was trapped."

He held his breath. "The men would have killed me if I had not crossed. You risked everything to save me. I owe you my life."

She stroked his brow. "I was terrified that the weight of both of us would be too much and that you would be left behind. When they hit you…" A huge lump wedged in her throat. "You were too heavy for me. I was convinced I had lost you forever."

He pressed his grazed palm to her cheek. "I am really in the future? With you? The blow to my head has not made me insensible?"

She pressed a soft kiss to his lips. "You're really here. With me." She drew back to turn off the taps. "This is ready. Should I leave you in peace, or stay?"

"I want to say stay. I never want to let you out of my sight again. But that would not be proper."

"Hm. Neither was the other night." She smiled as he blushed. "You know, I'm fairly sure I will see you undressed again. It's not so improper in this time."

He fidgeted, discomfited, and she relented. "Okay. I'll leave you to it. There's a towel to dry yourself here, and hopefully Joe's clothes will fit well enough. Just pull the plug out when you've finished. The water will drain away. Yell if you need anything."

He caught her shoulder, stopping her from leaving, his face suddenly serious. "I owe you everything."

She kissed him gently. "Sh. Enjoy your bath before it gets cold."

The scent of bacon and eggs wafted up from the kitchen, along with the bitter tang of coffee. Ellie picked her way downstairs and sat at the table as Joe bustled about making food. Her eye caught the pamphlet from the cafe, propped next to the salt and pepper.

"Read it," said Joe, slicing some tomatoes, ready to fry them. "You'll love it!"

She pulled the sheet of paper towards her and read. After a couple of sentences, she turned to Joe, astonished. "It's all changed!"

"Oh, keep reading," said Joe over his shoulder. "It gets even better."

1762. The year of a most heinous crime. A year of murder, lies, and an ANGEL!

In 1762, the brutal murder of a beloved young lass, who lived right here, in this very building, **rocked** the village of Masham.

The local magistrate, Hugh Ellis, **violated** Janet Shaw, a pretty, innocent young woman. His heinous assault left her pregnant. Ellis thought his crime would never be known, but Janet threatened to tell the priest what he had done.

Desperate to protect his reputation, Ellis **murdered** the poor, innocent young woman, then tried to blame it on the local blacksmith, Christopher Greenwood.

Christopher Greenwood was an upstanding, hard-working man who was a good friend of Janet. When Janet confessed to him what Hugh Ellis had done to her, he promised to keep her safe and to marry her, to protect her reputation. But her very existence was a **threat** to Ellis. How could he let her live when she could damn him and ruin him by telling what he had done?

And so, he **stole** one of the blacksmith's hammers and **murdered** Janet, leaving her body discarded at the side of the road, and laying the blame at Christopher Greenwood's door. Ellis accused Greenwood in front of the entire congregation after church one day and sent his men to drag Greenwood from his house to face justice.

Before Greenwood could be found guilty of a crime he did not commit, he escaped. The men chased him to his forge, but he **vanished** before their very eyes, rescued by an **angel of mercy**, who appeared in a rainbow and snatched him away to safety.

Ellis might still have got off scot-free, laying the blame for his **crimes** on Greenwood, but a **witness** stepped forwards. Hugh Ellis had been **seen** bludgeoning the poor Janet Shaw to death, before abandoning her corpse at the side of the road.

Hugh Ellis was tried and **hanged** for his crimes. And the ghost of poor Janet Shaw still walks in this building, wailing for the man who had been prepared to save her.

Christopher Greenwood was never seen again, but his brother erected a stone, commemorating his rescue by the angel. It still stands in the churchyard nearby.

Ellie finished reading, then laid the paper down, laughing. "Wow. I think the writer missed a trick in the 'overblown' department. And I'm apparently an angel."

Joe poured her a treacly coffee. "At least Janet's story was told."

Ellie pulled her phone out and did an internet search on Hugh Ellis. Gone was his knighthood. Gone was the portrait of a florid, overweight gentleman. Instead, the only entries about him were from a history of Yorkshire, which told, albeit in a less lurid fashion, the story of him raping and murdering Janet and attempting to blame Kit. There was no mention of any angel of mercy rescuing Kit. She scrolled through her photos. Her picture of Kit's 'disappeared stone' now showed an entirely different inscription.

In memory of Christopher Greenwood, taken by an angel, 6 September 1762

She held the phone out to Joe, who read it and grinned.

The adrenaline of the rescue had worn off and reality settled in. She put her phone down, her hands shaky. Would Kit settle in to life in 2022 okay? It would be so strange for him.

Joe slid into the chair across from her. "You okay, sis?"

Her fears made her stomach clench. "I hope I'm enough."

Joe raised a brow.

Ellie swallowed. When she spoke, her voice trembled. "He's left everything to be with me. And he had no choice. What if he regrets it? What if I'm not enough, and he's utterly miserable here?"

"Ellie, I saw the way he looks at you. Trust me. You're more than enough. He adores you."

A sound on the stairs made them both turn. Kit picked his way down, dressed in Joe's clothes, still limping slightly. Joe's trousers fitted him well enough, but the rugby shirt was stretched taut over his shoulders, and he plucked at it. He stopped at the threshold of the kitchen, his gaze on Ellie, his face full of uncertainty. Ellie hurried over to him, and he pulled her into his arms, holding her tight to his chest.

"You risked everything to bring me here," he whispered. "I hope I do not disappoint you."

She leaned back in his arms. "Never. I hope *I* don't disappoint *you*."

He smiled softly. "Never."

Joe coughed softly. "Kit. Bacon? Eggs? Tomatoes?"

Kit peered around Ellie and nodded. Ellie led him to the table and ushered him to a seat, then poured him a mug of coffee. She hesitated as she put it in front of him. "Kit, do you drink coffee?"

He scrutinised the dark liquid, frowning, wrinkling his nose a little at the smell. "I have never had it. Is it like tea?"

"Oh. Um, no. Not really. Okay, try it black first, then we can add sugar and milk. Or I can just make you some tea."

He had a sip of the coffee and grimaced. "May I just have tea, please?"

"Of course."

While Ellie made him tea, Kit sat quietly, his gaze flitting nervously around the room. Every time it settled on her, he smiled, and some of the tension left his shoulders, but as soon as he looked away, it crept back. Ellie chewed her nail.

"This must be so strange for you." She put a fresh cup of tea in front of him.

"It is very different." His face softened. "I will need lessons."

Joe put a plate of food down for him. "Bacon and eggs are still bacon and eggs. Eat."

Kit laughed and tucked in. Joe picked up the local paper to read.

As soon as Kit had cleared his plate, his shoulders tightened again. He stared into his tea, his breathing rate rising.

Ellie brushed the back of his hand. "You alright?"

He pinched his lips together. "What will I do here? I only know how to be a blacksmith, and the forge is long gone. How will I support you?"

"Sh. We'll figure something out. Relax."

Joe looked up from his paper, grinning broadly, then leaned back to grab a pen from the worktop behind him. He circled something in the paper, then put it down in front of Kit.

Kit drew the newspaper towards him, and Ellie peered over his shoulder, wondering what Joe had marked.

Local blacksmith to retire after more than 50 years.

Bill Dawson is finally hanging up his hammers after over 50 years as the blacksmith at Fearby. With no one in the family to take over, the area may be without a blacksmith for the first time in centuries.

"It's a real shame," said Bill. "This forge has been in my family for generations, but I've only daughters and nieces, and they don't want to take it on. It breaks my heart to have to sell everything. I just hope that there's someone local who might take over. There's so many horses around here… I don't know what they'll do if there's no blacksmith."

Ellie's heart soared, and she beamed at Kit. "Shall we go and make him an offer?"

45

Six Months Later

Ellie poured a mug of strong tea for Kit and grabbed a couple of biscuits. She added her mug of coffee to the tray and headed out of the back door. Despite trying coffee several times, Kit had never taken to it, but he could drink tea by the gallon. And eat biscuits by the plateful.

Outside, in essentially the same location as it had been in 1762, stood Kit's forge. Between them, Kit and Joe had built the fire in exactly the same place, along with a workshop. They had bought absolutely everything from the retiring blacksmith – from the anvil, down to every last tool – and the tools now hung from nails in a batten running around the workshop, just as they had in 1762.

When they'd visited Bill Dawson, Kit had almost dropped one ancient-looking hammer when he read 'KG' stamped on it.

"Is it yours?" Ellie had whispered.

He'd nodded, his eyes shining. "Thomas must have sold my tools to this man's family."

Kit had acquired the blacksmith's client list, as well as all of his equipment. A client list that had expanded rapidly as word spread about the excellent young blacksmith who had a real way with horses.

Kit stood to one side of his workshop, resting his hips against his workbench, talking to a woman. A freshly shod chestnut horse was tethered to a ring in the wall of the forge: his last customer of the day. The scene took Ellie back to when she'd met him in his

248

time. He might be wearing modern cargo pants and boots, with a warm sweater on the top, and he'd had his hair cut, but he was still the same. He caught sight of her as she approached, and his face lit up. She would never tire of his smile.

"Hey," he murmured.

"Hey. Tea and biscuits for you. Hi, Caroline. How are you?" Ellie called across to the horse. "Hello, Teddy. Are you behaving yourself today?"

Kit chuckled. Caroline sighed.

"No. Well, he *was* being a real pain until we got here, then Kit, as ever, worked his magic, and now he's just butter in Kit's hands."

Kit strolled across and stroked the horse's flank. "No. You are a good fellow, hey?"

The horse snickered, lowering his head and bunting his nose gently against Kit's shoulder.

Caroline rolled her eyes. "See! Butter! He was dancing about in his box and kicking the sides when we got here."

Ellie put the tray down on the bench. "I was just bringing Kit a tea. Did you want a cuppa? I made a pot."

"No, I'm fine thanks. Is that one of your designs?" Caroline jutted her chin towards to the cabled sweater Kit wore. His leather apron hid half of it, and the sleeves were pushed to his elbows, but the cables twisting into intricate Celtic knots were just visible across Kit's back and chest.

"It is indeed. I actually knitted it for Joe, but it was a bit too big on him and he never wore it." Ellie rested her backside against Kit's workbench and blew on her coffee.

"It's fabulous. If I could knit, I would get the pattern."

"I'm running another learn-to-knit class soon. It's not nearly as difficult as you're thinking. Trust me."

Caroline wrinkled her nose. "Oh, I'd be terrible."

Ellie laughed. "Come along and have a go. Or pop in to the house next time you're over with Teddy, if I'm around. I can teach you while you wait for him."

"I may take you up on that. But be prepared for me to be hopeless at it."

Kit left Teddy and joined her at the bench, slipping his arm around her hips. Caroline beamed at them.

"You two make *such* a great couple. I don't know where you found him, Ellie, but he's a keeper!"

"Local lad. Born and bred," quipped Ellie, making Kit dip his chin and chuff softly.

Caroline picked up her bag. "Right. I'll be off. See you both soon."

"I will send the bill," said Kit. "Teddy, be good now for Caroline!"

She laughed and led Teddy away to his horse-box, parked at the front. Once she'd gone, Kit tugged at Ellie until she stood in front of him, and settled his arms around her waist.

"Thank you for the tea. And biscuits."

She snuggled closer. "I only came out because it's warm out here with the fire."

He snorted. "I chopped and carried enough wood into the house for you to have the stove burning for many hours."

She wriggled her nose. "Okay. There *may* have been another attraction out here, as well as your fire."

He kissed her, his unruly waves of hair falling around his face. She pushed it back, and he laughed. "Yes. It was easier when I tied it back. Sometime I regret getting it cut."

"No other regrets?"

He tipped his face up towards the roof, pursing his lips as if thinking hard. "I have a good business, a warm house, and the most wonderful woman in the world in my arms. No, I have no regrets." He looked back down at her. "You?"

"None. Well, only that we're both so busy that we don't see each other so much."

"Have you finished making all the packages you needed to?"

"The kits? Yeah. I got them finished just after lunch, although I put them up on the website and I've already sold half of them, so I need to make up some more."

The kits of Ellie's designs, paired with locally sourced yarn, had been a roaring success, and there were plans to extend the range.

"Oh, various payments came in for you," said Ellie, though she'd made notes for him in the study. Kit still struggled with online banking, preferring to keep a handwritten ledger. "The gates you did, the new weather-vane for the church, and for

250

shoeing Dapple."

"Did you pay Joe?" he asked, scrunching his brow up.

"Yep. That's all the money we borrowed for the forge paid back now." She wormed closer. "The next payment will be the first one towards buying his half of this place off him."

Kit brightened. "Good."

Joe had sold his old house and had recently moved into a place on the other side of Masham. Ellie didn't think it would be long before he proposed to Liz. The two were inseparable in their free time.

"What time are Joe and Liz arriving?" asked Kit.

"Soon."

"Time for me to get washed, and change my clothes?"

"Should be."

She waited in the forge while he made the fire safe and tidied up, then the two of them returned to the house. He scooted upstairs, and Ellie finished the last preparations for dinner.

Just as Kit appeared in the kitchen, his hair still damp and tousled from his shower, the doorbell rang.

"Early, as ever," Kit said, making Ellie laugh.

"Can you grab the wine and the glasses and take them through for me? Thanks."

She kissed him as she passed, and hurried to the front door.

Joe stood on the doorstep, beaming from ear to ear, a large parcel in his hands. Liz was a pace behind him, also grinning.

"Hello. You're early."

Joe bent to kiss his sister's cheek. "I know. Sorry. Want us to go away and come back?"

"Don't be soft. Come on in."

She led them through to the cosy lounge. Shadow stretched out in front of the stove, warming a fat belly, a toy mouse next to his head – the closest he got to mousing now, much to Kit's annoyance. Kit followed them in, carrying a bottle of wine and four glasses on a tray. He put the tray down on the steamer trunk.

"Hello. How are you both?"

"Fine, fine." Joe gave him a one-armed hug, then handed him a parcel. "Happy birthday, Kit."

"Happy birthday," added Liz.

251

"Wine, everyone?" offered Ellie.

Everyone nodded, and she poured. They all sat down, Joe and Liz on one sofa, Kit and Ellie on the other. Kit peeled the brown paper from the gift, then laughed. Inside was a large slate sign, engraved with: The Forge.

He looked up at Joe and Liz on the sofa opposite. "Thank you."

Joe shrugged. "Well, there never *have* been many roses here."

"What did Ellie get you?" asked Liz.

Kit smiled. "She got me two books on the history of Britain. Some of which would have been my future. And a vast slab of chocolate." He mimed the size of it with his hands, holding them shoulder-width apart, mock-appalled.

"Mm. I've been *trying* to convince him that gifts can be frivolous! It's an uphill battle." She hooked an arm around his neck and scruffed his hair up. He batted her away good-naturedly.

"A toast to the birthday boy?" said Joe.

"Boy?" Kit murmured, tidying his hair with his fingers.

"Just a phrase," Ellie said gently. She raised her glass. "To Kit. Who is technically 288 years old today. But I must say, Kit, you're looking absolutely *fantastic* for your age!"

They all laughed. "To Kit!"

They clinked glasses, then Joe caught her eye, a slight sadness in his. "Today would also have been Granny Molly's birthday. I'm sure she is looking down on us from Heaven, feeling completely vindicated about everything. I *have* found happiness here, and Ellie *has* settled down with her tawny-haired ghost, even if it was a bit touch and go getting him here." He raised his glass again. "Happy birthday, Granny Molly. You really *could* see the future."

"Granny Molly."

Kit slid his arm around Ellie's shoulders, and she snuggled in against him. He brushed a kiss over her forehead and pressed something into her hand, his eyes shining. "A gift for you."

She frowned. "It's your birthday, not mine."

She opened her palm to find a single filigree wire, twisted into one continuous sentence, and her heart sang.

"My soul is at ease, for with you, I am home."

If you enjoyed reading Ellie and Kit's story, I would be enormously grateful if you would leave a review – on Amazon or Goodreads or wherever – to help other readers find them. Maybe talk about them on social media? Or perhaps have this as your next book-group book?

Thank you!

The Guardians of The Realm series

Book 1: Aegyir Rises

She's living her perfect life until a demon mistakes her for the warrior that imprisoned him. Now he's set on revenge.

Can she stop him before everyone she loves is slaughtered?

Reagan just wants to land her dream job and live quietly with her boyfriend, but her happiness is shattered when an accident releases an ancient creature who believes Reagan is someone else entirely.

All of her life, she's been plagued by dreams of being a warrior in a different world. Can these dreams really be memories of another realm?

When people all around her start dying mysteriously, Reagan realises she needs to figure out who she really is.

Because if she doesn't, no one will survive.

Aegyir Rises is the first book in the thrilling new-adult contemporary fantasy series The Guardians of The Realm.

Buy **Aegyir Rises** now, and lose yourself in a world of soul-stealing demons, warriors, and the fight of good versus evil.

★★★★★ "There's nothing out there as intriguing, tense and unputdownable in the urban fantasy genre that I've come across in a very long time."

★★★★★ "Oh my god! I have cried and been on the edge of my seat!"

About the Author

Amanda Fleet is a physiologist by training and a writer at heart. She spent almost 20 years teaching science and medicine undergraduates at university, but now writes full time.

Amanda lives in Scotland with her husband and her cat. She can be found writing, walking and running.

If you want to keep up to date with all the latest news, go to:
www.amandafleet.co.uk

Instagram: @amandafleet

Facebook: https://www.facebook.com/AmandaFleetWriter/

Twitter/X: @amanda_fleet1

Acknowledgements

There are a lot of people who helped me cope with all the blood, sweat, and tears during the writing of this, and I apologise profusely to anyone I miss out here. First and foremost, I need to thank the fantastic circle of writing friends I have, who have held me together and supported me when things have been difficult, and who have been there to celebrate the successes. There are too many of you to list individually, but I need to thank Jackie McLean and Ally Brady in particular. I also need to thank my writing buddy, Stuart Lennon, for all his advice and help (and for keeping me supplied with notebooks!). Thank you to my wonderful beta-readers: Daisy Ship, Annalisa Crawford, Leanne Caplis, and Cathy Adamson. Your words of encouragement kept me going. I must also thank my running buddy, Michael Caplis, who had to listen to so much rubbish from me out on our runs, but who was a great sounding board. My thanks also to GetCovers, who did such a great job with the cover. And last but most certainly not least, my love and thanks to my husband, Colin, without whom none of my books would have happened.

Made in United States
Orlando, FL
19 July 2024

49215159R00143